NEW YORK TIME
CATHERINE BYBE
MACCOINN

SILENT VOWS

"For being the stuff of folklore, the storyline is
surprisingly convincing…"
~ Romantic Times

"…absolutely brilliant and hilarious."
~Affair de Coeur

"Silent Vows" earns an unequivocal five stars
because it is just that much fun to read!… a light,
fun, absorbing read that disappoints only because
it ends."
~TJ Mackay~Goodreads

BINDING VOWS

"Binding Vows whisked me into an adventure I
was sorry to see end."
~Romance Studio

"…full of all the things I love, action, romance,
history, and a knight in shining armor."
~Night Owl Reviews

"…you cannot help but feel completely
mesmerized."
~Coffee Time Romance

"Catherine Bybee does an exceptional job of
making her time travels come to life."

Discover other titles by Catherine Bybee

Contemporary Romance
Weekday Bride Series:
Wife by Wednesday
Married By Monday

Not Quite Series:
Not Quite Dating

Paranormal Romance
MacCoinnich Time Travel Series:
Binding Vows
Silent Vows
Redeeming Vows
Highland Shifter

Ritter Werewolves Series:
Before the Moon Rises
Embracing the Wolf

Novellas:
Possessive
Soul Mate

Erotic Titles:
Kiltworthy
Kilt-A-Licious

SILENT VOWS

BOOK TWO

BY

CATHERINE BYBEE

Silent Vows
Catherine Bybee

Cover Art by Crystal Posey

Publishing History
First Edition, Faery Rose Edition, 2010
Second Edition, Catherine Bybee, 2013

Published in the United States of America

Dedication

For Sandra, the grammar queen and
constant cheerleader for every word I write.

For Fran, my editor and friend.
Thank you so much for your hours of work and
love for this project.

Chapter One

My life is over.

Myra MacCoinnich sat astride her horse, marching toward death, death of her life as she knew it.

Why?

Why were the Ancients, the benevolent Druid spirits, dictating her destiny by sending her into the future now?

Beside her, her sister-in-law, Tara graced her with a wry smile, a grin holding enough doubt to leave Myra with a giant hole in her heart.

"'Tis far enough," her brother, Duncan, announced as he brought their horses to a stop.

Sliding from the back of the mount, Myra gave her mare a final pat.

"This isn't goodbye, Myra. You'll see her again," Tara lifted an arm to Myra's shoulders in support.

"Are we doing the right thing?"

"Have your mother's visions ever been wrong?"

"Nay." Her mother's clear vision had warned of Myra's death if she stayed in 1576.

"Say 'no', Myra. The twenty-first century will be hard enough without tripping on words from the sixteenth-century. If Lara's visions have never failed, then we must believe you aren't safe here. You're going to love my time." Tara sent her a much more convincing smile.

"'Tis time, lass," Duncan called.

"Remember, 'Lizzy' is short for Elizabeth. Elizabeth McAllister."

Myra nodded, understanding Tara searched for any missing detail about her sister that would help Myra in the future, or so they hoped.

"If for any reason she won't listen, find Cassy. Cassandra Ross."

"You've told me all of this. I won't forget." Myra removed the heavy cloak covering the twenty-first century style pants and shirt. "Here, I won't be needing this." She couldn't believe she'd soon be walking in public with the clothes she wore.

Tara's eyes glistened with unshed tears.

Duncan's fierce hug filled Myra with warmth. She remembered the last words her younger sister Amber had uttered to her the night before. Tara was with child, yet neither of them knew it. Amber always knew such things. Much like their mother's visions, Amber was never wrong.

"Congratulations, brother."

"For what?" he asked, drawing away from her embrace to glance down at her.

"You'll see."

Duncan moved from her arms to spread the sacred stones in a perfect circle. He touched each one, lending them part of his Druid power to help them move Myra through time. Pulsating energy beat within the stones, waiting.

Myra placed one unsteady foot in front of the other, and found herself in the center of the stones. She repeated the chant in her head. Energy built.

"Godspeed," Duncan lifted a hand.

The wind started to turn, and heat, along with light, shimmered and burned from each stone reaching far above her head in a kaleidoscope of colors.

"Hey, Myra?" Tara yelled out in an obvious attempt at distracting her.

"What?"

"Have Lizzy take you to Magicland. The rides don't compare to this, but you'll love it."

Myra clenched her sack to her chest. Air within the circle thinned making breathing difficult. "Magicland, I'll remember."

She wanted to run, flee away from the stones, away from the power that started to surround her body; instead, Myra raised her voice and chanted. "Ancient stones, and Ancient power, take me safely to Lizzy this hour. Keep me safe and from harm's way, from prying eyes and the light of day. If the Ancients will it so, take me now and let me go."

The earth trembled beneath her feet. She stepped forward, fear slammed into her from all sides. Air filled her lungs before expelling in a near scream.

From the corner of her eye, she witnessed Duncan draw Tara tight to his chest.

The power within the circle, held steady by the stones entrusted only to her family, roared. She couldn't escape. This was her destiny. Dread slid up her spine and burst in her head, followed by an eerie sense of calm.

Myra squeezed her eyes shut. *Magicland, Elizabeth McAllister, oh, God.*

The earth fell from her feet and time swept her away.

~~~~

Amnesia. Who believes in that shit?

Some woman woke up on the Island of

3

Atlantis, smack dab in the middle of Magicland before the first employee arrived, and Todd needed to take the report. It sounded like a case for an ambulance chaser.

Scammers came in all shapes and sizes. This one had scammer written all over her. Someone was always searching for a way to make a quick buck.

Officer Todd Blakely asked the elderly woman at the reception desk of Anaheim General Hospital where the ER had taken Jane Doe, then made his way to the elevators.

He walked past the nurse's desk and smiled at the blonde behind the counter who eyed him up one side and down the other.

Obviously, she liked what she saw.

He didn't know if it was him or the badge and uniform. The department called them Badge Bunnies. Women who went out of their way to gain the attention of anyone in a uniform, police or fire, they didn't care which. The men often took advantage of the women's attention, which explained the high divorce rate among the ranks.

Todd walked toward room number 840 to visit Jane Doe.

Behind the slightly open door, he heard a small laugh. The sound was a little happy for someone who woke without a memory.

He glanced through the doorway, and saw Miss Amnesia sitting up in bed. The flat screen television, held on to a platform by a C-arm, swiveled in front of her. Her hair, the darkest shade of brown fringing on black, traveled down past her shoulders all the way to her elbows. Her deep umber eyes sat atop beautifully shaped cheeks and plump lips that smiled about whatever she watched.

Todd felt the air leave his body. Jane Doe was drop-dead beautiful.

Impulsively, Todd straightened his shoulders and forced his jaw into a hard edge. He would have to watch his step. Women as stunning as the one in front of him had a way of disarming the strongest of cops.

The woman in the bed hid a smile behind her hand.

Todd's mouth ran dry. *Sweet Jesus!*

~~~~

The pressure behind her eyes slowly disappeared. The nurse called the little white pills ibuprofen, not that she understood what that was exactly, but she consumed it nonetheless. All of Tara's coaching worked thus far, leaving her to believe all else would fall into place.

Myra sat back and once again replayed the conversation she and Tara had shortly before leaving the sixteenth century.

"They will probably take you to a hospital and run a bunch of tests. Let them, and for God's sake don't act like they're trying to hurt you. They aren't. Amnesic patients remember day to day things, just not who they are or the people around them."

"But I won't know those day to day things," Myra said.

"I know. When in doubt of what to say, say nothing. Act innocent. You don't remember anything. Name, home, family...nothing! Someone will eventually call the police, tell them my sister's name, and they will take it from there."

"I'm frightened, Tara."

"I know, I was too when I first came here. Lizzy will help. Give her my letter. You can count on her."

The sound of a dog barking on the TV shook the memories from Myra's head. How the peoples' images made their way into the small box, she had no idea, but it would be a great help in studying the people of this time.

She laughed at the pictures of dogs chasing their tails and falling over each other with long wet tongues.

Someone watched.

Myra felt his presence before glancing up to see blue eyes staring at her. The frown on his face worried her almost as much as the imposing clothes he wore, stripes and angles, with a belt that looked like it weighed ten pounds. A metallic badge glistened proudly on his pocket.

The stranger wore his hair long on the top and short at the nape of his neck. His age was close enough to hers to send a slight wave of awareness over her. Yet, his firm jaw was set in a way that told Myra she needed to be careful about what she said. A strange fluttering sensation formed deep in her stomach.

"Hello." Myra pushed the button that turned off the box, and then smiled at the ease of the task. "I didn't see you come in."

"No problem." He nodded toward the TV. "I'm interrupting."

"Nay. Excuse me, I mean no. Of course you're not. Please take a seat." Myra indicated a chair with her hand. Being alone with a man, a stranger, in her room wasn't something Myra was accustomed to. The way this man gazed at her, she wondered if she had reason to worry. Her eyes slid to his again, his attractive face and smooth speech caused her heartbeat to rise.

"I'm Officer Blakely." He extended his hand to shake hers.

Myra offered her hand. With his touch, the fluttering in her stomach grew. Her hand trembled in his as energy flowed through her fingers. She snatched her hand away hoping the man hadn't noticed the heat in her palm. Myra suddenly realized she felt more vulnerable under his eyes than she had all day with the doctors and nurses poking her with their strange objects.

"I'm here to take a report on today's incident." He remained standing while he removed a tablet of parchment, or paper as Tara had called it, and a writing device. Thank goodness Tara schooled her in modern day writing and reading before her journey. Otherwise, the simple acts of the people in this time would have been quite foreign to her.

"I've gone over this already." She counted off the number of people who heard her story. The daunting man from the theme park asked her everything twice, the medic in the ambulance on the way to the hospital asked once, an emergency room nurse, an emergency room Doctor as well as a Neurologist. Myra wondered if anyone in this time spoke to one another.

"Not for us, Miss." He flipped the pages to an empty spot. "I'm told you 'woke up' at Magicland. Can you tell me what happened?"

Officer Blakely breathed suspicion. She couldn't tell if her Druid's blood told her this or his body language did.

"I woke up on the small island surrounded by a moat."

"Atlantis Island?"

"That is what the man who found me called it." There were so many questions she had about the place she'd landed after her trip through time. Why were there ships in a moat? Where could they possibly go? Why had the beautiful village been abandoned? Where were the people who lived there? But she didn't ask.

Keep it simple! Tara's mantra for Myra's visit to the twenty-first century repeated in her head. "I think I hit my head. Although the doctors are not finding any injury to correlate with my lack of memory."

"You don't remember going to Magicland?"

"Nay."

"How long were you there?"

"I don't know. I woke up and found a kind man who called others to help me. They asked questions like you, but I couldn't give them any answers either."

"What do you remember?"

"I woke up, met the kind man who called the people from the hospital who eventually brought me here."

"Uh-huh." He turned the page. "Okay, let me just fill in a few blanks for my report." He sat down.

She relaxed slightly.

"Are you married?"

"No," she said automatically.

His eyes shot up, catching hers. "How can you be sure, if you have no memory?"

Her stomach twisted. "I'm not sure. It just

doesn't seem right." She watched her fingers clench. "Maybe I am. I should remember something like that, shouldn't I?"

He didn't answer. Instead, he stared.

"I do remember a name," she said quickly, trying to divert his attention away from her slip.

"Whose name?"

Myra fumbled with the blankets. The fluttering, which wasn't all together unpleasant only a few minutes ago, now felt like a lump in the back of her throat. "I'm not sure." She took a breath. "I remembered the name Lizzy McAllister a short time ago."

He scribbled the name on his notebook. "It isn't your name?"

"I don't think so, but I thought maybe if I said the name enough it would assist my memory as to who she is."

"Has it?"

"I'm afraid not."

"I'll check out the name, see if your picture pops up in any missing persons reports. Is there anything else you'd like to add?"

"No."

He blew out a breath before he stood. He placed his book in his pocket and prepared to leave.

"You don't believe me do you?" Now why had she asked that? She knew he didn't.

"It isn't for me to believe or not, Miss. I only have to write the report."

"Why don't you believe me?"

He walked over to the room's window, pulled back the shade, and exposed the skyline of the city.

She hadn't noticed the sky grow dark, or how

9

the lights from the surrounding buildings glowed. The sight was awesome, mystifying to the point where Myra didn't hear his next words until he repeated them.

"I said, the world is full of opportunists. Any person found *hurt* on property owned by a corporation as large as the Magicland theme park is going to be under suspicion."

"And I am under that watchful eye?" She pulled her gaze from the panoramic view and met his. *Opportunist?* He thought she was after something from him, or whoever owned the land she'd been found on.

He didn't believe her lies. She would ponder the irony of that later. "Why should I care if you don't believe me? 'Tis the truth."

"Sitting in this deluxe hospital suite on someone else's dime would certainly give one that feeling."

"What do you mean?"

"Who do you think is paying for all of this?" He spread his hands at the room. "You're sitting in a private room in an overcrowded hospital. These cherry wood furnishings and plush blankets aren't exactly standard hospital issue." He walked over to a bank of electronic devices. "There's even a CD player in here," he mumbled.

The comfortable room was small by her standards. Her room at home was three times as large. Perhaps she was receiving special treatment and didn't know it.

If someone else paid her way, he or she might not be able to care for themselves or their family. In her time, one would be happy to care for the sick or injured if able, but Myra wasn't sick and instantly felt guilty for her lies.

"Perhaps, I should leave." She tossed back the blanket to get out of the bed and noticed her bare thighs and naked feet, then quickly covered herself back up. "If you'll excuse me?"

Officer Blakely held her gaze, his emotions masked. A slight tremor went through her when he didn't budge.

"Where will you go?" he asked.

She opened her mouth only to shut it without uttering a word.

"Listen, lady, I'm sure your overnight stay in the hospital isn't going to break anyone's bank." He moved closer to the door. "Twelve hours will give me time to look up this name, maybe something will come up. Or you'll remember who you are in the morning."

She wasn't listening. Her eyes gazed beyond him.

"So are you staying?"

She closed her eyes. "Do I have a choice?"

"I'll be back tomorrow. If you remember anything, call this number." He took out a card, walked back to the bed, and handed it to her. His fingers barely brushed hers.

A vibration went up her arm at the contact. The lump in her throat eased into submission.

He pulled his hand back in alarm. His surprised expression met hers the instant their fingers touched. "If I'm out, the department will contact me."

She studied the card.

When he turned to leave, she stopped him. "Officer Blakely?"

He peered back with a thoughtful stare.

"I truly have no idea where to go." She spoke the truth.

The blue in his eyes glistened, his gruff expression shifted. She peered closer, her Druid gift sought his thoughts. For a brief moment, Blakely believed her. He said nothing, nodded, turned and left the room.

Chapter Two

'Believe none of what you hear and only half of what you see.' That was a cop's motto.

Todd had clocked out, changed clothes and drove to his favorite watering hole. He sucked down a longneck beer and pondered Jane Doe. Next to him, Jake sipped his Scotch and tried to get Todd to change the subject.

"Let it go until tomorrow. It's not like she's going anywhere." Jake had a few years on Todd and one failed marriage under his belt. His two kids visited him every other weekend and for one month in the summer. Even with alimony payments, he still felt the need to find wife number two. Fortunately for Todd, no candidate was sitting in the seat at the bar next to them or Todd would have been talking to himself. With an eligible woman in the room, Jake's attention span was nil.

"Something isn't right," Todd continued.

Jake rolled his eyes and shook his head. "What isn't right?"

"Her story is bogus. Who wakes up in the middle of an amusement park? No one saw her go down. It isn't like Atlantis Island is that big. Someone would have noticed an unconscious woman."

"But someone found her there, right?"

"No, she was found wandering the streets near the Gods of Mythology attraction. She only said she woke up on the island. I'll check their surveillance tapes tomorrow."

"I'm sure the lawyers already have them. You might need to check with the boss and subpoena them." Jake ordered a second round.

"Possibly."

"So she was found in the park, no injuries and no signs of sleeping in the elements?"

"Right. No forced entry, she could have found a corner and hid in it until the park closed."

"She would have been picked up on a camera somewhere. I know I wouldn't be able to stay in one place all night long in the middle of that park. I've always wanted to climb on top of the T-Rex."

Todd took a long drink, sat back and scratched his five o'clock shadow. "The thing is...I don't think she has any idea about Magicland's worth or influence."

His partner grunted his disbelief.

"No, really. She threatened to leave the hospital when I told her someone else was footing her bill."

"But she didn't," Jake said.

"Because she had nowhere to go. You should've seen her. Something in her eyes spoke the truth when her mouth didn't. Weird and doesn't fit with the rest of her story."

"Could be a domestic violence thing, and she's trying to get away from the old man."

"Maybe." Todd's head started to pound despite the beer. After hours of investigative work, he was no closer to the truth behind Jane Doe.

"So, tell me about your date with Sheila." Todd changed the subject.

~~~~

A large, dark-skinned woman shuffled her way into Myra's room first thing in the morning. "I'm Keisha from social services."

"Good morning," Myra pushed her plate of food away and diverted her attention to the woman at her bedside.

"I see they have chorizo today," Keisha nodded toward the food. "Not the healthiest breakfast served in the hospital, but it is one of the better tasting."

"'Tis quite spicy."

"And terribly fattening, too, I'm sure. Not that you have to worry about that."

"I suppose not."

"The doctors aren't ready to release you yet, but when they do I have a list of shelters in the area which might be of service." She handed Myra a piece of paper with names and addresses on it. "There's an abuse center on the list if you need it."

Myra peered into the woman's mind and sensed a lack of trust.

"The lawyers from Magicland agreed to accommodate you for awhile."

"No. They have helped enough."

The social worker gave her a puzzled look before she gathered her things. "Either way, there are people who can help you."

Keisha stood to leave.

"Thank you for your concern."

Keisha walked away shaking her head.

It took a lot of willpower to stay put. Every fiber of Myra's being told her she had no right to stay in the hospital when someone else was paying her way.

Officer Blakely said he would return.

15

Hopefully he would bring Lizzy and Myra would have her problems solved.

Over twenty-four hours had passed since she'd left 1576 and taken her first trip through time. The scared and lonely part of her needed to be battled down continually. The other part, the excited fraction of her brain, wanted nothing more than to jump out of her sickbed and explore. From the first ride in the ambulance to the gadgets surrounding her, everything was new and different. Having an uncertain future kept her from enjoying the pleasantries of this time. Well, not all of them.

Myra slipped out from under the cotton sheets, tiptoed into the bathroom, and enjoyed her second shower. "Oh, Tara. Ye were right to have Fin working on this luxury at home," she murmured to herself. To shower indoors with heated water at the Keep would be heaven.

Later, she sat by the window and watched the people come and go. There were so many of them.

Some resembled her family and the people of the village outside MacCoinnich Keep, but others were simply different, from the clothes they wore to the girth of their waistlines.

The faces, dear lord, their faces with eyes shaped in small slits to foreheads flat and large. Even their hair was different and shaded in every color of the rainbow. One woman even had a pink streak running through her blonde tresses. Myra did her best not to stare.

~~~~

Todd and Jake arrived at Jane Doe's room after three in the afternoon. After one jaw-dropping glance, Jake elbowed Todd in the ribs and lifted his eyes in approval.

"How are you feeling today?" Todd asked.

"The same, thank you."

"This is my partner, Officer Nelson."

"Miss..."

"Doe," she told him. "Apparently my name is Jane Doe number 33." She fingered the name band she wore on her wrist. "Why so many numbers? Are there that many women who don't remember their names in your village?"

"More like unidentified bodies..."

Todd shot Jake a disapproving glare.

Jane Doe's smile fell. "Oh." She stood and moved to the bed. "Please sit."

Once they were all comfortable Todd started. "We found the name Lizzy McAllister, well actually her name is Elizabeth McAllister."

"And?"

"It appears that Miss McAllister is on vacation. Her employer isn't expecting her back for a few days. We can question her then to see if she knows who you are."

She let out a disappointed sigh.

"Her name appeared on a police report filed last summer," Jake relayed. "Her sister went missing. Does the name Tara McAllister mean anything to you?"

Todd watched Jane's expression and noticed a flicker of recognition, which she quickly hid. He had done his homework. The woman sitting in front of him didn't match the pictures of the missing woman, but he couldn't help wonder if they were in some way connected. Missing persons and people showing up without an identity sounded related to him.

"No." She looked down at her hands.

"What about the names Duncan and Fin? Ring any bells?"

Myra's first thought was, what did bells have to do with it? "No." She denied knowing her own brothers.

"How about the name Gwen Adams?"

"Adams?" Myra shook her head. "Gwen Adams." Tara had referred to Grainna as 'Gwen' many times. Did they mean Grainna? Cold crept up her arms making her hair stand on end and her flesh crawl.

The men exchanged looks.

She circled her arms over her body searching for warmth.

"The name means something?" Todd asked this time.

"Maybe." What did these men know of Grainna? She wanted to ask, but feared the answer. Had they contacted her when Lizzy wasn't available? Was she on her way there now?

"Gwen Adams disappeared the same time McAllister did."

A sharp breath escaped from her lungs. Grainna must have followed her brothers and Tara back in time. That was why her mother's vision warned them of Myra's death if she didn't escape into the future. Everything started making sense. Her family was in grave danger.

Her head started to spin. She closed her eyes, desperately trying to hide her emotions, but it was impossible. A burning ache punched her chest with worry.

"Are you okay?" Todd asked.

Myra rolled her head on her shoulders, and

squeezed her eyes together, then tried to push away the concern, anxiety and terror from her face. "I don't know."

Myra's eyes met Officer Blakely's. Starring directly into to them, she said, "I don't know what to do." Tears glistened. She caught her lower lip with her teeth and moistened her dry lips.

"We will do what we can to help, Miss..."

"See, that is a problem. What do you call me? Miss Doe?" A tear fell, and then another. Good God, she wanted to go home and knowing Grainna wreaked havoc back in her time forced her to face why she couldn't. Grainna would kill Myra for her virgin blood.

Todd peered into her eyes, the eyes of a liar, and she was ashamed, conflicted, torn between telling him the truth or continuing with her lies.

~~~~

Victims had their reasons, their need to remain silent. In his experience, he discovered most liars or victims hid something either due to an irrevocable act of their own, poor judgment in boyfriends, or spouses, or as the consequences of a stupid act in a drunken state. Then there were the others, like the woman in front of him, one he believed kept her silence because of the act of another.

A true victim didn't bring anything on him or herself, they were simply in the wrong place at the wrong time. Without a doubt, Todd knew Jane's misery was because of someone else. Someone she had a great dislike for, and most likely a damn good reason behind it.

The nurse's aide knocked on the door and brought her dinner tray in. "Hey, gorgeous. How are you tonight?" The aide's nametag said 'Joe'. He smiled at his patient and ignored them.

Tears flowed from Jane Doe's eyes. "Hi, Joe," she managed to choke out.

Joe's flash of anger surprised Todd when he finally looked at them. *Interesting, she's already managed to find friends.*

"Hey, if you want to have me kick these guys out, I can," Joe said.

"We were just leaving."

"She's been through enough, don't you think?" Joe blurted out, his jaw set in tight anger.

"Thank you for your protection, Joe," Myra told him. "It's not their fault."

"All right. But if you need me, just call." He set the food tray on the table, walked away and glared at Todd.

She pushed the tray to the side.

Jake asked her, "Our sergeant asked us to take a picture of you. Would that be okay?"

She nodded and flinched when the flash of the camera went off.

"We'll run this through the system, see what comes up."

~~~~

She waited until the staff finished their rounds for the evening before she took out her bag and emptied its contents on the bed.

The sacred stones that moved her through time looked like ordinary rocks, ones found on any plain in the Highlands. Closer examination revealed words written in Gaelic, identifying them as something sacred, something cherished.

Wrapped in linen were a set of candlesticks beautifully carved and encrusted with precious

20

stones. They were a sacrifice for her family to part with, but Tara had insisted that she come to the twenty-first century with something to barter for currency.

"My world runs on money, without it you have nothing," Tara had said. After many hours of watching the television, Myra understood what Tara meant.

Myra decided to leave the hospital in the morning. The list of places taking in people like her, people with no family or home, was long. She'd surely find a place to stay among them. Myra fingered the list of shelters.

With any luck, she could find a buyer for her wares and be able to pay her way.

Having a plan or at least a direction in which to move, Myra put all her belongings back into the bag, sat in the chair next to the window, and waited for sunrise.

~~~~

The next day was Todd's day off, but instead of kicking back with a football game, beer and pizza, Todd sat at his desk cross-referencing the names he and Jake had uncovered in their Jane Doe investigation.

Gwen Adams had several hits on the internet, mainly in reference to the Renaissance Fairs she ran throughout the country. A few photos of the woman came through, none of which were flattering. Her identification card and social security number had different birthdays, indicating that maybe Ms. Adams was trying to conceal something.

He looked again at the picture of a woman well in her 80's, and racked his brain over what

21

she could possibly be hiding.

Either way, her disappearance occurred the same weekend in July that Tara McAllister vanished, the only fact connecting the two women. Now Jane Doe showed up with an accent matching the men with whom McAllister was last seen. The puzzle had just become more complicated.

Too many coincidences made for connections.

Instinct told him he was on the right track. Jane's ghostly expression when he mentioned the old woman's name sent a chill down his spine.

Todd's eyes started to blur. He sat back, rubbed the back of his neck, and reached for his coffee.

On the way home, he turned his car in the direction of Anaheim General. He would question why later, but for now he needed to see her again. Her expressions the night before haunted his dreams and kept him awake most of the previous night.

He walked the familiar path to her room, this time in a sweatshirt and blue jeans. The badge bunnies who ogled him less than fifteen hours before didn't give him a passing glance.

He eased open the door in case Jane was sleeping, but the room was empty. The bed was stripped of its linen and the counters void of clutter. Only a housekeeper was there, mopping the floor. "Excuse me, where did they move the woman from this room?"

The Hispanic woman stopped, and replied in broken English, "She not moved, she discharged."

Discharged? His brows turned in. "Discharged where?"

He strode back to the central desk where the

staff congregated, flashed his badge, and demanded, "Where's the patient from room 840?"

"I'm not sure." The nurse shuffled her feet. "After report I went on my rounds and she was gone. She did leave a note."

Todd felt his pulse jump. He shoved his badge back in his pocket and waited for the nurse to find the note in the chart. He removed his cell phone from his pocket, noticed he didn't have a signal. Frustrated, he muttered under his breath and flipped it closed.

"Here." She handed a paper to him. "I told the doctor she eloped. She wasn't on a 5150 or anything," she told him.

"No, she wasn't being held," he said before reading the note.

To the Lovely and Caring Nurses, Staff and the owners of the land in which I was found,

Thank you for all your kindness and care. I appreciate everything you have done for me. If I can find a way to repay you, be assured I will do so.

It was signed, *Jane Doe 33.*

Todd slammed his fist on the counter, all those behind it jumped. "Can I get a copy of this?" He handed the paper over to the nurse.

As soon as he cleared the hospital doors, he was back on his cell calling his partner.

"Dammit, Nelson, she's gone."

"Gone?" Jake asked, the volume on the TV in the background lowered. "Where would she go?"

"I don't know. I have a list of shelters the social worker gave to her. I'm going to check them out."

"Why? We don't have anything on her. No one filed charges."

Todd ran across the street to the parking garage where he parked his Mustang. "She wouldn't last a single night in a shelter, Jake. They'll eat her for breakfast."

"Maybe. But there isn't anything we can do for her."

"I can't sit and do nothing."

There was a pause on the other end of the line. "You're getting too involved, Blakely. She's not a stray cat you put out cream for."

He let out a long sigh. "That's my point. We're kinder to stray animals than we are to people." The phone cut out, ending their conversation.

Todd slammed the car into reverse and drove in the direction of the first shelter on his list and growled, "Sonofabitch, where the hell did she go."

~~~~

Myra walked down the crowded street, looking at all the faces. Unlike her village, where people smiled and waved a greeting, everyone here seemed in a hurry. She smiled and said a quick hello to some of those who passed by. Only the elderly returned her greeting, the others sent her puzzled looks or avoided her eyes altogether.

The constant hum of the town deafened her ears. The cars driving by at such a fast pace, both fascinated and amazed her. One step into traffic and she quickly realized the cars wouldn't stop to let her pass. She followed the crowd and learned what the lighted signals meant and when it would be safe to cross the street.

Myra, buzzing with excitement, realized she

was alone in a crowded town. No one asked where her family was, or where she was going. Simply walking a busy street in her time could prove dangerous. No one here appeared to mean her any harm.

For the first time since she'd arrived, she relaxed and enjoyed the freedom of exploring this fascinating time.

She passed places of business that sold everything from clothes to household wares. Furniture stores and places to buy food, both ready to eat and not, were on every corner.

She wandered aimlessly for quite a while before she asked a shop clerk for directions to one of the addresses on her paper. He sent her a puzzled stare. He eyed the band she wore around her wrist from the hospital and stepped back.

He thinks I'm mad.

"The mission is down on central."

"Where is that?"

He pointed her East. "Four blocks that way, take a right. You'll see it."

"Thank you, sir."

"Whatever." His eyes followed her as she exited his shop.

Once outside, Myra removed the hospital band and stuck it in her sack.

The Mission was a stark white building covered with letters and symbols. Inside, a woman sat behind a desk, her skin the caramel color of the social worker at the hospital. "Can I help you?"

"Aye." Myra looked around at the people sitting in the chairs scattered around the lobby. The smell coming from their un-bathed bodies nauseated her. Their eyes watched her movements. "I was told you provide shelter here."

The woman took in the full length of Myra's body. "We do. You need a place for the night?"

Myra nodded and glanced over her shoulder and noticed a man staring at her. He was scarcely more than a lad; the markings on his arms had names and numbers along with pictures in dark colored inks. She had never seen such a sight before. She looked up at his face, noticed the smoking stick hanging from his mouth. His tongue licked his lips as his eyes raked her body. Frightened, she forced herself to turn her back on the man.

The woman had her sign a registry, and then laughed when Myra wrote down 'Jane Doe'.

She led her to a large room littered with cots. A curtain separated the men's side from the women's. "You can put your stuff here, but if you have any valuables I wouldn't leave them."

"There are thieves here?" Myra clutched her bag closer.

"You're kiddin' right?" She didn't wait for an answer and went on. "They just finished up lunch. If you're hungry I'm sure they'll find something for you. Otherwise dinner's at six o'clock." The woman left and returned to her desk.

Myra sat on the cot and looked around the room. So many of those she watched were sick in their minds. Some talked to themselves while others rocked back and forth.

Women with small children stared desperately at the blank walls, hardly existing in their miserable lives. Children, knowing no better, bounced on the cots and played with broken toys and forgotten boxes. *These people have nothing.*

As night approached, Myra became more aware of the people around her. The men from the lobby who watched her throughout the day now stalked closer.

She opened her mind to catch glimpses of the men's thoughts. None of them tried to hide. All of them meant her harm. A tremor of terror washed over her. She wouldn't last the night in this place if their lustful, evil thoughts came to be. These men were thieves. They would use her and take her things. Even if she did survive, her belongings would be gone before the sun rose, and with them her ability to go home.

She took her bag, made her way to the bathroom at the front of the building, and kept her eyes to the floor.

~~~~

It was dark. His first three stops at local shelters were futile. No one had seen the woman from his picture. Her frightened expression on the paper had him worrying over what she looked like now. Jane Doe was in trouble. He knew it. He scanned every alley and every street.

Nothing.

He changed direction to the south side of town, the side of town even the toughest of the tough didn't go unless they had to. Drug dealers and prostitutes made their living on these streets.

He tried to think of what might be going on in her head. She wouldn't know this side of town wasn't safe. Then again, maybe she did. Doubtful.

Her big brown eyes and her words flashed in his memory. *"I don't know where to go."*

So he searched, and would search all night if he had to. She was out there somewhere. Alone.

~~~~

Night fell in around her. The deafening sounds from earlier in the day diminished into a dreadful eerie silence. The occasional car drove by, headlights shining in her path.

The hum of machines that heated the buildings attempted to fill the silence but failed. Only the soft pat of her feet hitting the pavement kept her company.

She slipped away from the mission shelter almost as easily as she had the hospital earlier in the day. The trouble was she didn't know where to go. Where she would find safety?

She walked the deserted streets. The cold night air oozed into her bones. "Where are those warm nights, Tara?" *I'll keep walking. It will keep me awake and warm.*

Piercing cold prickled up her back and made the hairs on her neck stand up. Myra felt the eyes long before she saw the face.

Cruel, black eyes watched her.

She used every power within her to see inside the man.

Within his darkness, she saw herself as he did. *Easy prey!* His mind shouted.

She braced for attack.

Out of nowhere another man, at least one hundred pounds heavier than her, stepped into her path from the darkness of an alley.

She turned and moved in the opposite direction, never making eye contact with her foe.

Remain calm. She heard Tara's words whisper in her ear as if she was standing by her side. *Don't show fear.* Myra tried, but the day's events rushed into her mind.

Fear blossomed and grew.

She quickened her pace and walked directly into the path of a second attacker.

This one, lanky and thin, had skin that held a deathly hue of green. He undressed her with a look, chewed on his tongue, and licked his ugly, sore-covered lips.

Keep moving. She attempted to walk around him.

The vicious man blocked her path.

Scooting to the side, she stepped past him.

He laughed.

"Excuse me." She moved again, her heart raced.

He stood close enough for her to smell stale tobacco and something else she couldn't identify.

"Lookie what we have here, Cutter." He reached out and touched her hair. "Now ain't you soft an' pretty."

Frozen in place, she felt his fingers whisk past her cheek. She pulled away.

"Now what could you possibly need out here at this time of night? Whatcha need? A hit?"

Myra started to breathe faster, her heartbeat soared as she battled her losing fight with fear.

He grabbed her waist and shoved.

She landed against his vile companion. His smelly body heat suffocated her.

"Where you going, lil' lady? We're just gettin' this party started."

Looking over, she saw the sneer from the man standing behind her. His partner laughed.

Trapped, her mind raced to find a way out.

Myra saw a garbage can across the street on the sidewalk. With little more than a glance, she focused and raised it five feet into the air with her mind. Then she let it drop.

It crashed to the sidewalk with a bang.

Both men turned.

She stomped on the instep of the one who held her.

He roared in pain and let go.

She ran, her legs pumping faster than any time in the past.

Footsteps pounded the pavement in pursuit.

Headlights of an oncoming car shot out of the darkness.

Myra ran toward it and waved her hands for help.

Brakes screeched when the car almost slammed into her.

To her dismay, it swerved around and didn't stop. The driver leaned on the horn as he drove away, leaving her alone with her enemy.

Myra ran into the dark alley. It was a dead end. There was no escape.

The men were a few feet away. Fear gripped her throat. *They're coming...*

Chapter Three

He missed her by half an hour. Jane Doe #33 registered into the mission on the wrong end of town. The staff gave a positive ID and men he recognized as known felons out on parole told him she had been there.

She was gone. No one saw her leave.

It was past ten, and the streets were bare except for those people who lived on them.

He drove with his windows opened so he would hear each sound. He followed every noise. She was out there somewhere in the urban jungle. Those who would stalk her would be no less deadly than a jaguar or lion.

A horn blasted his thoughts. He heard a woman's scream. With his heart racing, Todd gunned the engine in the direction of the desperate outcry.

~~~~

They advanced on her slow and steady.

Myra gritted her teeth and nestled into their heads. Repulsive images of violent hands moving over her naked body sprung forth in her mind.

They laughed.

With no place to run, her mind raced and bordered on complete panic. She forced herself to calm down. It was the only way to survive what they had planned.

No knights who served her family would hear her cry or come to her rescue.

CATHERINE BYBEE

She could only depend on herself and her magical Druid gifts.

"If you turn around now, I'll let you go," she said, her voice wavering.

They looked at each other and broke out in laughter.

"And if we don't?" the big one asked.

She watched each of them, trying to see which one would attack first. The smaller man's movements were jerky and unpredictable. Cutter held lust and murder in his eyes, his intent clearly written in his thoughts. His eyes told her he had killed before. "God's teeth," she muttered.

Again they laughed. The lanky one ran toward her. Closer...

She pushed the wind from beneath his feet.

His unsuspecting frame hit the ground, halting his laughter.

Myra tried to dart around Cutter, but he grabbed her arm in a deathly grip.

She screamed—surprising them both. When she tossed out a hand, the garbage piled up next to the drain on the street burst into flames. With a flick of the wrist, the fire leaped toward them.

She ducked even though her arm was still in Cutter's grip.

The flame caught Cutter in the chest. He let her go and started beating the flames off his shirt. He danced around in circles yelling.

Clutching her bag to her chest, Myra ran again. When she looked back to see if they followed, she stumbled straight into the chest of another man.

~~~~

Myra burst out of the alley as if the devil

himself chased her. Todd caught her around the waist, and at the same time leveled his gun at the men who followed her.

"Police!" he yelled, halting the man and silencing the woman's scream.

The skinny one was in his sights, but the larger man heaved himself over the chain link fence and moved out of firing range.

Todd shifted his eyes to the top of the woman's head buried deep into his shoulder. In that second, the scrawny guy made his escape.

He would have given chase if he'd had back up. Instead, he holstered his gun and focused on the woman trembling in his arms. He didn't know who was more startled, her or him. Renewed fear for her safety quickly replaced his relief at finding her.

She held on to him. He found his arm inching around her waist and pulling her close. She let out a slight whimper that reminded him of a wounded animal scared and alone.

"They're gone. Shh... It's okay now." His hands stroked up and down her back.

Her body relaxed and the tears started to flow. She mumbled something in a language he didn't understand.

He couldn't tell if it was an oath or a prayer. He pulled away and looked at her. "Did they hurt you?"

She shook her head. "If you hadn't come..."

"They're long gone and can't hurt you now."

Nodding, she sucked in a deep breath in what Todd thought was an attempt to control her emotions.

He kept his arm around her and walked back

to his car parked half on the curb with the driver's door open and with the engine still running. "Let's get you out of here."

He helped her into the passenger seat and then took his own.

"Buckle up," Todd told her before putting the car in reverse.

The car moved. Her hand clutched her bag in a white-knuckled grip.

"Buckle up," he told her again.

When she responded with a blank gaze, he assumed she was in shock. He reached across her chest, pulled the strap over her lap, and clicked it in. She still trembled.

"Hey, you're safe now." Todd placed his hand on hers. Heat surged with the connection he tried his best to ignore.

She gazed up at him with her innocent, trusting eyes.

Thank God she's safe.

"What are you doing out here, Officer Blakely?"

Her words stopped him from staring at her. "Todd," he placed his hands on the wheel and maneuvered his car onto the street. "Call me Todd."

"What are you doing out here, Todd?"

"Searching for you."

"Why?"

Why? Dammit. Wasn't that the same question he had been asking himself over the past nine hours? He stopped at a red light. "Because you don't belong out here." Her hair was escaping the rubber band holding it. Her dirt smudged face held those big Bambi eyes that resembled a deer in the headlights of an oncoming car. No. She didn't belong on the streets.

"I'm not going back to that place, that mission. The minds there are sick."

"True."

"And the hospital is for those who are ill."

"True." *Now what?* He hadn't thought farther than finding her. Now what was he going to do with her. He knew of a women's shelter, but they closed their doors after ten, it was going on eleven now.

Not that she'd be any safer there. The women in those places led hard lives.

"So, where are you taking me?"

He let out a long-suffering breath, and hoped he wasn't making a huge mistake. "Home."

~~~~

Todd's home was a small bungalow nestled in an older part of town. The streets were tree-lined and quiet. The yards were small, but not so much that he could hear every conversation his neighbors had, just the ones when voices were raised.

He walked around the car and opened her door. She either was accustomed to this, or had no idea how to open it. By her expression, he wasn't sure which was true.

Once inside, he tossed his keys on the table by the door and switched on the lights.

She walked behind him and glanced about the room. It was sparsely furnished with an old worn leathered sofa and two side chairs. He had a small fireplace that hadn't been lit in years, and a flat screen television hanging above it.

Todd disappeared around a corner and called

35

out. "Make yourself comfortable. Would you like something to drink?"

What the hell am I doing? He twisted the cap off a beer. The woman standing in his living room had been lying to him since they met, and yet he still brought her here, to his home.

He was breaking the ultimate rule of police work and getting personally involved. She wasn't a suspect in any crime. Not that it made him feel any better. "I have beer, wine or soda if you like."

"Wine would be nice." Her voice moved closer. Todd's gaze took in his bright kitchen and the few dishes sitting in the sink and a forgotten newspaper on the counter. What a mess.

She walked into the room and smiled.

He removed the wine from his refrigerator, poured her a glass, and handed it to her. "Have a seat. I'm going to make a sandwich, want one?" He'd missed lunch and dinner.

"Nay. This is fine."

He watched her eyes close as the wine went down her throat. Her features started to relax for the first time since he found her. "Feeling better?"

"Aye, I mean yes. Thank you."

"You really are from Scotland, aren't you?"

"Yes." She stopped the glass before it met her lips. "I mean, I think I am." She put the wine glass to the side and settled into one of the tall chairs.

"Uh-huh..." He watched her nerves return, and her lies. "Right." He tossed bread, lunchmeat, and lettuce on the counter.

"You live here alone?" she asked.

"Yeah." He stacked ham between the bread with a slice of cheese. "I tried roommates, but they didn't work out."

"Why not?"

"Different lifestyles, I guess. Some were pigs, never cleaning up after themselves. Others wanted to party all the time." He put his plate on the counter and moved to sit next to her.

"No family?"

"No." He took a bite.

"You don't have a housekeeper?"

"No."

"You do your own cleaning?" She sent him a puzzled look, as if she didn't believe him.

"You sound surprised. Did you grow up with housekeepers?" he asked without thinking.

He noticed when she opened her mouth to answer, but bit back her words.

He took another bite of his sandwich, chased it with beer, never taking his eyes off her.

Nerves dangled on her sleeve like fringe. Lying was new to her, but like any practiced art, she was getting better at it.

"Just tell me one thing." He looked away, giving her an out if she wanted to take it. "Are you in trouble with the law?"

"God no."

"Don't you mean, 'you don't think you are?'" he mocked.

She shifted in her seat. "I'm not in trouble with the law."

Her second honest answer. Maybe he was stupid for believing her, but he did. Then again, he needed to have his head examined by the department shrink after his actions on this day. He tempted his luck and asked her more. "What's your name?"

She reached for her drink, struggled with her

answer before she spoke. "My name is Myra."

"Myra what?"

"Please, Todd, I can't. You wouldn't understand."

"You would be surprised at what I understand, Myra." When she didn't give him any more he asked. "You're running from someone. Who? An ex-husband?"

"Nay, I've never married."

"Then who?"

"I can't tell you." She finished her wine and stared into the empty glass.

"And I can't help you if you don't tell me what you're running from." He wanted to be angry, and a part of him was, but the fear he sensed from her and his crazy need to protect her overshadowed his annoyance. God he hoped his dick wasn't interfering with his good sense.

"If you want me to leave I will. But I can tell you no more. I'm sorry. Truly, I am. You wouldn't understand." Her eyes leveled with his, challenging him.

He kept her gaze for a full minute before he pushed his plate aside, no longer interested in eating. "It's late. Let's get some sleep."

Myra followed him. "The bathroom's down the hall. If you need anything let me know." He watched her set her bag on the bed. "I'm just down the hall."

"Thank you."

You can thank me by trusting me. He wanted to scream, but didn't. Instead, he wished her goodnight and walked away.

Before he made it to his room, he heard her whisper, "I've already told you too much." He stopped dead in his tracks and looked back at the door to her room. It had been a long night, one he wouldn't soon forget. Maybe he could get her to open up more tomorrow.

Leaving his door slightly open, he listened to her movements. He heard the soft click of her door and the creak of the bed as it gave under her weight.

Now what the hell am I going to do?

~~~~

Myra woke early and lingered in the hot shower she was quickly growing to love. The endless supply of hot water washed away her trepidations.

She had slept better than in the hospital. In fact, she'd rested more than she had in weeks. Glancing at her reflection in the mirror, she ran a finger over the fading circles beneath her eyes. She had been so nervous about her journey into the future she hadn't slept for weeks prior to the trip.

There were so many things Tara had prepared her for, and so many she hadn't. Her wait for Lizzy was unexpected. Pulling a brush through her hair, she thought of the men who attacked her. They scared her more than she wanted to admit. The harsh reality of life without her family crushed down on her in those moments in the alley.

Yet the family was right in sending her to the future. Grainna needed a Druid virgin to break her curse and would have done everything within her power to capture Myra, and kill her.

She was on her own.

Except for maybe Officer Todd Blakely, who had acted as gallant as any knight. More so when she realized they shared a home for a full night and never once did she feel her virtue threatened.

Todd Blakely was no ordinary man. He knew she lied and still helped her, asking nothing in return. Well, perhaps a few answers, but that was all.

I'll make it up to him, she vowed silently.

After dressing in the only change of clothes she brought, she cleaned the clothes worn the previous day and placed them above the shower to dry before leaving the bathroom in search of food and Todd.

Todd stood in the kitchen making coffee. Closing her eyes, Myra savored the rich aroma. She was beginning to love coffee. No wonder Tara put it on the list of things to bring back with her when she went home.

Todd moved slowly, his eyes half open, appearing as if he had just stumbled out of bed and into the kitchen. His bare muscular chest narrowed to lean hips covered by a pair of baggy cotton pants made her instantly aware of the man. She'd seen knights remove their shirts on occasion after an intense battle or during heavy training, but Todd? Todd's ease with his nudity had her swallowing saliva down a dry throat. She licked her lips and prayed he wouldn't notice her unease.

~~~~

Watching from lowered lashes, Todd took in her bare feet and wet hair.

God she was beautiful. Fresh. He tried not to stare, but her face was a magnet. His body reacted recklessly, just like his mind had done the night before.

He hadn't slept well with her in the next room. It wasn't until the predawn hours that his lids finally shut. Now, he hovered over the coffee pot wishing the machine would move faster. He needed something to do with his hands other than picturing them on her.

"Good morning," she offered.

"You look rested."

"I am, thank you." She cleared her throat. "Your home is very quiet."

"Humm...coffee?" he asked when the pot was half full.

"Oh, yes, please. I just love your coffee here." She took the cup.

"They don't have coffee in Scotland?"

"Nothing like this I'm afraid." She smiled over the rim and pulled in the scent, savoring it.

"I thought Folgers was everywhere."

Myra sent a coy smile, but didn't add anything.

He moved around the kitchen, completely aware of her stare. His baggy sweat pants and full day and night's growth of beard had him squirming under her gaze. What was she thinking?

"Are you working today?"

"No. I go in tomorrow." He handed her a bowl of cereal and watched as she took her first bite. Surprise lit her face as she started to chew. "Don't tell me you don't have cereal in Scotland either?"

"I just can't get over how different everything tastes." She told him truthfully.

"Even cereal?"

Chewing, she avoided his question.

They ate in silence. Her peculiar behavior was laced with lies, but Todd wasn't awake enough to play verbal roulette.

She was going to answer some questions

today, he told himself. He would give her time to tie her tongue in knots, then pounce and get what he needed. If her silence were any indication of her wavering will to remain untruthful, then it wouldn't take long to crack her open.

"Do you know of an antique dealer near by?" she asked, catching Todd off guard.

"Antique dealer?"

"Aye."

"Not personally, but I'm sure there are a few. Why?"

"I have something that might be worth a bit of coin to sell. To help pay my way."

Interesting choice of words and it wasn't just the singing way she spoke. "What is it?" *And is it stolen?*

"I'll go get them." She left and returned with two objects covered in a cloth. She unwrapped an elegant pair of candlesticks.

He knew nothing about antiques. The ornately carved objects in front of him were beautiful, but he had no other appreciation for them than that. The jeweled bases were flashy and he imagined that if the stones were real they would be worth a lot of money. "Are they old?"

"Oh, yes. My family has owned them for many years." She gazed at them with loss.

"And they don't want them anymore?"

"My need to sell them outweighs the need to own them."

He picked one of them up. It was heavier than it looked. "This family of yours agrees with you?"

"Yes, they're the ones who told me to take them with me." She watched him examine her family heirloom. "They're not stolen, if that is what you're thinking."

He wasn't trying to hide his thoughts and wasn't surprised when she guessed his next question. "Can't help but wonder, me being a cop and all."

She snatched the stick from his hand. "I'm not a thief."

"Didn't say you were."

"But you thought it." She wrapped them both back up.

"True." He got up to pour them both more coffee. "What am I supposed to think? You've been lying about everything since I met you."

"I've never stolen anything in my life."

Placing his hands on the counter, Todd looked directly into her eyes. "Let's go over the facts as I see them. Here I have a beautiful, well-spoken woman who fakes amnesia to avoid questions. She has such a strong conviction about whatever it is she's hiding that she takes to the streets in a city she is unfamiliar with." He moved around the counter and stood next to her. "She has a family somewhere, but is unwilling or unable to ask for their help."

She looked down at her hands to avoid his eyes.

He touched her chin, forcing her to look at him. "This woman shows me a pair of candlesticks that look expensive, and I'm supposed to believe they aren't stolen? I'm gullible, Myra, not stupid."

"If you think so little of me, why are you helping me?" she whispered.

He watched her eyes dart back and forth between his. "I don't know." He moved closer, his hand left her chin and rested on her shoulder. He really should walk away but her scent drew him in.

"I promise you, I didn't steal them."

"Prove it."

~~~~

Myra swallowed hard. "I can't." She stood up and backed away from him. He was cutting off her air. His nearness conflicted with her body and brain.

"Why?"

She gave him her back, and tried to collect herself. "You wouldn't understand."

"Try me."

"This is going nowhere. I should leave." Myra started toward her room.

He reached out and pulled her back and into his arms. His free hand caught her wet hair on the back of her head and held it. His eyes searched hers for a brief moment before he swore, "Dammit." Then his lips crushed down to hers.

She hadn't expected it and stood stunned and unable to move. His assault on her mouth was as torturous as it was pleasant. His hungry kiss was laced with anger. No one had ever kissed her like this, no one would have dared.

When his other hand swept up to hold her head in place, she swayed toward him. His tongue probed hers, demanding. Once her lips parted, he moved in deeper. The intimacy of their kiss, his complete possession of her senses, had her swimming. Butterflies exploded inside of her when his kiss went on.

Stunned at first, she simply let him in. Yet as the kiss grew, her own desire swept over her. Her timid hand, clutched at her side, moved to his waist.

Todd groaned and pressed her to the wall.

His hard frame brought awareness to every crease of her body. Myra's fingers touched the bare skin of his warm welcoming chest. A surge of heat pooled deep in her stomach and caused an aching deep within the folds of her sex.

He moved away almost as quickly as he had taken possession.

Breathless, her eyes stayed shut, afraid to look at him. She was embarrassed somehow, even though she had nothing to be embarrassed about.

"That shouldn't have happened," he spoke through the fog.

"Aye, you're right about that." She dared a look. Saw understanding eyes.

"You drive me to do things I wouldn't otherwise."

"I'm sorry."

"No, you're not." His expression searched hers again. "Give me something, Myra, something to start the trust."

His request sounded more like a plea.

"MacCoinnich, my surname is MacCoinnich. My home is in Scotland, but I cannot return there yet."

Todd nodded and took a deep breath.

"I'm going to take a shower, Myra MacCoinnich, and then we can find an antique dealer to see what it is you have."

She glanced toward the door, wondered briefly if she should leave, but knew she wouldn't.

"Promise me you won't go."

Did he read her thoughts? "I promise."

Chapter Four

After visiting two antique shops, and finding them operated by average minimum wage clerks, Todd decided to take their chances at an auction house that specialized in antiques.

He knew he was in the right place the minute they went through the alarmed door with a security guard standing by.

Todd immediately asked for whoever bought items or commissioned them to sell. While they were waiting, Myra walked the floor.

A candelabrum stood on one of the massive tables in the center of the room. Her fingers lingered on the piece as she sighed.

Todd watched her touch the ends of it and smile. "You would need a big room to fit that piece."

"Yes, you would."

"I wonder why it's so large." It stood almost four feet tall and had room for over a dozen candles.

"Back when this was made, it needed to light a large dining hall or room. We, er, they didn't have lights like you do today."

"Ahh, just what I love to hear, someone who knows mid-century art." The proprietor wore a three-piece suit and an extra fifty pounds. His beard was neat, short and just like him. "Welcome to Graystones." He extended his hand to both of them. When he turned to Myra he said, "You look very familiar, have we met before?"

"No, I'm afraid not."

"My mistake. My name is Robert Harrison. I was told you were looking for me."

"Are you in charge of buying antiques?" Todd asked once they sat down next to the man's desk.

"Some we buy, some we commission for sale. What is it you want to sell?"

Myra removed the candlesticks out of her bag and un-wrapped them one by one. "I hate to part with them, but I find I must." She lovingly put them on his desk.

He reached for his glasses, set them on the end of his gin blossom nose, and proceeded to stare. "Amazing. Where did you get them?"

"They've been in my family for years."

"Your family is from Scotland?" he asked.

"Aye."

"You can tell that by looking at those?" Todd questioned.

"That and the accent gave it away." Mr. Harrison laughed at his own joke. "See here?" he pointed to markings on the base. "Celtic. And here you see words, most likely Gaelic. I'll need to look up their meaning."

"North, south, east and west," Myra told them.

Both men gazed at her. Todd continued to stare when Harrison went back to his examination. "Yes, most likely you're right." He switched his glasses for a glass one used to examine the stones. "Fabulous."

"What?" Todd moved to the edge of his seat.

"The gems are not only real, but rare and of the finest quality. My guess is it was made sometime in the fourteenth century."

"Twelfth," Myra corrected.

"My dear, I do know my centuries, and this is likely fourteenth or even fifteenth century." His tone was condescending yet softly spoken.

"You're mistaken. My great, great..." She stopped, shook her head. "A distant relative commissioned those made as a wedding gift for his wife. The story has been passed down in my family for generations, generations dating back to the twelfth century."

"Well, we'll have to see about that." He sat them down and removed the eyeglass. "Are you sure you want to sell them?"

Todd interrupted before she could speak, "We want to see what they're worth." If they were stolen, and he couldn't help but wonder if they were, selling them could cost him his badge, and land her in jail.

"That may take a few days. We'll do a carbon dating and cross reference them. Would you mind leaving them with me while we do that?"

Myra's attention turned to him, uncertainty written on her face.

"I assure you they are safe here, Miss. We have a form for you to fill out and our insurance is secure as is our building."

"All right." Todd took the clipboard from him and filled out the questionnaire. "Feel free to call me as soon as you know what they're worth."

They stood to leave. Todd thanked the man again, and then asked, "So if you had to venture a guess, what would you estimate their value to be?"

"Ah. Well, don't quote me, but I'd estimate their worth around one hundred thousand."

Todd felt his jaw drop.

"Each."

Once the outside air hit their faces, Todd grabbed her elbow and silently marched her down the street to where he had parked his car.

She practically had to run to keep up with his pace. The dark glasses covering his eyes kept her from seeing his expression. But if she had to guess, she would say he was upset. Very upset.

"What's the matter?" she asked.

He said nothing.

"You're hurting my arm." Myra stopped and tried to pull out of his grip.

He rounded on her in fury. "What the hell have you got me into? Two hundred thousand dollars?" He glanced around and lowered his voice.

"Is that a lot of coin?"

He jerked off his sunglasses and stared at her. "This is no time to joke, Myra."

"I'm not."

"If those candlesticks are stolen, not only will I lose my job, but we, and I emphasize *we*, will both end up in jail."

His hand still held her arm, his fingers gripped into her flesh. She took her free hand, placed it on his, and added a little spark. Instantly, he let go.

"They are not stolen!" She put two feet between them. "I don't appreciate you calling me a thief. Or haven't I made myself clear?"

He studied his hand. "Yeah, well, excuse me for having a hard time believing a woman who has made an art-form out of lying since I met her. Now that my face is associated with yours, and those antiques, you'll have to forgive me for being concerned about my reputation, not to mention my freedom."

"If you're that concerned, why help me? Is there some law, Officer Blakely, forcing you to assist me? Forgive me for not knowing." Two could play at sarcasm, and his was making her angry. "Poor little Scottish me, doesn't quite know all of your American laws." She placed both hands on her hips, her hair fell to her waist.

People gathered around and watched their exchange. Todd tilted his head at a man he noticed leering. He grabbed her elbow once again.

Instinctively, Myra clasped his hand and willed more fire into her spark, forcing him to let her go.

He jumped back this time, waving his tingling hand. "How the hell did you do that?"

"Just one of my many secrets, Officer Blakely. Now if you would be so kind as to take me back to your home so I may retrieve my belongings, I'll be getting out of your life."

"Fine!" He reached for her again, but stopped when her eyes warned him not to touch her. Instead, he opened the car door and waited for her to sit before slamming it shut behind her.

~~~~

He drove in circles. Had in fact passed the same In and Out Burger three times before he stopped the car.

"What are we doing here?" Myra asked.

"Eating." He got out of the car and waited for her to follow. When she didn't, he jerked open her door. "Coming?"

"Nay."

"Get out of the car, Myra."

"Nay."

"Dammit, woman, you are driving me to drink." He reached down to pull her out.

"Don't you touch me." Her voice was ice. "I'm not accustomed to being man-handled, and I don't want to hurt you."

"Ha! You hurt me? I don't think so."

She pushed the car door wider, and stepped up beside him. "Try me. Try me and let's-just-see-how-far-you-get." With each word, she tapped his chest giving him a little jolt.

His face sobered. As did his mood.

"I see I've made my point." Myra shut the car door, and stormed toward the restaurant.

"Where are you going?"

"To eat. Fending off unwanted hands takes a bit of energy, and since you caused it, you can pay." She marched into the red and white checkered building, leaving a stunned Officer Blakely behind.

He ordered for them both, then took pity on her when she tried to make the soda come out of the machine. Once seated, Myra watched everyone but him.

When the food arrived at the table, she stared at it. It wasn't until he started eating that Myra followed his lead.

With the first bite of a double cheeseburger with all the trimmings, her eyes closed.

A small part of him wanted to remain angry with her. Yet, when she sat across from him looking like she could spark fire out of her eyes one minute then completely enthralled with her meal the next, he all but melted.

The dimple on the right side of her cheek peeked out. He hadn't seen that since the first day he had met her, and made a mental note to try and cause it to happen more often.

"So, how do you do that?"

"Do what?" She picked up a French fry, popped it in her mouth.

"You know," he pointed a finger at her, made a tapping gesture and added, "that shocking thing?"

"Oh, that."

"Yeah, that."

"I picked it up when I was a child." She sipped her soda and wiggled her nose. "How did you learn to be so untrusting?"

"I picked it up when I became a cop."

"I tell you what." She wiped her face and put the napkin back in her lap. "No more lies. If you ask something I can't answer, I'll tell you so."

"You mean won't tell me."

"Okay, won't tell you. I have my reasons, Todd, and they are bigger than you, me and everyone around us. 'Tis the honest to God's truth." Her eyes never left his.

"All right. But you have to promise something."

"What?"

"That you will tell me the truth, all of it, at some point."

"You won't believe me. But if that is what you need to hear, then I'll make that promise. Before I return home, I'll tell you my story."

"So you plan on returning to Scotland?"

"Yes. When I can do so safely."

"It's not safe now?"

"If it was, do you think I would be here?"

Good point. "Have you ever been to California before?"

"Nay, 'tis my first time."

"How did you end up in Magicland?" He saw her struggle with an answer.

"That I can not tell you."

And he probably didn't want to know. Breaking and entering was a crime, one he couldn't ignore. Or at least shouldn't.

He gathered their trash and stood to leave. "Well, since you haven't been to California before, I suppose you might like to see some of the sights."

Chapter Five

Todd started with the beach, always a popular destination spot for tourists. Myra was no exception. Deserted, except for the occasional die-hard surfer whose wet suit kept them warm in the cold waters, they had the beach to themselves.

Myra pointed and asked what the men did in the water on their boards.

"Don't they have TV's where you come from?"

"There are no TV's in my home."

"What about neighbors?"

"We live far in the country."

He accepted her answers, explained the art of surfing, and enjoyed the play of expressions cross her beautiful face. She kicked off her shoes and let the cold winter ocean foam around her pale skin.

Todd knelt in the sand and dug his hands in. A sand crab emerged in his palm. She squirmed when he placed the small creature in hers. It moved quickly, causing her to squeal and drop it. The creature burrowed into the sand at an unimaginable speed.

"Where did it go?"

"Hiding from the big giants I think."

Todd took her hand and helped her stand, then kept it in his. A slight blush rose to her cheeks. He wondered if she was as innocent as she seemed. When he'd kissed her earlier, she felt virgin shy under his lips, which made him draw back when all he really wanted to do was plunge forward, consequences be damned.

Where was her family? Why had they deserted her? He would have his answers, one way or another.

They walked along one of the many boardwalks and peeked into some of the shops. At the third one, Todd realized Myra pined for some of the clothes hanging from the racks.

"You should get that." He held up a blouse she noticed. "It would look good on you."

"Maybe after the candlesticks are sold."

He had forgotten she didn't have any money. "You need clothes. And mine won't fit you very well." He took several items off the rack and thrust them at her. "Here, go try them on."

"What do you mean?"

"You know, see if they fit."

"I don't have any means of purchasing them." She thrust the clothes back to his hands.

"I do."

"No. I can't."

"You can pay me back."

She looked at the copper colored skirt and matching blouse. "Are you sure?"

"Go." He pushed her toward the dressing rooms.

She went in and out several times. He met each outfit with a nod of approval or a shake of the head.

The clerk happily made choices and brought them over for her to try.

Todd sat back as she paraded the clothes for him. Once in a while, she giggled and sometimes she blushed. More than once she stayed in the dressing room stating the dress 'simply isn't appropriate.' Todd couldn't remember enjoying watching a woman shop as he did her.

At the counter, the clerk helping Myra added a few under-things that she 'really did need'. Todd handed over his credit card and smiled.

Wearing a calf length skirt, a blouse, and a pair of shoes to match, Myra posed, seeming more at ease. "This is lovely. How can I ever thank you?"

Her dimples showed again, making his heart beat a little too fast. "You just did."

"Once Mr. Harrison calls back with a price, I can pay you back for all of this."

He grasped her hand, pointed to a large fish tank in a store window, and changed the subject. He wanted her worry-free. He might not be able to keep her that way for long, but he would try.

At dinner in an outside café, they talked about the difference between the weather in Scotland and California.

Myra asked questions about everything she saw. He attributed her curiosity to being from another country. Once in awhile, he thought her questions were a little strange, but he kept his observations to himself.

When they finally made it home, it was almost midnight.

"I had a wonderful time," Myra said as they walked through the door.

Todd followed her to her room, and tossed the bags on the bed. "Good, I'm glad." He turned to see her studying him.

Her gaze skirted to the floor. "Thank you."

"You're welcome."

She didn't look up. "'Tis late."

"Yes, time for bed."

She blushed brighter than he had ever seen. "Oh, ah..."

"Good night, Myra." He lifted her chin, brushed his lips against hers in a brief caress, and then left the room.

~~~~

"Good night," she whispered when he was gone.

It took forever to fall asleep, and once she finally did, Todd was waking her up.

"Hey," he sat on the edge of the bed. "I'm going to work."

Her eyes drifted open. The sun hadn't risen, and Todd stared at her strangely. "What?"

"Work. I have to go to work."

"Oh..." Myra tried to sit up in bed, only to have his hand keep her in place.

"You sleep. I'll call you in a few hours."

She stopped trying to sit up, leaned back against the pillow, and smiled up at him. He wore his full uniform and looked every bit an officer of the law.

"Make yourself at home." He brushed a hair from her face and got up to leave.

"Sir Blakely?" she murmured.

"Yes."

"Be safe and Godspeed."

~~~~

The day might have been the longest of his life. It began with a mound of paperwork, starting and finishing with one subject, Myra MacCoinnich. Of course, according to the record, she was still Jane Doe #33, and he had yet to correct it.

Jake sat at his desk, going over his own pile of papers. "So, did you meet up with Melissa over the

57

weekend?"

"No." Todd had broken it off with Melissa several weeks ago, but since Jake liked his ex-girlfriend, he kept asking about her.

"So? What did you do?"

"Not much," he lied. Jake would never understand why he took in Myra. Hell, he hadn't even figured it out yet.

"Not me, I watched the game with Jim and the boys, then spent some quality time with Sheila. If you know what I mean." Jake laughed.

"I know what you mean."

"I had a fantastic weekend."

"Glad to hear it," Todd said out of the corner of his mouth.

"Nelson, Blakely," Jim yelled from the door to the room. "Someone's here for you two."

A tall, thin, attractive woman stood next to Jim. She wore a smock over a pair of jeans and a t-shirt. The smock was covered in what appeared to be paint. A small smudge of green must have missed the apron and hit her chin. She didn't seem at all concerned about her appearance when she marched over to them.

"I came as fast as I could." Her paint-laden hand thrust out in greeting.

Dumbfounded as to who she was, Todd said, "That's great. Who are you?"

"I'm sorry, I'm Liz McAllister. Do you have any word about my sister Tara?"

~~~~

It was a marvelous day, one Myra would never forget.

After waking, and one extraordinarily long shower, she padded around Todd's kitchen snacking on almost everything. Although his cabinets were only half-full, everything in them was new and exciting.

She left the television on while she explored Todd's home. At the Keep, she occasionally helped the kitchen staff, but nothing in this kitchen looked the same as the one from her time.

His freezer had boxes of food she had never seen before. Lasagna, Pizza, Thai Chicken with Noodles. She couldn't pronounce the names of the dishes, let alone know what they contained. There were directions printed on the boxes. She fingered a dish called a Chicken Bake and felt confident she could prepare a meal from this century for Todd. Once she found everything she thought she needed, she smiled with an overwhelming sense of pride.

She turned off the television set, and fiddled with the black box that sat next to it. Out of nowhere, music blared into the room.

Startled, Myra almost knocked over a lamp in an effort to lower the volume. Once she turned the correct knob, a nice, steady, quieter beat pulsed out of the smaller boxes around the room.

It was pleasing with a quick-tempo, much different than the music she was used to. The man who sang with the music had perfect pitch. Without thinking, Myra found herself moving to the beat.

Tara had been right about the music, she would miss it when she went home. For now, she danced, smiled and giggled at some of the words in the song.

~~~~

"Have a seat, Miss McAllister," Todd offered.

59

She looked between the two men, apprehension written on her face. "This is about Tara, isn't it?"

"Not directly, no." Jake sat to her side, Todd behind the desk.

"Then what?" Disappointment laced her words.

Todd brought out the picture of Myra he had buried in papers on his desk. "Have you ever seen this woman before?"

Liz glanced at the photo. "No."

"Take a good look."

"Who is she?" She studied the picture before handing it back. "And what does this have to do with my sister?"

"We're not sure who she is." Jake took the photo, tossed it at Todd. "She ended up in a hospital a few days ago with amnesia. The only thing she remembered was your name."

"My name? Why? I've never seen her before in my life."

"We were hoping you could help us with that. Since you don't recognize her, maybe you can't."

Todd let his partner do the talking.

"You said this didn't have anything directly to do with the disappearance of my sister. What do you mean by that?"

"Just a hunch really," Todd finally spoke. "This woman." He held up the picture. "Has a very distinct Scottish accent. Your sister was last seen with two men with similar accents, isn't that right?"

"That's what I was told." Hope filled her eyes. "Do you think she may know something about Tara?"

"She has amnesia, Miss McAllister. She doesn't remember anything," Jake said.

Liz McAllister clutched her hands together and rubbed them hard. Todd had seen the action many times in the past. "Can I talk to her?"

"That might be a little difficult. She left the hospital two days ago."

Obviously disappointed she asked, "Where did she go?"

Todd had to keep his mouth shut and let his partner go on. He told her they had no idea where she was, and no authority to spend valuable resources to find her.

"But if she knows something about my sister, you need to find her."

"We don't know if she has information about her."

"And you don't know if she doesn't. Please..." Liz stopped and lowered her voice. "You have to find her."

The woman seated across from him was obviously tormented with the loss of her sister. What did Myra know about Tara McAllister's disappearance? If she knew anything? Was he harboring a fugitive in his home? *Damn.* All these unanswered questions rolling around in his head were giving him a headache.

"I traced her to a shelter, but she left. Maybe she'll go back. We'll let you know if we find her."

Liz stood to leave and shook their hands again. "Please call me." A heavy sigh escaped her lips. "I'm desperate. I was told every day that passes since my sister disappeared is a day closer to her death. If this amnesic woman knows me, even if I don't know her, maybe she knows something." Liz McAllister blinked back tears and walked away.

~~~~

The phone rang. On the second ring, Myra heard the metallic click of Todd's machine sitting by the phone. Through it, she heard his voice. "Myra, pick up."

"I'm here," she called out to the machine.

"Pick up."

Myra held the small black box and pressed the TALK button. Tentatively she placed it to her ear. "Hello? Todd?"

"There you are, what took you so long?"

"Ah, well."

"Never mind." His voice was curt. "How is everything there?"

"Good, fine." Something was bothering him, Myra could sense it. "I'm getting ready to cook dinner. What time will you be here?"

"About four-thirty."

"I'll see you then."

"Yeah. Hey, Myra, do me a favor. Stay in the house."

"Is it not safe?" she asked.

"Yes, no. I'll explain when I get home."

"Okay."

"I've got to go."

"Todd?" Myra wanted to ask what bothered him, but changed her mind.

"Yes?"

"Be safe."

"See you at four-thirty."

~~~~

What happened? She had read the directions, and still the smoke billowed from the oven. The boxes of food melted into the wire racks. She had obviously missed something vital for the success of the meal.

Even though the meal smoked dangerously, she hadn't burned the house down. The dishtowel that caught on fire didn't really count. Who knew the heated rod in the oven would be so hot? Besides, the water flowing through the pipes in the sink quickly put the fire out. However, the windows needed to be opened to air-out the room, and that made the whole house cold.

She rummaged in the refrigerator until she found the makings for sandwiches. Not the meal she had planned, but it would have to do.

Myra brought in a few logs Todd had drying by the back fence for a fire. Myra set them in the hearth and opened her hands. Flames caught on the log and brought a smile to her face.

Chapter Six

Todd thought he stepped into the wrong house. Music played on his stereo, a fire blazed in his fireplace, and there was the smell of something cooking coming from the kitchen. Not cooking so much as burning. The unmistakable scent of burnt plastic filled the room.

He spent the better part of the day trying to structure a speech to lay on Myra about how she needed to be straight with him or she would have to leave. Now seeing all she had tried to do made him forget every last word of his prepared speech.

In the kitchen, she bent over the oven, and he admired the view. She wore one of the outfits he bought for her the day before. A simple pair of blue jeans fit snug to her hips and made the most appealing sight he'd seen all day.

He shook his head. That kind of thinking wasn't going to get him anywhere except deeper into whatever trouble she was in.

"Hey."

Myra turned and noticed him staring. Her dimples broke out along with her smile. He could get used to that.

"You've been busy." He moved to the counter, set his sunglasses and keys on it.

"A little." She moved to the refrigerator, pulled out a beer and handed it to him. "I hope you don't mind."

No woman had ever made him a meal in his

home. Sure, he'd been invited to dinner by women at their place, but never his. It was an unwritten rule of bachelorhood not to let a female anywhere near your kitchen. If you did, they would move right in and before you knew it, you would be saying 'I do'. And Todd didn't.

"Did something burn?"

His eyes circled the room, and her ears glowed red in what Todd quickly identified as embarrassment. "I'm not as adept in the kitchen as I thought," she told him. "I did the best I could. I hope it's okay?"

"Of course. I am going to change clothes."

~~~~

Myra stared after him, wondering what she had done wrong. She thought he would be pleased to come home and not have to cook for himself. It was the least she could do to repay him for all his generosity.

She finished setting the food on his table, poured herself some wine, then waited for him to return.

The meal was full of awkward comments and difficult moments. Gone was the previous day's lightheartedness and fun. Something was bothering Todd, and he wasn't ready to talk about it.

It got to the point where they both ate in silence. Finally, when they were cleaning the dishes, she summoned up the nerve to ask, "What's bothering you? Did something happen at work?"

He stared out the window avoiding her eyes. "Yeah, something happened."

"Do you want to talk about it?"

He looked up. "Elizabeth McAllister came into

the station today."

She flinched.

"How do you know her?"

"I don't."

"Then why did you give us her name?"

Myra put their dirty dishes in the sink. "I was told she might help me when I got here."

"By whom?"

She waited a beat and turned toward him. "I can't tell you."

"Why not?"

"Because I can't, not yet anyway."

"Dammit, Myra, why not!" He dropped the plate in the sink. It broke into several pieces.

"You wouldn't—"

"Understand," he finished for her. "Well understand this—Elizabeth McAllister walked into the station today holding out hope that we had some word where her sister is, and thought maybe, just maybe, we had some answers for her. How do I know you didn't have something to do with that?"

"I had nothing to do with Tara's disappearance."

"You say her name like you know her."

"I do."

"How can I believe you had nothing to do with her vanishing into thin air?"

"I didn't," she cried.

"You're lying!"

"I told you I wouldn't lie!" she yelled back.

"Where is she?"

"I can't tell you."

He had backed her into a corner, verbally and literally. She felt the wall, and saw his hands shoot out, caging her in. "Then you know where she is."

66

"Aye."

"Is she alive?"

"What do you think I am? A monster?" Her eyes poured fury on him. "Of course she's alive."

"Why hasn't she come home?" He fired questions faster than she could process them, forcing her answers before she realized what she said.

"She can't."

"Why not?"

He moved in closer, she couldn't catch her breath. "It isn't safe. Don't you understand that? 'Tis dangerous for Tara to return here." She trembled, and cursed herself when she felt a tear fall out of her eye.

Spent, she stood there shaking, and unable to control it. *Damn him!* Damn him for pushing her like this.

He cursed himself under his breath and tried to gather her close. She held herself stiff in his arms. "I'm sorry."

She didn't cry, not really. A few tears trailed down her cheeks, but she refused to fall into the abyss of depression.

When he let her go, she put distance between them and started to clean up the broken dish in the sink.

"Let me get that."

She stopped, her words void of emotion. "If I had somewhere to go, I would leave here this minute. If I could go home safely, I would pop out of here in the blink of an eye." Literally, she thought. "But since I cannot do either, I'm stuck. So unless you are going to make me leave, can you please give me a little peace so I can gather my thoughts? Or would you still like to interrogate me?"

Maybe she wasn't being fair to him under the circumstances, but she'd had just about all she could take for one night.

~~~~

He left her alone and stood next to the fire. Flames lapped up the wood, bringing a nice warm glow to the room. He couldn't remember the last time he lit a fire. It would have been nice if he wasn't so miserable.

Sometime later, Myra returned to the room holding a piece of paper. "This is a letter from Tara to her sister. I promised Tara I would give it directly to Lizzy as soon as I could. You obviously don't trust me, so here." She handed him the letter sealed in wax. "I trust you not to read it." She swallowed hard. "Take it to her."

Todd grasped the letter. The paper was unlike any he had seen before. He had no idea how much information he held in his hand, but if he opened it and read it himself, Myra would know.

"Why are you giving me this?"

"Because I want you to trust me. Because I'm not the monster you think I am."

He wanted to stop her when she turned to leave, but didn't know what to say if he did. The misery etched in her eyes was something he knew he put there. Knew he couldn't erase.

~~~~

He was gone when she woke the next morning. He'd left a note by the door asking her to meet him at a nearby park at twelve-thirty.

She was never one to exercise patience. Left with nothing to do but wait and worry, she

68

manufactured a dozen reasons why Todd wanted to meet her outside his home.

Did he want her to leave? Was this his way of making her? Could he have her imprisoned for not revealing where Tara was? More importantly, would he?

She thought of his lips on hers during their one shared moment, remembering how quickly he melted her resolve. She wanted to believe he would trust her now, even if she had given him so little to trust.

Once again, she pined for her family, and for her mother's counsel.

~~~~

Todd asked Elizabeth McAllister to stop by the park on her lunch hour, thirty minutes before Myra was supposed to meet him.

His plan was simple. Give Miss McAllister the letter, and let her read it. If she wasn't satisfied with its content, he would arrest Myra when she arrived.

His stomach clenched at the thought of putting handcuffs on her, but she left him no choice. *She knows where the missing woman is and refuses to tell me.*

He pulled the letter out twice, fully intending to read it before giving it to McAllister. Each time, he put it back after picturing Myra's striking brown eyes asking for his trust.

At exactly the time Myra should have been leaving his home, he stood in the park waiting for Miss McAllister.

Liz looks like her sister, he thought, watching Elizabeth walk toward him. Her hair was shorter than the photos he'd seen of Tara, and Liz's was strawberry blonde. She was terribly thin, most likely from the stress. Having a missing family member probably took away her appetite. He couldn't help feeling sorry for her.

"Miss McAllister, thank you for meeting me." Todd shook her hand, and asked her to sit.

"You know something, don't you?" She left her sunglasses on and stared at him.

"I might."

~~~~

Liz looked at Officer Blakely and saw a torn man. She had a feeling when he called her an hour ago that she was finally going to hear something about Tara. It had been over five months since her sister dropped off the face of the earth, leaving a gaping hole in her and Simon's life. "I'm listening."

He drew in a long, audible breath then let it out slowly. "The woman in the hospital, the one who gave us your name, claims to know where your sister is." Todd reached into his pocket for the letter. "She asked me to give this to you."

Liz looked at the sealed paper with her name written on top.

A trembling hand went to her lips, covering the cry that escaped, "My God."

"What is it?"

She finally sat and took off the sunglasses clouding her view. "It's Tara's writing."

She ripped off the seal, pulled out the uneven parchment, and started to read.

Dearest Lizzy,

I have started this letter four times now, unsure of how to tell you what you need to know.

Forgive me if I leave things out, and listen to Myra, as she will fill in all the blanks.

First, know that I am safe. I can only guess at what you and Simon have been through since I left. And for that I am so very sorry. But I am safe, and oh, so happy, Lizzy. I have found my Knight in Shining Armor. The one you always told me to wait for. He is the most wonderful man and I cannot imagine my life without him. His name is Duncan MacCoinnich. He is the same man who I'm sure by now the police are looking for in regards to my disappearance.

I could go on and on about him and the life we are living. I can't go into details in this letter in case it gets into the wrong hands. Besides, if I wrote everything that has happened, you would toss this letter in a fire and claim it was forged. Again, I ask that you listen to Myra. She is my sister-in-law now, and more than that, a blood sister by choice. Remember?

Myra needs your help, Lizzy. It wasn't safe for her to stay here, so her family sent her there. I know you won't turn your back on her and in turn, on me.

The Gypsy woman from the Renaissance Faire, the one Cassy and I attended, is very dangerous. I'm sure you can find her picture, look at it, study it, and I beg you to stay away from her. If she ever comes near you or Simon, run.

She is, in part, the reason I cannot return to you, at least not at this time.

Paper is sparse here, and I can't write any more than I have. Know I love you with all my heart. Let Simon know Auntie Tara is happy, and if I can, I will visit someday.

Love, Tara

Todd watched her silent tears fall. Slowly, she read the letter. An occasional gasp or sigh was all she uttered. She read it twice before shutting her eyes and giving into emotion.

"Are you okay?" What a stupid question, of course she wasn't okay.

"She's alive. Thank God, she's alive."

"Can I see the letter?" Todd put out his hand.

Liz shook her head and put the letter in her purse.

"That could be evidence."

She was getting up to leave, and Todd was desperate for answers.

"If you thought that, you wouldn't have brought it to me without reading it," she concluded. "Where is Myra? I have to talk to her."

He looked around the park, spotted her staring at them from the far side. When Liz's eyes found her, her lips lifted in a smile.

"How do you know you can trust her?" he asked.

"Tara told me to."

~~~~

Myra saw him sitting on a bench talking to a very attractive woman. In the time it took for her heart to lunge in her chest, she realized it was Lizzy sitting next to Todd.

He had given her the letter, just as she asked. Maybe he trusted her after all.

The two exchanged words, and even from a distance Myra could see Lizzy wiping tears from her eyes.

When they both looked up and saw her, she

took it as her cue and walked toward them with a calmness she didn't feel.

Myra spoke first. "You are just as Tara described. More beautiful in fact."

"Is she okay? I know the letter said she was, but is she really?"

"Oh, Lizzy. She is better than okay, she and my brother make a lovely couple. She misses you so much."

"Call me Liz, no one calls me Lizzy, except Tara."

"Then I must call you Lizzy. We are sisters, all of us."

Liz glanced over her shoulder where Todd stood silent, watching them. "I have so many questions."

"You will have more before this day is done."

"Ladies?" he interrupted them. "Would either of you mind telling me what is going on here?"

Myra watched his eyes shift between them both, waiting for one of them to speak. "Thank you, for trusting me."

His jaw started to twitch. "Don't thank me yet, Myra. I'm not sure I've done the right thing. Miss McAllister here seems to think everything is fine after reading that letter. Would either of you mind telling me what it says?"

They both stood silent.

"Great. That's just perfect." His police radio squawked in his ear, taking his attention away from them. "I've got to go," he said after a brief contact with the voice on the other line. "But I'm not done with this yet. I'll see you when I get home." He pointed an accusing finger at Myra then ran off to his squad car.

"You're living with him?" Liz asked once he was gone.

"No...well, I guess..." His car sped off, with lights and sirens blaring.

"Cute. Very cute."

Myra gave a quick laugh. "You sound just like your sister."

They both sat on the bench. "Where is she?" Liz jumped right in.

"Scotland. With my brother and the rest of my family."

"Why can't she call?"

"There are no phones."

Liz started to ask another question, Myra stopped her.

"Let me start at the beginning. But I warn you, some of what I'm going to say will be difficult to believe. You might even think me mad before I am done with my story."

Liz took a deep cleansing breath and settled in for Myra's tale.

"My family, and now Tara, live in MacCoinnich Keep in Scotland. In the year 1576."

Lizzy laughed. A short explosion of disbelief.

"Please, hear me out. I know this sounds crazy, but please listen. We are Druids. All of us, even Tara and you. We have certain gifts, powers, which separate us from all others. Grainna, the woman Tara warned you about, is the most powerful evil Druid who ever existed. She murdered countless people in her quest to gain more power. Many years ago, the Ancients stripped that power and sent her to this time. My brothers were sent here last summer to stop Grainna from finding a Druid virgin and regaining those powers. Tara's life was in danger in this time, so Duncan and Fin brought her to our time to keep her alive."

Lizzy put her hand up, stopping her from going on. "You want me to believe that my sister is sitting in some castle in the sixteenth century?"

"Aye. She is."

"And you're some type of witch with powers?"

"Druid, not witch. My gifts are part of who I am. I was born with these gifts, like both you and Tara."

"I don't believe you." Lizzy got up to leave.

She expected that. "If I can prove it, will you listen to the rest of my story?"

Arms laced defensively across her chest, Liz turned to her. "Prove it."

"All Druids have some abilities. Each person's is different from the next. My strongest gift is the movement of the wind." Out of nowhere, the wind around them swirled, causing Myra's hair to pull back as if she faced a storm. Just as quickly, it ceased.

Lizzy's mouth gaped, then shut. "How do I know you did that?"

Myra looked around to see if others watched. Two women sat on a blanket a few yards away while their children tossed a ball back and forth, an elderly couple walked hand and hand beyond them. Being careful not to draw attention to them, Myra stood and took two steps away from the bench. "Please sit down."

The bench moved half a foot in their direction. Enough so that Lizzy saw it, but no one else would. "I speak the truth. When we are alone I can give you a better demonstration. It isn't safe out here where we could be spotted."

Speechless, Lizzy sat.

"My mother has visions, visions the Ancients use to communicate with our family. Shortly after Duncan and Tara married, her vision warned us about my safety."

"So your family sent you here, away from the danger." Lizzy's words were more a statement than a question.

"Aye." Myra swallowed hard. "I believe Grainna managed to escape back to my time and is there now searching for a virgin."

"And since Tara is married, she no longer fits the bill."

"Fits the bill?"

"Sorry, I mean Grainna can't break her curse by killing Tara."

"Exactly. My family sent me because—"

"You're still a Druid virgin," Lizzy finished for her. She stood and started to pace.

"Aye."

"This is really hard to swallow. I mean believe," she said after catching Myra's eye.

"I understand your hesitation, but I swear all I say is the truth. Tara's letter should offer some measure of proof."

"So, what is it you want from me?"

Myra cast her eyes to her hands resting in her lap. "I need shelter while I'm here. I welcomed Todd's generosity, but feel as if I'm overstaying my welcome."

Lizzy swept a trembling hand over her face. "I have a son to consider."

"Simon. Tara told me of him."

"Then she must have explained my need to

keep him safe."

Myra stood and stepped closer, grasping Lizzy's hand. "Please don't worry yourself. I've delivered a wagon-load of information for you to absorb. Think of what I've told you, what I've said. Todd will not leave me on the street."

"Okay. Damn this is crazy. You believe I'm a Druid? As well as Simon and Tara?"

"I know you are."

"I can't move objects with my mind."

"All our gifts are unique, different to each of us. Surely, you must have noticed some extra sense. A calmness or knowing something without being told?"

"Not me. Simon maybe," Lizzy's voice trailed off in thought.

"Tell me."

She sat back down and stared in the distance. "Simon said from the beginning that Tara was alive. When Cassy realized Tara wasn't coming home, Simon stared us both in the eye and said, 'A visitor would come and tell us where she is.' Holy shit, that's you."

"I look forward to meeting your son."

"Yeah, well, not today." Lizzy stood, dusted her hands on her pants, and took in a deep breath before pushing it out. "I need to think about all of this."

"I understand." The sting of rejection held tight in Myra's chest. She shouldn't have expected Lizzy to run to her with open arms.

~~~~

Accessory after the fact. At the very least, that was what he was if Tara McAllister was a kidnap victim. Even if she wasn't, he was keeping vital information from his superiors on an open missing person's case.

He didn't even want to think of the candlesticks, which were at this very moment undergoing an appraisal. They may well be stolen, and then what would happen to his career?

How had Myra come into the country? She had no passport, no identification. Her name didn't come up on any database in the States or Scotland.

He added harboring an illegal alien to his list of crimes.

With his head in his hands, Todd closed his blurry eyes.

The sound of a video hitting his desk brought his attention to his partner. "What's this?"

"This." Jake added five more to the pile. "Is our evening's entertainment. The executives from Magicland sent them over. They're surveillance tapes of the night and morning our Jane Doe washed up on Atlantis Island." Jake laughed at his own joke.

"Why so many of them?"

"They show the entire day before she showed up. Their security couldn't find her on any of the tapes, except right before she was found."

"So, they want us to see if we can spot her?"

"And anyone she might have come in with. Very few people go to Magicland by themselves."

"Why are they pursuing this? She isn't trying to sue them."

"A lawsuit is always possible. Nobody wants to miss anything in case Jane Doe comes back to haunt them."

With his finger on the fast forward button, Todd and Jake watched the first two tapes, both pointed toward the island from different angles. Once the sun went down, it was increasingly difficult to see who left the island. They stopped allowing people on the island at dusk, and neither Todd nor Jake saw even a glimpse of Myra.

Chapter Seven

Later that night, from the window in Todd's living room, Myra enjoyed the twinkling lights people hung on their houses to celebrate Christmas. The effect was magical, and something she'd never forget.

The lights of Todd's car shined through the window when he turned into the drive. She stood there in the dark, waiting.

She heard him come in, and knew he hovered watching her.

"Why are you standing in the dark?"

She almost flicked her wrist to light a fire in his hearth, but stopped. *Probably not the best way to show him about my abilities.* Not the right time. "The lights outside are so beautiful. It seemed a shame to dilute them."

He came to her, cautious. "Would you like to see the rest of the lights? There are more up the street."

"I would enjoy that."

He helped her into one of his coats and locked the door behind them.

The night was brisk, but not bone chilling. Such a contrast from her home at this time of year.

The lights sparkled from almost every home, filling her with joy, making her forget her problems. It was Christmas time. The first she would spend away from her family, and she hoped it would be the last.

"Why don't you put up lights?"

"Christmas isn't my time of year."

"How is that possible? Isn't Christmas for everyone? Even in this day?"

Todd sent her a puzzled look. "Not everyone has the same feeling about this time of year."

"But it is a time for hope, love."

Todd gazed at the waving Santa sitting in front of a pile of cotton designed to look like snow. "My Dad..." He sighed. "My Dad was killed in the line of duty three days before Christmas. I was seventeen at the time. Shortly after, my Mom got sick. I didn't know a broken heart could kill, but she was gone within three months of his funeral."

"I'm so sorry." She stopped. "It must have been awful."

He pushed them forward by placing an arm around her waist, and kept it there even after she kept walking. "It sucked. Without a brother or sister to help absorb some of the impact, it made it even worse. Growing up an only child, I thought I had it made. Never needing to share even the simplest of things. TV, bathroom, toys, even the front seat of the station wagon." They turned the corner to a street that took lighting for Christmas to a whole new level. "I never knew how much I needed a sibling until the day my parents were gone and I was alone."

"I can't imagine life without my family."

"How many siblings do you have?"

"There are five of us. Duncan is the oldest, Fin, myself, Cian and Amber. My parents made sure we had each other, so when the time comes, we can bind together."

"You're lucky to have such a large family."

"I am." Myra leaned her head against his shoulder. They walked in silence for awhile. Todd's fingers held her waist, sending a shiver down her spine. The touch wasn't meant to be intimate, yet it was.

A group of children stood out in front of one of the homes singing carols. They stopped and watched.

"Todd Blakely? Is that you, lad?" A voice from one of the homes called.

They both turned at the mention of Todd's name. An elderly man stood in the doorway where the carolers had just been.

Todd smiled and pushed Myra up to meet his neighbor. "Hello, Mr. McGregor. You've outdone yourself this year. Has Abby kept you buying lights all year?"

"It gives me something to do, with the kids off and gone. Who do you have here?"

"Max McGregor, this is Myra MacCoinnich, a friend of mine." He stumbled on his introduction.

Myra smiled, greeted him first in Gaelic then in English. "Happy Christmas," she said in both languages, as was her custom.

His smile went beyond his eyes and up into the receding hairline. "Ah, lass, I've not heard that since my own grandmamma was alive. Happy Christmas to you."

"Max! Have you lost your manners? Ask them in, it's cold out there." Abby called from the hall, "We have warm cider if you like."

"We're enjoying the lights, Mrs. McGregor," Todd told the aging woman.

Myra warmed into the smile of the older man, thinking how the elderly moved like honey, thick and slow, on a cold winter's night.

There was no getting out of a few minutes with the McGregor's. They sipped apple cider on the front porch and enjoyed the crowd gathering around the neighborhood to look at the lights. Myra and Todd listened to the couple banter.

"So, you're from Scotland are you?"

"Aye, I am." Myra said without worry. Abby's smile was sincere and welcoming.

"She spoke in Gaelic, Abby. I didn't know anyone spoke that anymore."

Myra smiled and moved closer to Todd on the bench they shared. "If no one speaks it, then how do you recognize it, Mr. McGregor?"

"Good point, lass."

"Still, it is nice to hear," Abby added.

"And 'tis nice to speak," Myra said in Gaelic, then translated in English for Todd's benefit.

Todd smiled down at her, taking her hand in his.

Mr. McGregor talked about his grandchildren, and how they were going to travel to Texas to visit them over the holiday. Myra heard little of it. She concentrated instead on the way Todd held her hand, how his fingers stroked the inside of her palm. Small shock waves traveled up her arm, making her whole body tingle. How could so innocent a touch make her body yearn? Make her want? What?

~~~~

He couldn't stop touching her. He had given it a college try for a solid five minutes when they first sat down, but with her so close, and her scent taking hold in his brain, he couldn't help himself.

She actually flinched when he first took her

hand, but now she relaxed beside him, and spread her fingers so he could weave their fingers together.

He envisioned her opening up to him like a rose did for light. He pictured her beneath him in his bed, and then his physical reaction forced him to shift uncomfortably in his seat.

After promising to come back to visit, Todd and Myra left their hosts and continued their walk.

Lights were strung across the street from one house to another. Some twinkled, others stayed lit. Several neighbors had small camp stove fires lit in their driveways and greeted the passers-by who came to enjoy the decorations.

They walked in silence, with only the occasional comment on a display or the people they saw.

Todd looked ahead and noticed a couple stealing a kiss under some mistletoe hung beneath a mass of lights. Purposely he stopped when they reached that point and turned to Myra. "Do they have mistletoe in Scotland?"

"Aye, we have mistletoe."

"Do you kiss under the mistletoe?"

Myra's ears grew red again, answering his question. "Only if the lad can pluck a berry can he receive a kiss. Once the berries are gone...well, no more kisses for him."

Todd slipped one hand around her waist. "Well, here in the States our traditions are a little different." He looked up. "It seems all the berries are gone, but one kiss is still allotted to the lad that catches the lass."

He liked the wave of color spreading up her

neck.

"I suppose since we are in America we should abide by your customs."

"I think we need to oblige or face the consequences of bad luck."

She stumbled over her words. "W-well, I wouldn't want to cause you any bad luck."

Her eyes were open when he lowered his mouth to hers. Tenderly, he captured her lips, thankful to finally be there. When her lids fluttered closed he moved closer, bringing the whole of her frame up against his. Every curve, hard and soft, molded to him in a perfect fit.

Molten lava rushed into his belly and slid lower. Her hands crept up into his hair, holding him hostage.

They stood in the middle of the sidewalk, surrounded by houses and people, oblivious to it all.

Todd came out of the fog first, gasping for air as if he'd been sucker-punched. "I want you," he whispered in her hair, not willing to break their contact.

She stiffened when his words registered. "I don't—"

"You want the same thing, Myra. Don't try and deny it."

"I don't know what I want. I've not ever..." She didn't finish her sentence.

"Not ever what?"

"No one has ever kissed me the way you do. Let alone anything more."

A virgin? Was that even possible? "You mean you've never...?"

"Never." She lowered her head and removed

her hands from his shoulders.

"Hey." He caught her gaze. "It's nothing to be embarrassed about." He kissed her again, briefly, then placed a protective arm over her shoulders and walked her home. "So are the men in Scotland blind?"

She laughed. "Nay."

"What then?"

"My father is very protective."

"Does your father know you're here?"

"Much to his dismay, but we had no choice."

Interesting, a protective father who sent his daughter away to a different country without any money. Something wasn't lining up.

Both kept silent, stuck in their own thoughts. They were within a block of his home when Myra stiffened, and all color washed from her face. She stopped and spun in a slow circle.

"What is it?"

"Someone is watching us."

"Some of the neighbors are busybodies."

"No, Todd. The one that watches wants more than to gossip."

Now the hair on his neck stood on end. It wasn't so much what she said, but the complete certainty in her tone that alarmed him. He moved his hand to where his gun normally was. He'd left it on his nightstand in his room. "Let's get you inside."

She needed little encouragement and within a minute was safely tucked behind his locked door, while he and his gun checked-out his yard.

He didn't like the fear he saw in her eyes. The uneasy feeling they were being watched was hard to shake off. With his gun in front of him, he circled the house twice, poking around his garden tools in his shed and behind the fences to neighboring properties.

If someone had been there, they were gone now.

He found her, curled up, clenching a butcher knife in her hand. "He's gone," she whispered.

"I didn't find anyone out there."

"But you felt him, didn't you?"

A denial was on his lips. "Maybe. Who do you think might be watching us?"

She started to shake.

"Hey, hey. Stop that." Todd pried the knife out of her fingers and gathered her in his arms. "It's okay. Nothing is going to happen to you. Shhh..."

He held her until he felt her body heat up and the shaking stopped. It took him some time to calm her down, but once he did, he tucked her into her bed.

He left her bedroom door open and slept on the sofa.

~~~~

Michael pulled back, into the darkness just as he had been taught by Grainna. Following Tara's sister had paid off at last. She'd finally lead him to the young Druid virgin. When Grainna returned, and although he didn't know when, he knew his mistress would, she would be pleased with what he had discovered.

He considered taking the young Druid woman and holding her until the solstice, but the cop she was staying with was a problem and he decided to wait a bit longer.

Grainna would know what to do, and she would have him do it when she returned.

He placed a cigarette to his lips, covered the tip with his hand, and lit the end without a match or a lighter.

~~~~

She was running and the woods surrounded her. Vines reached their spiny fingers around her ankles tripping her, causing her to fall to the forest floor.

She opened her mouth to scream, but no sound came. His hands crawled over her body, pinching, probing. Female laughter crackled from the shadows, damning her body, laying claim to her virginity. 'You will break my curse, and in return I will end your life quickly. The others will suffer.'

"Noooo!"

"Wake up." Todd shook her torso, avoiding her hands when they clawed at him. "Myra, wake up."

She woke to her own screams. Todd's grip held her firmly in place. Her breath came in small gasps. Her heart raced. "She is coming for me."

"It's just a dream." A damn scary one from what he could tell.

"No, it's more than that. She's coming back. I'm sure of it."

"Who's coming, Myra? Who are you so afraid of?"

"Grainna."

He couldn't get any more out of her. She stopped talking and rocked.

~~~~

He called her so often over the next two days, he might as well have stayed home.

She tried, unsuccessfully, to reassure him she was fine, but he could tell her nerves were on edge. As were his.

He tapped his pencil while watching the videos for the third time. "What do you think that is?" He pointed to the flash on the screen just before dawn. "Lightning?"

Jake spit out a sunflower seed shell and hit rewind. They watched the clip again. "Might be. Although I don't remember any rain last week. I'll look up the weather pattern online, see if I come up with anything."

He watched the video of Myra walking around the island, appearing lost. The static on the screen annoyed them both. Then they saw her riding the raft over to main park. "Aren't those on tracks?" Jake pointed to the raft in question.

"Everything in the water is on tracks, except the canoes. Do they still have them?"

"Don't think so."

Jake pulled himself out of his chair and flipped on the lights. "We're wasting our time. We can't tell when she went to the island, and there's no other way but by that raft. Unless she swam."

Todd remembered their conversation the day they spent on the beach. She vowed she had no idea how to swim. "Someone would have noticed a woman in the water."

"Well, she couldn't have gone unnoticed for two days. What does that leave? She appeared out of thin air?"

A head poked around the corner and told Todd he had a call. He flopped down at his desk and grabbed the phone, "Blakely."

"Mr. Blakely, this is Mr. Harrison over at Graystones."

Todd shifted in his chair, moved the receiver from one ear to the next. "Hello, Mr. Harrison."

"I am so glad to have gotten a hold of you. I have stunning news for you and your companion."

"And what might that be?"

"First, I want to apologize to Miss MacCoinnich. She was right about the year these pieces were made. In my defense, I have never seen antiques so well taken care of from that time-period outside of a museum. Why even our people didn't believe it until it was dated by our expert in Renaissance." He took a breath and continued to ramble on about how rare and exciting it was to have such marvelous examples of early twelfth century art, and how the pieces would likely bring a bidding war amongst the many galleries in Los Angeles, New York and London.

"Mr. Harrison," he interrupted. "What's the bottom line?"

"Oh, my, I guess I do go on, don't I? Well, you will be happy to know that my earlier estimate was entirely wrong. As a matter of fact, I wouldn't be surprised if the pieces sold for three times what I quoted you." Harrison was almost giddy. "That is if you are still willing to sell them?"

Todd cleared his throat, and only managed to choke out his reply. "How soon do you need to know?"

"Take your time, Mr. Blakely. We don't want to rush anything. Of course it is a great deal of money we are talking about, not something one would have sitting around on a coffee table, if you know what I mean."

Chapter Eight

"This is crazy!" Liz closed the book in her lap and tossed it aside.

Her hours of research and reading on Druidism and medieval times made her head ache, but the real kicker was she believed it. Believing it either made her crazy or stupid. She laughed when she closed her current study material.

Crazy! Definitely crazy.

The digital clock blinked out nine-thirty PM. It was late, but that didn't stop her from picking up the phone and dialing.

~~~~

Todd passed the phone off to Myra with few words.

After she hung up the phone, Myra smiled for the first time in several days before resting her head against the doorframe where she stood.

"Is everything all right?"

"Better than all right, I think." She placed the receiver on the charger. "I'll meet with Lizzy tomorrow to fill in some of the details she wants."

He swung his feet off the coffee table and turned off the television. "And what about me? When will you trust me enough to fill in some of those details?"

Except for the feeling of being watched, which they both felt and talked about often, everything else they discussed was superficial. They had both avoided the important subjects over the last few days. Todd hadn't asked or demanded any details, and Myra hadn't offered them.

"I do trust you. Yet, I'm afraid."

"Of what?"

He had taken care of her every need since she arrived. He had pulled her into his arms, kissed her senseless, then demanded no more when he learned she was a virgin. His concern for her well-being was evident in every phone call he made. Every risk he took keeping her under his care.

She knew they had no future together, but she still worried he would walk away when he learned who she was. Learned what she was.

Most people ran from things they couldn't explain. Would he? Was she willing to risk him rejecting her when she told him the truth? Every day she grew closer to him. Even now, the possibility Lizzy would consent to her moving in, had Myra concerned. She couldn't imagine not seeing Todd daily.

"I'm afraid you won't believe me," she finally said.

"I've learned from my years on the force that life is often stranger than fiction. I haven't pushed you for the answers I know you have, but that doesn't mean I don't want them."

"If I ask you to believe something I cannot completely prove, will you believe?"

He walked up to her, took her hands in his. "You told me you're a virgin. I believe that without proof."

She laughed, despite herself. Closing her eyes, she offered a silent prayer. "We should sit down."

Rigid, with her hands in her lap, she sat and tried to find the words to tell him her story. Her fingers fidgeted together, nails against nails, continually making clicking noises and filling the silent room with sound.

"My parents are Laird Ian and Lady Lora MacCoinnich. I reside in MacCoinnich Keep in Scotland, with my brothers and sister."

"That is where Tara McAllister is?"

"Aye, but she is Tara MacCoinnich now, wife to my brother, Duncan."

"Duncan is the man from the pictures? The man at the Renaissance Faire she was last seen with?"

"Aye, and the other man, Fin, is my older brother."

"So if Miss McAllister... I mean Mrs. MacCoinnich is safe in Scotland, why hasn't she contacted her sister?"

She closed here eyes and took a leap. "Before last week, when I traveled here, I lived my life in the sixteenth century. The century in which I was born. The century in which Tara now lives."

Whatever he thought she was going to say flew out of his mind. By the look on her face, he knew it showed. He started to say something only to be silenced by her hand.

"That part I cannot prove. Not yet anyway." She stood and started pacing. "I come from a family of Druids that date back from the 800's. We are often misunderstood and keep our heritage secret to avoid persecution."

He couldn't sit. She was so serious in her delusion. He put his hands on her shoulders and turned her around to face him. "Myra, there are people who can help you."

Her smile placated him. She knew he didn't believe her. "Just listen, before you condemn me as mad. I know how all of this sounds."

"But..."

"You wanted the truth, Todd, and I am giving it to you now."

He nodded and watched her as she continued.

"All Druids have some power. Gifts. Abilities beyond what you are used to. I am no different."

She took a step back and opened her hands to his fireplace. "Our powers stem from nature. The elements of life. Fire is the easiest." She pushed her hands to the hearth and flames leapt and caught on the logs. A small blast of hot air shot out. She didn't turn to see if he watched.

"Jesus." His jaw dropped, his breath caught in his throat.

"My greatest gift isn't fire however, 'tis air. Or wind really. Moving the air gives me the ability to move things. Objects both small." She lifted the remote control off the table from several feet away and gently set it back down. "And large." She waved her hand, and the coffee table moved across the room.

Todd jumped back a foot, his eyes wide. He blinked several times, then mumbled a curse when she put the table back with nothing more than a flick of her wrist. If he thought his pulse couldn't beat faster when he saw the logs catch fire, it was nothing compared to the rapid tattoo beating in his chest now. "How the hell did you do that?"

"With my mind." She took a step toward him, he stepped back. She grounded her feet and stood poised and waiting. For what, he didn't know.

He put a distance of several feet between

them. What the hell was she? Every word she spoke repeated in his mind, every strange comment about food, clothing or objects. Every bit of slang he'd explained, he'd checked off to her being from a different country, not a different time. "Why are you here?" Not that he believed in the time travel thing. The jury was still out on that.

She stepped back, her expression guarded. "You refer to her as Gwen Adams. Her real name is Grainna. She is centuries old, condemned to live her life in an old and virtually powerless body. She too is Druid. But evil. Evil beyond even your worst criminal in this time." Myra moved to the window and refused to look at him. "I believe she followed Duncan and Tara back to my time and is there now trying to break her curse."

"How does that involve you?"

"I am a virgin and Druid. The combination is what she needs to break her condemnation. 'Tis easy to assume Grainna is there. My mother had a vision that I would die if I stayed in my time."

"You want me to believe you were sent here from the sixteenth century to avoid being a sacrificial virgin to some cursed old lady?"

She winced. "Believe what you like, I am simply telling you the truth. Tara was at risk from Grainna when she was here. Duncan and Fin were sent to keep Grainna from finding Druid virgins in this time."

"So, what? All the missing women on the books have been sent back in time?"

"No, only Tara. There are few Druids left in this world."

Todd went to his liquor cart and poured two

fingers of the nearest open bottle. He downed it in one swallow then poured another. "Tara's a Druid?"

"Aye."

"That would mean that Lizzy is..."

"And her son Simon."

"And does Lizzy know this?"

Myra shook her head. "I told her the day at the park."

"Did she believe you? No questions asked?"

She trembled. "No, she has questions, but she is now open to hearing the answers."

He had questions, but knew himself well enough not ask them, yet. If Myra was sucking him into her delusions, asking her for more crazy answers would only feed her madness.

Slowly Myra turned. "I told you I would reveal everything and I have."

"Hummph."

~~~~

Myra had gone to bed hours earlier. Todd sat with a bottle of whisky and stared into the fire flickering in the night. Instead of chasing away the shadows overwhelming him, he kept picturing how the fire had been lit.

He searched for every conceivable loophole in her story, struggled with her explanations and her examples. If he only believed half of what he witnessed, he had to believe she had some telekinetic ability. Mind over matter.

The fireplace could have been rigged, but the table? The remote?

Dammit! He couldn't wrap his mind around what he saw, or how easy her explanations fit with the facts as he knew them.

Why did it matter? Why did she matter? Had she put some type of hex on him? Some Druid spell that left him dangling? Is that why she had burrowed under his skin to the point where he dreamed of her every night?

Todd prided himself on keeping women at arms' length. He refused to allow anyone to get close as long as he worked the streets. It wasn't fair to a woman to stay up all night worrying about his well-being. He remembered the long nights as a child when his mother waited anxious by the phone, waiting for his father to call. He promised himself he wouldn't do that to another person. Ever. Yet here he was, all but living with Myra. She made him dinner every night, albeit mainly sandwiches, but he didn't really care. She answered the phone when he called, wistful and happy to hear his voice. Now this. He had a boatload of shit piled high on his doorstep.

Todd didn't know what to believe.

He downed the Scotch, looked at the glass, and then let out a miserable laugh at the irony of his choice of drink.

~~~~

Lizzy was over half an hour late. Holiday shoppers filled the crowded mall. Christmas carols blared through the speakers of each shop and courtyard. Harried parents pushed children around in strollers and dangled bags upon bags of merchandise.

If it wasn't for the sinking pit Myra felt in her stomach, she might have enjoyed all the sights and sounds. But with every passing child wailing in protest at being dragged into yet another store, Myra felt their agony as if it were her own.

Todd left early in the morning even though he wasn't due to go to work. He didn't leave a note or any word of what was going on in his head. She thought the worst.

Myra sat at the far end of the overstuffed mall, completely out of place, with no idea what her future would hold. Maybe Lizzy had decided against their meeting, against believing her story, maybe she'd avoid her just as Todd was doing.

With her head in her hands, she tried to block out the noise around her and concentrated on what to do next.

A huge swell of relief exploded when Lizzy sat down next to her, chatting away as if they were in the middle of a conversation. "Sorry I'm late. Traffic is a bear out there. I had to park a mile away." Liz glanced her way. "Hey, are you okay? What happened?"

"I didn't think you were coming," Myra managed.

"I told you I would. Geez, get a grip," Lizzy teased.

Myra's laugh threatened to turn to tears.

"Man, there's no need to cry. I'm not worth all of this."

"It isn't only you." Myra sat a little taller, drawing courage she didn't feel. "Todd doesn't believe me."

"Doesn't believe what?" Lizzy hauled her bulging purse to her lap.

"Everything! Anything... Oh, I don't know. He thinks I'm crazy."

"Did you tell him everything?"

"Aye. All of it."

"Did you show him your little..." Liz waved her

hand in the air. "Gift?"

She nodded. "Now he won't even look at me."

"Oh. Well. It's a lot to believe. Even for a boyfriend."

"Boyfriend? What is that?"

"You know. Companion. Lover?"

Eyes wide, Myra shook her head. "It's not like that. He isn't a boyfriend." She lowered her voice to a mere whisper. "We don't..."

"Right."

"No, really."

"Has he kissed you?"

"Yes, but..."

"Are you sleeping with him?"

"No!"

"But you are living with him." Liz smiled.

"Only because I had no other place to go."

"But his opinion means something to you?" With a nod, Liz continued. "You told him absolutely everything?"

"Everything."

"Then give him some time. If he doesn't haul you off to the funny farm, then he believes you. Or he's crazy about you. Either way you have nothing to be concerned about."

"He isn't crazy about me."

"What makes you think that?" Liz opened her purse and took out her cell phone, glanced at it then tossed it back in her purse.

"He hasn't tried to kiss me since I told him I was a virgin." Myra moved over slightly to give room for an elderly woman to sit.

Liz's jaw dropped slightly.

"Don't look so shocked. 'Tis expected where I come from."

"Oh, yeah, I forgot about that. Grainna needs a Druid virgin. Man, you and my sister. Are you positive Grainna is in your time?"

"'Tis the only thing that makes any sense. If she is in my time then my life would have been in danger if I stayed."

"I've heard about running from your enemies, but this is a bit far, don't you think?"

"True. But my coming wasn't our choice. There are other forces that lead our lives."

"You mean the Ancients."

"Yes."

Liz shrugged. "Well, I think life is what you make it. Both good and bad. I would have stayed and kicked some serious ass."

Myra laughed. "I bet you could. I however, have never kicked anything."

"So what are you going to do now? Lose your," she lowered her voice, "lose your innocence and go home? Or stay here?"

Myra pushed a long strand of hair over her shoulder, grateful the conversation had come back around to the future. "Best I do nothing at this point. I have to believe I will know what to do when the time comes."

"But you will go back, eventually?"

"Aye, I will." Myra's eyes leveled with hers.

Liz's jaw clenched. "If I help you, I need you to promise me something."

"If it's in my power."

"Take us with you. Simon and me."

Myra felt a rush of air, uncertain of what to say.

"I don't mean to stay, just a visit. I need to see that Tara is alive and happy with my own eyes."

"I don't know—"

"Please. Think about what you would want if you were in my place. I need to see her."

"We don't travel for our own personal wishes."

"And whose rules are those?"

"The Ancients," she said.

"Have you ever met them? These Ancients?"

"Of course not."

"Then how do you know they don't want me to go back with you?" Liz was reaching, and Myra sensed it, but she didn't blame her. "Maybe it's all part of some master plan."

With no one to ask, no family to make the decision for her, Myra searched in her heart for the answers she needed.

She didn't look far. She knew she would return with Lizzy and her son. There was no reason not to. "All right. You may both come. But if my family feels you need to return immediately you must."

"As long as I see Tara."

"You will see her. I promise."

"Thank you."

They both stood and started walking the mall.

"I need to do a little Christmas shopping while we're here. Simon has been bugging me about some new video game he wants."

"What is a video game?"

Lizzy squeezed her eyes and gave a very long-winded answer to Myra's question.

Myra asked about everything she saw. From the teenage boy with spiked purple hair, to the mechanical merry-go-round in the center of the mall.

They talked as if they had known each other for years instead of days.

"Have you spoken to Simon yet?"

They were walking out of the massive building into a sea of parked cars. "I'm going to sit him down tonight and explain what I can."

"Do you want me to help?"

"No. I can manage. Simon's a great kid. I don't know how much of this he'll believe. Hell, I'm having a hard time believing it myself."

"I'll stay one more night at Todd's then." Myra's skin stood up when she thought of how that night would end. Would he even allow her to stay?

"If he gives you a hard time, call me. I'll come and get you."

Liz drove Myra to the antique dealer who needed her to sign a few papers for the sale of the candlesticks. As expected, there was a bidding war, and the antiques were sold for over half a million dollars.

Mr. Harrison was very accommodating, and if he questioned why the check for the sale was to be made out to Elizabeth McAllister, he didn't let on. He smiled. "If you have anything else you would like to sell, Miss MacCoinnich, please call on me again."

"That I will, Mr. Harrison. 'Tis been a pleasure doing business with you."

He walked them both to the door where a security guard stood to escort them to their car. "Are you certain we haven't met before, Miss MacCoinnich?"

"Positive."

"And you, Miss McAllister? Have you been to us in the past?"

"Sorry. I'm not into antiques."

"Ah well, my mistake. Thank you again,

ladies. And Merry Christmas."

It wasn't until they were back in the car that Liz explained exactly how much money half a million was.

"So, it's enough to buy the material I need to bring back with me and all the spices?" Myra fastened her seatbelt and sat back in her seat.

"You could buy out an entire Superstore with that kind of cash."

"I will spend what I need and leave you the rest. After I pay back Todd for all he has done."

Lizzy laid into the horn when another driver cut her off. "I can't accept that much money."

"Of course you can. And will. You never know what you might need, family helps family."

"But—"

"Stop. I won't hear an argument. Your coin will do me little good in the past. Think of it this way. If any of us need something from you in the future, we will ask for your help without worry that you cannot afford it."

"Fine. But I'm not spending it."

"As long as you have it in case of an emergency," Myra said smiling. The right decisions were always the easy ones.

~~~~

Myra walked into Todd's home, as she had so many times in the last week. Only this time it felt different. After placing the key he had given her to lock up his home on the table, she took a deep breath and proceeded to the living room where Todd sat. Waiting.

His back was rigid. He didn't move when she entered the room.

"You decided to come back?" he said.

Myra circled the sofa, and with great care eased herself into the chair across from him. "For tonight."

"Then what? You'll move in with Lizzy?"

"I never intended to impose on you this long. Or at all for that matter. 'Tis for the best, I think."

"That's it? Hi, let me take over your life for a couple weeks, turn it upside down, and make you take cold showers. Then you give me some far-fetched tale about being from a different time, sent here to save the world from some evil witch, and I'm supposed to believe that? And that's it?" His tone was cold, bordering on cruel.

"What do you want me to say?" she cried. "I know you don't believe me, and there is nothing more I can do to convince you that what I say is true. All I can do now is thank you for helping me." Myra slowed her breathing. "But it isn't enough, is it?

"No, it isn't," he spat out. He spent the entire day going over the Magicland tapes, searching for any sign that what she said was a hoax. Instead of being able to debunk her story, he found everything lining up.

All of it.

Her story behind her arrival, Tara McAlister's disappearance, the question behind who Gwen Adams was. He re-studied every piece of evidence so many times his eyes were crossed. He came up with no other plausible explanation, except that what she had vowed to him was the truth. Twisted, crazy, un-deniably insane truth. A truth he had to be nuts to believe.

That wasn't the worst part.

The worst part, the absolute most horrendous part was the fact that he sat in his home unable to get a hold of her for the last couple of hours, worrying that maybe she'd left. That she'd returned to her time without as much as a goodbye.

He'd never desired a woman as much or with such fierceness as he did Myra. What in the hell was wrong with him?

"I should go to bed." She moved passed him.

His arm shot out, stopping her.

"No." His tone was deadpan. Slowly, he backed her into the wall. She wasn't going to walk away, not yet. Not when his blood pumped the way it did when she was around.

Unable to form a single coherent sentence, he did what he had wanted to do every night since they met.

He took.

Chapter Nine

His mouth came down in a searing assault, sending endless shock waves through her limbs. She hadn't had time to think or process what he was doing. The simple fact that he was holding her, kissing her and branding her as his own was overwhelming. He wanted her. The way his hands roamed over her body, crushing her to him felt desperate, stronger and more fierce than any other time he had touched her.

As his hands thrust through her hair and his mouth probed hers for entry, she felt his hard mass lean into her soft fragile curves.

Then something turned on inside her. Like a switch, her body ignited into flames, burning him and engulfing her.

Her lips opened to his, welcomed his warmth, his moisture. Without thought, her hands traveled to his back, pulling him closer. She hesitated briefly at his waist, not certain how much liberty she should take in his arms. Where were the rules dictating what she should and shouldn't do? She felt his hands skim down her neck. His thumb traced the outline of her breast.

"Oh, God," she moaned when his lips left hers.

It was then she realized there were no rules, only passion. Their bodies reacted, guiding them to do what came naturally. God help her, she wanted what came next.

When she dropped her hands lower and

brushed down his thighs, heat punched his stomach, leaving him breathless. When he filled his hand with her breast, she didn't pull away but molded into his caress. She moaned at his touch.

He pulled her shirt from her pants, desperate to touch her flesh, to feel it against his. He wanted to devour her in one long gulp. His day of pacing and fear powered his adrenaline now. He managed to shed her of her top.

"Beautiful," he whispered. He trailed his lips down and feasted on her breast.

She didn't push him away, instead she seemed as anxious as he to shed her clothing.

He started to move toward the sofa, backing her up. They should go to his room, but the thought of walking that far disturbed him. He wanted her there, now.

Somewhere, in the back of his mind, Todd told himself to slow down. This was her first time, and he wanted her to taste heaven, needed her to enjoy every pleasure he knew he could give. But she was tugging his shirt out of his jeans, and he was helpless, lost to her.

A deafening crash outside the front door was like ice-cold water tossed over an open flame. Her nails, clawing at him in passion, suddenly gripped him in fear. Her gasp edged toward a scream.

His head shot up while the rest of him froze. He looked down at Myra and put a finger to her lips demanding silence when the second crash came.

He tugged her to the floor. Staying low, he inched over to her shirt and thrust it into her hands.

Myra hurriedly dressed and wedged herself

between the wall and a divan.

Todd crawled on his hands and knees to where he left his gun. Crouching on the balls of his feet, he clicked off the safety on his nine millimeter and clasped it with both hands. With his weapon in front of him, he edged his way to the side of the massive picture window.

He saw a large shadow and pulled back. *What the fuck?*

"Stay here," he whispered as he passed her. "Stay down." He ducked into the kitchen and headed to the back door.

~~~~

Cowering in the corner and completely helpless, Myra shut her eyes and opened her mind. Her head ached with a familiar pain of someone looking in. Whoever stood outside was crawling around in her head like a parasite, sucking up information. Instantly, she shut him out. He was powerful. Druid or witch, she wasn't sure, but his intent was evil.

She felt his presence hiding in the shadows, she saw the stranger looking at a brick he held in his hand. Waiting and wanting to hurt them.

The chain that latched the back door slid open. Myra knew Todd was walking into a trap. Rushing to the back door, she screamed. "Stop!"

Todd turned, and pulled her down when she reached him. "I told you to stay."

"Shhh..."

Another crash outside had him covering her body with his. Myra closed her eyes and concentrated, opening her mind to the intruder outside.

Her breath came out in a rush, as if she had

held it for hours. "He's gone."

"What?"

"Thank God." She rested her forehead on his arm and caught her breath.

Everything outside grew quiet. "How do you know he's gone? Don't tell me you can read minds?"

"I can see intent, feel emotions. He wanted to harm you. Oh, God." The warm adrenalin rush now spent left a chill in its place. "He was in my mind," she declared, trembling. "I feel violated and dirty."

"Do you think he's like you? A Druid?"

"I don't know. He held power. He watched us, Todd." She searched his eyes making sure he heard her. "He wanted us to stop."

Todd's jaw clenched as he stood and pulled out of her arms. "I'm going to take a look, just to make sure he's left."

Trying her best to ward off the chill, Myra wrapped her arms around her body and waited for Todd to return.

"He's gone, tripped over the trash barrels on the side yard, but other than that I didn't see a thing."

Todd pulled her off the floor and walked her to the couch. She watched as he went around locking doors and shutting curtains. Once he returned, she curled up into his lap and did her best to calm down, all the while trying to figure out who would be watching them and why.

"You're cold." He rubbed his hands over her arms. "How about a fire?" He pulled away and smiled at her.

"What?"

"You can light it faster then I can," he said.

Surprised he was suggesting she use her gift, she asked, "Are you sure?"

The slight twitch in the corner of his eye was the only clue that he was a little nervous. She opened her hand to the hearth and watched as the flames leapt from the embers.

To Todd's credit, he didn't even flinch. "Is there any way you can teach me that trick?"

She smiled and rested in his arms. Perhaps there was hope for him. Maybe he'd learn to accept who and what she was. "Sorry. It's in the blood I'm afraid."

"Too bad. That could come in handy."

"It does."

His hand stroked her hair, calming her down. "Who do you think was out there?" he asked.

"I don't know."

"Could someone have followed you from the past?"

"I don't think it's possible, but I don't know for sure. All I do know is he felt evil and wanted us to stop."

"Then that wipes out a voyeur."

"What is that?"

"Someone who wants to watch lovers..." He stopped from finishing his sentence.

"Grainna would want us to stop. But it was a man out there. Of that I'm certain.

"Maybe he works with this woman. Or does her bidding."

"I hadn't thought of that." Myra knew Grainna had men serving her every need when she lived in this time.

"Last night you mentioned a curse," Todd said.

"Aye, a curse that bound her powers and left her in an old body for decades." Myra repeated the curse aloud for Todd's benefit. "A virgin's blood of Druid descent, only of age to give consent. Virgin blood will set you free, this is your curse from us to thee." She shifted, moved closer. "The Ancients sent her to this time knowing few virgins existed. Let alone Druid virgins."

"But you're a Druid virgin. Her ticket to power."

"'Tis why I was sent away when she went back to my time."

Todd shook his head. "Sending you years into the future seems like a lot of trouble to go through, for something so easily fixed."

"What do you mean?"

He stroked her arm. "You're a very beautiful woman, Myra. I'm sure the men in your time would be lined up to rid you of your virginity."

Heat filled her cheeks. She lowered her head. "Maybe for a woman in this century. In mine, 'tis expected I go to my marriage bed a virgin."

"Your virginity isn't worth your life. If this woman is as evil as you say, then she will stop at nothing to get what she wants. The criminal mind hasn't changed over the centuries, even if the thoughts about sex have."

Was that all it was? Just sex? Did the feelings and desires he pulled out of her mean nothing more than a physical act?

Her head started to ache. It was so simple an hour before, in his arms. Wanting desperately for him to make love to her. Wanting him to love her. And to what end? She would be leaving him eventually, and although she was prepared to lose her innocence, she desperately wanted it to be more than a physical release.

"I am constantly at a loss as to what I should do."

He smoothed her hair back, pushing her head onto his shoulder. "It's painfully obvious to me what you should do, but since I'm the only man in the room, I'm biased." His chest rumbled with a little laugh.

"Being with you, having sex...would take away the threat." She cleared her throat, uncomfortable, "'Tis an option." But was she willing to exercise it?

"I would happily oblige, but I don't want you regretting it in the morning. Because I wouldn't."

"You confuse me," she confessed.

"I can beat that. You scare the hell out of me."

His blatant honesty made her laugh. "How?"

"Oh, come on. One wrong move from me and wham, ball of fire."

She leaned back, playfully swatting at his arm. "It's a good thing my family is not here."

"I can only imagine."

"Nay, I don't think you can. There was a boy once, when I was all of fourteen. He was much older than I."

"How much older?" His face grew serious.

"Well at fourteen, he was practically a man at sixteen. He had already started his training with my father and brothers, so he could be knighted and ride in battle when he came of age. Anyway, Daniel took a liking to me, but because of who I was, he kept his distance."

"What do you mean, who you were? Did he know you were a Druid?" Todd played with her hair.

"No. No one knows that. I mean because I was Lady Myra MacCoinnich. His family wasn't from a great home or land, and his pursuit of me wouldn't have been accepted."

"So what happened?"

"One day, on his return from exercising his horse, he found me in the stables. I was tending one of our pregnant mares and waiting for him in all honesty. I had never been kissed and knew he wanted to do so. We talked for a short time then finally he kissed me."

"And?"

"Nothing really. I worked it up in my mind to be something bigger than it was. There was no spark. I thought maybe we needed to do it again, that I had done something wrong, so I kissed him back."

"Was there a spark the second time?"

"Not from me. He, on the other hand, must have felt something, for he didn't hear my father when he walked around the corner and found us."

"Poor Daniel." Todd faked a sympathetic pout.

"Poor Daniel? Poor me! My father shot lightning out of the sky, nearly catching the stables on fire. He was so angry." She shook her head, remembering. "It rained for a solid week."

"Your father can control the weather?"

"Aye. His storms are magnificent," she told him with pride. "'Tis his greatest gift."

Clearly alarmed, Todd said, "I guess you're right about your family not being here. I wouldn't want to feel lightning at my feet."

"My father would do more than that at this point."

"More than killing me with lightning?"

"Killing is instant. Laird Ian would demand you marry me."

His hand stilled in her hair, his body stiffened.

"Relax, Sir Blakely. My father has no way of coming here." She giggled.

"I'm not a knight."

"That is where you are wrong. You may not have those titles in this time. But your actions are those of a knight. You've dedicated your life to righting people's wrongs. You uphold the laws of your land. Your chivalry would not go unnoticed in my time."

"Now you're making me blush."

"Make fun if you must. My father would reward you greatly if given the chance."

"Is that your way of asking me to come home to meet the parents?" It was easy to tease when the act was impossible to do.

"Would you?"

"Ha. And risk being shot by lightning? You're asking a lot from a mere mortal."

She realized then she asked too much. There was no way of knowing if he was able to travel through time. Only Druids were entrusted with the stones. Myra wasn't willing to risk his life to find out.

Firelight played off the walls, casting shadows over them both. Myra fell asleep next to him, and he didn't want to move. He watched the rhythmic movement of her chest and felt the small puff of air from her heart shaped, pink lips when she exhaled. He'd never watched a woman sleep before. Never wanted to.

When the last flame melted into the glow of

the ashes, both of them slept, content in the other's arms.

By its own bidding, her mind slipped into his. She was completely unaware that their dreams mixed. There she saw herself as he did. She stood in front of him in a gown of sheer silver, nearly transparent, and revealing of all her curves.

Her hair flowed free of any binding, and settled at her waist. She sensed his longing to touch it. To touch her.

He undressed her with his mind, caressed every curve. Her body arched in her sleep, her lips parted and gasped when his hands possessed her in his dream.

Todd didn't know what woke him, but when his eyes opened his body was fully aroused. Myra's hands clenched at his chest. Her lips parted and she murmured his name. "Please, Todd."

Unable to resist, he lowered his lips to hers, kissed her, half awake, half asleep. He told himself he would take only a taste, to wake her up and put her to bed, but her absolute surrender rendered him powerless to pull away. Like a man unable to quench his thirst, he returned for more. Needed more.

He moved his lips to the long column of her neck. Her timid hands ran through his hair. She captured his eyes, staring boldly through him before she forced his lips back to hers. He quivered. She was completely awake and kissing him back. Taking as much as she gave.

For a while, he simply kissed her, their tongues dueling. For a woman whose experience with men could be measured on one finger, Myra learned fast. Little mewling sounds from her throat encouraged bolder moves from him.

Her nimble fingers clasped onto his shirt and tugged it away from his skin. Todd sat back and met her passion-filled stare.

"Can I?" she whispered, her lip caught between her teeth while she waited his answer.

With a nod, Todd watched Myra remove his shirt from his shoulders, and rake her fingers over his chest in exploration. Ripples of pleasure shot to the pit of his stomach with an ache more powerful than any drug.

She brushed a tender kiss to his chest, then glanced up for approval. Todd swept her hair behind her back and slid his hands over her breasts. Myra pushed into his palm, and her head leaned back with a groan.

He inched her shirt over her head, exposing creamy white breasts and erect nipples. Bending his mouth to hers, he knew he was lost, drowning and almost past the point of no return. "Tell me to stop and I will. But do it soon if you have to."

He played with her nipple and watched it respond.

She didn't answer with words. Instead, she ran her hands over his body and rested on his groin. Bold move for a virgin, he thought. There she stopped and measured his length, tightly bound in the pants he wore. Lightly stroking him over the clothing was like taunting a wild animal through a cage. He groaned.

He had his answer, but he'd be damned if he would take her on his couch. He stood, lifted her, and carried her into his room.

Gently he eased her back onto his mattress,

and watched the emotions pass over her beautiful face. Todd stretched out alongside her, gathered her into his arms, and pressed his lips to hers again.

He slowed their pace, savored and enjoyed each touch, each caress, wanting it all to last. But she was so responsive to every touch it damn near unmanned him.

Myra arched toward him. His hands stroked down her back and lower, pressing her hips to his. His erection, bound in the clothes he wore, sat snug between her legs. She moaned with the contact and Todd smiled under her lips while they kissed.

She was a moaner, and unlike any woman he had ever been with before. Her body hummed with every caress, every noise they made. His lips found and tantalized her breast. "Yes," she said.

When her hands found him again, he stilled, bit back a groan.

"Should I stop?" she asked, completely unaware of her affect on him.

"God, no." He drew in a quick breath, caught her lip in his teeth. "Don't ever stop."

She laughed at his words and worked at the button of his pants.

Myra's movements were anything but virginally shy, and his body hurt under all his clothing. He shook off the rest of his clothes, and helped her with hers.

The darkness hid her blush, but Todd felt the heat in her cheeks when he cradled her face in his hands. He stretched out beside her. His erection pressed to her thigh and even that had him catching his breath. He was her first. The simple act of making love never held such power. He knew his time in her life may very well save it, but that wasn't what brought them to this point. No, this was something they both wanted. Never once did he feel she wanted him only to rid herself of the threat from Grainna. Myra was too pure for that.

Her touch was full of tenderness and, dare he say, love. Never had one woman's touch meant so much. "Are you sure this is what you want, Myra?" he asked, giving her one more chance to back out.

"When you touch me, I feel alive," she confessed. "This burning inside me is only sated when you touch me. I want this... I want you."

His fingers burned a trail down her sleek frame. Pausing at her hip, he waited for her to arch up. He didn't have to wait long.

Smiling, he kissed the pulse in her neck and pressed his palm to the triangle at her legs, slowly slipping one finger into her tight, hot folds. Her moan reached new levels that brought a wave of satisfaction down Todd's back. Her breath caught, her body went rigid, not in denial, but with the first throes of an orgasm hovering over her. She pushed against him, riding his hand. Myra stilled before she trembled and crested for the first time.

His devilish laugh of success played against her chest. "Amazing," he whispered, dragging his lips back to hers.

"Please, Todd..." she groaned. As if she were unable to stop her body's response from the spasms he gave her, she arched into him and moved. Her instinctive movements were his undoing. He opened his bedside table, ripped open the condom with his teeth, and slid it over his erection.

"What is that?" she asked.

"To protect you."

She didn't ask more, instead she stroked his length.

"Are you sure you'll fit?"

Like a glove. "Lets find out." He moved his body until he hovered over her. Her legs fell to the side offering him everything. He clasped his fingers with hers, captured her eyes with one penetrating look. In complete awe of the strength of their joining, he watched her as he slipped inside.

Expecting her barrier, he eased himself inside with slow degrees. Her tight passage expanded, inviting him in. Her eyes widened as he sheathed his length fully inside her. She didn't cry out in pain. Thank God. He didn't want her to hurt, which she must, he thought. He stilled his movements, swept his tongue into her mouth, and mimicked the act of making love.

Then she started to stir. Slow little movements of her hips arched to him, asking more of him. He moved slowly at first and watched her climb higher.

Her body closed around him, accepted every glorious inch of him. She whimpered as he drove them both closer to completion.

His movements quickened, along with their breathing, moisture pearled over their skin as they tumbled over each other, climbed toward the peak. "Todd," she cried as her frame stilled under his and her body clenched around him, gripping his seed from deep within to explode along with her.

In time, her mind drifted off the cloud he had

put her on. Tangled in sheets ruffled and moist with the evidence of their passion, she was helpless to move even a finger. His leg laid over her, pinning her to the bed, and beneath him. The weight of it comforted and reassured her. His body fit so perfectly against hers. Snuggling closer to keep from being chilled, Myra smiled in her contentment.

"Is it always like that?" Myra asked against his chest.

"If it was, no one would ever get out of bed."

She laughed, "I believe that was a compliment."

His mouth smothered hers in a kiss that threatened her soul. Breathless, he murmured, "A compliment it was, along with a request."

Her head fell back when his lips found the pulse beating in her neck. "Anything."

"More."

"Aye, more."

Chapter Ten

The sun shines brighter in the month of December, with its rays closer to the surface of the Earth. Neither Todd nor Myra could be bothered with waking despite its mighty power. They both were content to stay in the bed they shared as long as hunger held off.

Someone else had a different idea.

Pounding on the front door startled them both, and had them reaching for their clothes.

Alarmed because of the previous night's intruder, Todd reached for his weapon. When he heard a female voice calling Myra's name, he set it back down.

"Myra! Come on, it's cold out here, open up," Lizzy called while pounding on the locked door.

Todd tossed her his bathrobe that hung by his door then hurriedly tugged on his jeans. "What is she doing here?"

"I told her to pick me up this afternoon."

He ran his fingers through his hair. "She's early."

But when they looked at the clock they noticed the time read half past noon.

Myra tightened the belt around her waist, started for the door. Todd caught her, placed his lips to hers. "Good morning."

She could get used to that, she thought, his smile and morning growth of beard. The casual caress of a lover's hand reminded her with only a touch, of the night they had shared. "Good afternoon," she corrected.

She pushed past him when Lizzy's knocking continued.

Myra opened the door, Liz's frown slowly turned into a knowing grin. "Well now... What do we have here?" She stepped into the house.

Blood shot to Myra's face, glowing red at the embarrassment of being discovered.

Liz laughed, tossed her purse on the coffee table, only to pick up Myra's bra and let it dangle from her fingertips.

Myra snatched the evidence out of her hand just as Todd rounded the corner shrugging into his shirt. "I see you're right on time," he said, completely unaware of the crimson that flooded Myra's neck.

"Apparently I'm early."

"Oh, God." The gasp from Myra had them both showing pity on her.

Liz couldn't contain her mirth and laughed. "Why don't you go make us some coffee, handsome," she told Todd. "We girls need to catch up."

Liz circled around Myra, hiding her smile. "Maybe you should go and get dressed."

Thankful for the reprieve, Myra practically ran from the room. She tossed on the clothes she wore the night before and joined Liz back in the living room.

"So?" Liz wasn't exactly subtle in her questioning. "Want to tell me what's going on?"

Head down, Myra said, "We, ahh..."

"Yeah, I figured 'you, ahh...'"

Myra peered up into a face of acceptance and

not of scolding, not of judgment. In fact, she saw the face of a sister. "Oh, my God, Lizzy. I had no idea. Tara told me making love was wonderful, but I never imagined it was going to be like that."

Liz laughed, keeping her voice low when she asked, "Do you love him?"

Myra opened her mouth and nothing came out. Did she? Could she? "I can't love him, Lizzy. I can't stay here."

"Women always hold some love for their first. It's against our nature not to. So, how was it?"

Myra hid her face behind the tips of her fingers, smiling into them, and then launched into details women always told, but men seldom knew.

Giggling emanated from his living room, under hushed tones. Todd smiled into his coffee and took the time to reflect on the changes in Myra's and his relationship.

They had taken 'playing house' to a new level, but what surprised him was his lack of concern over the matter.

The intruder from the night before kept his mind from wandering back to the picture of Myra naked and aroused in his bed.

Myra's theory of the man being a part of some ancient ploy to take her virginity was only conceivable if he believed her story. He tried not to, but found himself losing the battle.

Since they'd slept together, the intruder should move on now if Myra's theory was correct. But how would their late night visitor know he and Myra had been intimate?

Worse, what if he was simply a stalker attracted to her, waiting for an opportunity to find her alone?

Todd didn't like any of the scenarios he came up with. He really hated the thought of her leaving the safety of his home and moving in with Liz. Well, that at least was easily fixed.

The two women clammed up the minute he set foot into the room. Todd handed a cup of coffee to Myra, ignored her shy glance, and said, "My ears were burning, hope you don't mind if I join you?"

He snuggled in beside her on the sofa, and lazily placed his arm over her shoulders.

"Hey, mom?" A boy's voice yelled from beyond the front door, before he took the liberty to open it.

"In here," Liz called out, directing her son.

Simon McAlister, at eleven years old, stood five feet five. His lanky body was stretched further by the skinny jeans he wore. His hair was unfashionably long for most boys his age. Todd noticed the skateboard hanging from Simon's hand and immediately understood his hair fit the intended image.

He hurried in the room and nodded toward Todd and Myra. "Hey."

Todd smiled, seeing himself at that age. "Hey," he gave back.

"Simon, this is Myra MacCoinnich and Officer Todd Blakely."

"Just Todd is fine."

"Hey." Simon glanced between them both, shrugged his shoulders.

"I've heard a lot about you, Simon. 'Tis a pleasure to finally meet you," Myra said.

"My mom said you know where Tara is. Is that true?"

"Aye."

124

"You're going to take us to see her, right?"

Myra glanced at Todd, then back to Simon. "I am."

"Cool." With that business out of the way, Simon moved on to much more important matters. "Hey, Mom, I found this on the driveway." He held up a cell phone and waved it for her to see. "It was just laying there. Can I keep it?"

"Let me see that." She held out her hand and issued another order. "Close the door, you're letting all the heat out." Liz turned the phone over and opened it. "Yours?" she asked, handing it to Todd.

He examined the phone. "No."

"Where did you find it?" Todd asked Liz's son.

"By the garage door. By the way, your garbage cans are all knocked over out there. Want me to clean them up?"

Liz shot a surprised look over her shoulder, as did Todd. What kid offered to do chores for a stranger?

"Five bucks." Simon held out his hand and let one of his dimples show.

"Simon!" Liz scolded.

"Smart kid." Todd reached into his wallet pulled out a five.

"You don't have to do that."

"I hate cleaning up after the neighborhood dogs."

Happily, Simon scrambled out to make quick work of his chore

"He's saving for a new skateboard. Sorry about that."

"Don't be." Todd looked at the phone.

"It's his isn't it?" Myra's face paled, her smile

faded.

"Probably."

"Whose?" Liz asked.

Todd went into the contacts function of the phone to see whose numbers were there. It was empty. He noticed the low battery and decided to wait to find out what information the phone might hold about its owner.

Todd stood and placed the phone on his fireplace mantle. "It wasn't dogs that knocked over the trash last night." He took the time to explain what happened to Lizzy.

"Do you know who it could have been?" Liz asked.

"Grainna had many followers in this time. It could be anyone."

"I've been thinking," Todd told both women. "In light of the situation, maybe it would be best for Myra to stay here, at least until we find out who this guy is."

"Do you think he'll come back?"

"We have to assume he hasn't gotten what he wanted. Perps always return to the scene if their business is unfinished."

"I hadn't thought of that. I don't want to bring any problems to you and Simon."

"I'm sorry Myra but—"

"Don't, you needn't explain. I understand." She turned to Todd. "Are you sure you don't mind me staying here a while longer?"

A wicked grin crested his face. "It's a sacrifice I have to make."

Liz rolled her eyes back, "Oh, puleeesse."

~~~~

Michael watched from a distance so the Druid

wouldn't see him. Wouldn't sense his presence. Only when people surrounded her could he risk probing her mind. She was too powerful and locked out any ability he might have had to eavesdrop on her thoughts.

She would have given Grainna her destiny. But he screwed up. He shouldn't have left the night he tried to keep them apart, but he had, and in turn he gave them the time they needed to consummate their bond. It was evident by the way the man held her, how his hand sometimes dipped too low on her hip, the way only lovers would touch.

When Grainna returned and discovered what had happened, he'd barely survive her anger. He knew her return was imminent. She didn't forgive without dispensing pain and consequence.

But he would endure her wrath, for power was the sweetest of rewards, and the powers he had gained at Grainna's hands were many. She needed him. So no matter what her punishment may be, it wouldn't be death. Her reward for bringing her pure Druid blood, virgin or not, would bring him closer to his ultimate goal. So he waited, watched and planned.

~~~~

Todd's days were filled with shopping, something he seldom did. Myra had the strangest things on her list. Books on plumbing, herbal medicine and gardening, were just the beginning. After the check cleared for the candlesticks, she purchased bolts of material with matching thread and more needles than one would need for a lifetime.

She bought packets of seeds for several types

of plants, fruits and vegetables. Jars of vitamins, Ibuprofen, and antibiotic creams were purchased in bulk. Reams of paper and boxes of pens made the growing stack bulge. She had acquired every possible item on her list and more. Some things Lizzy suggested, others he did.

Every day Myra prepared for the eventuality of her leaving. They didn't talk about when, but he knew it wouldn't be long.

Their passion filled evenings fell into a pattern, leaving him with less than a handful of hours of sleep. He should have been left tired and worn out, instead, his body and mind were more alive than ever.

Dinner out was going to be a surprise. Todd made reservations for all of them, keeping the destination to himself. His only hint was the evening's entertainment would be a history lesson for Liz and Simon.

"Where are we going, Uncle Todd?" Simon asked from the back seat.

The minute Myra came into money, the kid started sucking up to his newfound 'Aunt Myra'. "I'm not your Uncle and stop asking. It's a surprise."

Simon rolled his eyes, "Todd and Myra sitting in a tree..."

"Knock it off." Lizzy and Todd scolded at the same time. Only Myra was in the dark at what else he was going to say.

~~~~

Myra sat in the passenger seat, watching the world go by at a pace faster than any horse could take her. Her life had changed so much, and she surprised herself by adapting to it so easily.

SILENT VOWS

She stopped probing into Todd's thoughts when he asked her to. Not looking was hard at times, like now when he seemed so distant. Christmas was only a few days away and the solstice had passed. She knew he thought of her leaving. Like him, the thought of her going brought a heaviness to her heart. Their relationship was so new, so exciting, she couldn't bear the thought of not seeing him again.

Todd pulled into the parking lot of Renaissance Times. Myra, slightly baffled, had no idea where they were headed.

"I knew it," Simon said from the back.

"What is it?"

"It's a restaurant set up to look like a medieval castle. Inside they have a tournament with horses and everything."

"That is supposed to resemble a castle?"

"Yeah."

"Huh." It fell short. The cars were parked right up next to it for one thing, and every stone that made up the walls were too perfect.

Simon slammed his door and ran up ahead, not bothering to keep his voice low when he asked Myra his questions. "So this is like your home?"

Myra clenched her teeth, looked between Lizzy and Todd. "Not quite."

"What's different?"

"MacCoinnich Keep is much bigger to start."

Lizzy gave her a disbelieving look, "Bigger than this?"

"By three." She looked over Simon's head. "Maybe four."

The hostess was elaborately dressed in peasant garb, but the colors were too vivid and the adornments of ribbons were out of place. Her smile was pleasant enough, and when she addressed them as Lords and Ladies, Myra nodded her head in acknowledgment by habit. The woman gave her a puzzled look.

People filled the outside lobby, most holding large colorful glasses filled with different types of alcoholic beverages. Men dressed as knights were flanked by their squires. They walked with authority in the crowd, causing many heads to turn in their direction. Not very different from her home, Myra thought, although their costumes were more English than Scottish. Myra couldn't help but want to see a kilt or two in the mix. She was disappointed to see none.

She watched, tucked under Todd's arm, and asked her own set of questions when Lizzy and Simon headed off to where the horses were displayed. "What are we doing here?"

He looked between her and the two that walked ahead. "I thought if Simon was going to take a quick trip back in time," he whispered, so no one else could hear, "he might want to see what it's like. Or at least have the right questions to ask before he goes."

"That was very thoughtful of you."

"That's me. Mr. Thoughtful."

A woman, dressed from head to toe in a gown of gold and black, nodded and smiled when she walked by them. "I need to remind Lizzy to prepare to wear dresses like those."

"I have a hard time picturing Lizzy in anything other than jeans." Todd watched as the woman passed.

"What of me? Do you have a hard time

picturing me dressed as her?"

Todd stopped, caught the glint in her smile and placed a slight kiss on her lips. "I see you dressed in rich green velvet. The sleeves would flow to your fingertips, but off your shoulders, exposing your lovely skin. I see small flowers in your hair, brushed free and blowing in the wind."

She closed her eyes picturing what he described. In her vision, Todd stood beside her, attired as the knight she knew him to be, her family crest etched into the shield he carried. As lovely as the image was, it panged her heart in an ache she knew too well, an ache that would grow at the impossibility of their tomorrows. Their lack of a future.

"Hey, why the long face?"

She shook off her thoughts, her pain. He was still there, and Myra was determined to cherish every moment. "I will have my maid make a dress just as you describe. It will always remind me of you."

Her ache was contagious. Todd put a protective arm around her and moved closer to where Lizzy and Simon stood. "How exactly has Liz explained this all to him?"

"Delicately, I think. He seems to understand. Then again, maybe he thinks us all crazy and is just going along to save our feelings." Myra looked at a display of knight's armor and couldn't help but miss her home. Her family.

"Do you think he has a gift? Like you?"

"Most certainly. He told me of his love for animals, and how he befriends all he comes in contact with. Maybe that is his gift. My younger sister Amber has a way with everything in fur and feathers. There have been stories of my ancestors being able to read an animal's mind and even talk to them."

Todd watched one of the horses that stood behind a protective glass looking at Simon. "Why is it so easy to see him communicating with it? If I believe in time travel, a woman starting a fire with a flick of a wrist, and moving heavy objects with her mind, believing in Dr. Doolittle isn't so far fetched."

"Who is Dr. Doolittle?" Myra asked.

Todd laughed and explained while they walked into the arena.

A huge field of dirt for the tournament and games was set in the center of the room surrounded by an arena of stadium seating. Each section was clearly marked with colors so the crowd knew which knight to cheer to victory when they arrived on the field.

Todd and Lizzy flanked both sides of Myra. Both of them watched her more than what was happening around them.

A man dressed and acting as King made a great fuss over announcing dinner before the serving people came out. Their arms were laden with pitchers of ale and flasks of wine. A chicken dinner was served with no utensils, soup was given in a bowl fit to hold in your hand and the bread went unbuttered.

Myra whispered to Lizzy. "Tara has commissioned utensils made so this practice is quickly changing at home."

"Tara always had a germ phobia."

Several knights in many different coats of arms came forward to entertain the guests. The music accompanying them was loud and dramatic.

Games, showing the knights skills with a lance or bow took up much of the time on the field. Often Myra would lean over and whisper to either Lizzy or Todd how these games were played differently in her time.

The dancing horses took Myra by surprise. It wasn't common for such a display to take place at her home. The skill and showmanship was so much like a dance she hardly let her eyes stray from the beauty on the field.

Simon was in awe over the horses as any eleven year old would be. He put out a very quiet. "Cool."

The piped in fog and flashing of lights along with the booming music enthralled Myra. Todd held her hand, stroked the inside of her wrist, and watched the show along with her.

~~~~

He wasn't surprised when he followed them into the arena. What took him back a step or two, were the looks the boy kept passing over his shoulder. His fear of being discovered prompted him to retreat into the shadows.

He thought Myra was the strongest, but felt a pull from the boy indicating a strength he wasn't expecting. Even now, several yards behind him, the boy watched.

It was time to see how powerful his prey was. What better setting than a room full of people and animals?

~~~~

Myra sat on the edge of her seat when the page announced the falconer. Anxious to see what the man would command the creature to do in a stadium this size, she wrung her hands and waited. Simon switched places with his mom and asked questions under his breath.

"What's the big deal? It's just a bird."

"Nay, Simon, a falcon is a weapon in these times." She spread her arms to the arena. "They are used to hunt and scout for their master. Its talons are razor sharp as is his beak, and used because of his ability to kill prey many times its size."

"Wow." Simon glanced over his shoulders. Once the man on the back of the horse moved to the center of the room with the falcon on his arm, he sat back and watched.

Myra shivered, feeling a cool draft in the air. When her hands came up to rub warmth back into her arms, Todd took the liberty to put his jacket over her shoulders, then kept his arm there.

The falconer eyed the crowd and looked toward the eves of the building. "I ask you lords and ladies for your complete silence. The falcon will not discriminate if he thinks you are a threat. Do not call attention to yourself or call out to Ely as he soars above your heads." The rustling of movement in the arena quieted and a hush went over the crowd. With a short command, the falcon took to the air and soared above the crowd. He circled the room twice then returned to rest on his master's arm.

The falconer gave another command and the bird took flight again, this time to a perch high above the people, where he knew his food waited for him. But on his return flight, something caught the bird's eye, and he detoured off his predicted path.

Myra noticed the falconer's distress when the bird didn't go where he was supposed to. Twice he put out a signal for the bird to return, which the animal ignored.

A woman, sitting several rows behind Myra and her party, was wearing a flashing light in her hair. The falcon screeched, filling the room with his ominous sound when he dived toward the defenseless woman. Her arms instinctively went up to protect her face. The terror in her scream when the bird scraped her arms had those around her jumping out of the way.

Her screams alarmed the falcon more, causing it to dive at her again.

Myra jumped to her feet, and in a quick motion wrapped Todd's coat around her arm. She called to the bird, as she had heard her father do to his own. Her command was ignored. "Call him, Simon," she yelled over the noise of the growing chaos in the building.

Simon's eyes moved back and forth between Myra and the flailing woman.

"Call him," Myra yelled again.

He stood and said the bird's name softly. The bird's head jerked up and cocked to one side. Simon repeated his call again. "Ely, come."

The falcon abandoned his prey, circling both Myra and Simon. Much to everyone's surprise, Ely landed on Myra's outstretched arm.

Lizzy pulled her son close, baffled.

The falconer attempted to gain Ely's attention and failed. Myra spoke in her native Gaelic encouraging the bird to settle. The beast darted his eyes, confused by the mixed signals, then settled on the perch of her arm.

Myra walked to the center aisle, and anxious patrons parted giving her a wide berth. None of them uttered the smallest sound.

She made her way to the edge of the fence where the falconer waited. Graciously, she gave the bird to his owner. The trainer hastily covered the animal's head and with a short bow, quickly left the stage.

The attention she received after everyone settled down worried her. The management resumed the show as rapidly as they could, while those people sitting around them watched her actions for the rest of the evening.

The four of them said very little the rest of the night, knowing they were being watched.

Myra felt a chill fall over her again when she realized what she had done. It was tricky keeping her gift at bay in such situations. Coupled with her nature to help those in need, it proved almost impossible. But it appeared no one questioned how she got the falcon to come to her. Even Simon asked how she did it. "It wasn't me, Simon, 'twas you."

Simon kept the conversation up most of the way home. Todd said very little.

After they dropped Lizzy and Simon off, Myra turned to Todd and asked, "Why are you so upset?"

"That thing could have ripped you up."

"But it didn't."

"But it could have."

"Aye." She held on tight when he took the corner a little to fast.

"It was a stupid thing to do," he scolded her.

"I am not stupid."

"I didn't say you were stupid, I said it was a

stupid thing to do."

"I heard what you said. Tell me, Todd, would you rather have had that woman lose her skin?"

"Better her than you."

She paused, knew his anger came out of concern for her safety. "I'm sorry I upset you."

"You didn't upset me, it's just..." He shook his head and gripped the steering wheel harder. "Every time you use your..."

"Gifts."

"Yeah, gifts. I'm forced to believe everything you've told me. It would almost be easier if you were just a little crazy." He looked over at her. "At least there's medication for crazy."

"So you would rather I be mad than who I am," she said.

"I don't know what I want. You confuse me."

They drove the rest of the way in silence, both caught up in their own minds

Once home, Myra went straight to the room that had been labeled hers, the one she hadn't slept in since they became intimate.

Todd stopped in her doorway, watched her gather her nightgown and turn her bed down. "So this is where you want to sleep?"

"I don't want to confuse you," she tossed at him.

"Too late."

"There is no reason to pretend we have a future. If you can't accept me for what I am, then it is best we don't let anything more happen between us."

"How can we have a future, Myra? You're going back. I plan on staying here."

It broke her heart, hearing him map out their

groundless relationship. *Ask me to stay.* "Aye, I'm going back. I have imposed on you long enough." There was no longer a reason for her to stay.

Later, she sat on her bed alone in her room, and wept. She softly spoke her prayers and confessed her love for the man in the next room, and she choked back a sob at the unfairness of her life.

Her mind slipped into sleep, finding peace in oblivion as her tears wore out. In her dreams, she heard the chant she had shared with Tara. Unknown to her, the stones hidden in the folds of her bed started to glow.

In this day and in this hour, we call upon the sacred power. I choose to give my blood to thee, I choose that you are a sister to me.

Her dream shifted from the time she had pricked her finger and sat with Tara. She saw instead the image of Todd, naked and lying beside her, tangled in sheets moistened by their love. She held his head, looked into his mind and changed her chant.

In this day and in this hour, I call upon the sacred power. If you give your love to me, I will give you my love times three.

In her sleep, her body shuddered with the thought of Todd sliding into her.

Restless and tossing in his big bed all alone, his body stiffened with Myra's vision, mixing with his. Her body wrapped around his in his dream, pulling a gasp from his sleeping lips.

The stones from the Ancients hummed and lit, bringing both man and woman together in their sleep.

Chapter Eleven

It was Christmas Eve and Todd watched her from the doorway. Myra shuffled her things and packed them into glorified carpetbags. She wore a long skirt and simple shoes. Her hair fell free in front of her eyes each time she bent over to pack something new.

They'd barely spoken since their fight. When she had announced her departure date the night after they'd come back from Renaissance Times, Todd did his best to be agreeable. He spent more time at work, which made it easier in some ways.

Simon wouldn't miss any school and Lizzy had a week off for the holidays.

He knew the real reason she was leaving.

He couldn't blame her.

Myra tried lifting the mattress to get at what was underneath.

"What are you doing?"

She tossed him a look over her shoulder. "The stones are hidden here."

Todd lifted the mattress so Myra could retrieve them.

He sat on the bed and picked one up, turned it over several times and gave a short, "Humph."

"What?"

"I thought they would be...I don't know...gold or something. They look like ordinary rocks."

"Look closer." She placed a hand to the stone, giving it a small amount of energy. The words carved in it faintly glowed, almost causing Todd to drop it.

Does everything she touch light up?

Quickly, she placed all the stones in the sack, and then put out her hand in a silent request for the sixth one. Her hand brushed his when he gave it back. A small amount of static gave him a charge. He drew back.

"That's everything." Myra kept her eyes down when he got up to take a load to his car.

The night fog was dense driving up the mountain roads and into the Angeles National Forest. Streaks of white fog would sometimes glare the windshield, making driving difficult. Behind them, Liz followed with Simon in her car.

The road was almost deserted. Few people needed to drive it on Christmas Eve. Todd concentrated on his driving, and tried his best to keep his thoughts away from what was happening. A part of him, the skeptic part of him, didn't believe anything would happen once they were isolated and Myra set up her rocks.

The other part of him, the part he didn't recognize and had just started getting used to, realized she was leaving and he may never see her again. "Will you bring Liz and Simon back?" he asked unexpectedly.

"One of us will." She lifted her chin, refused to look his way.

But not you.

~~~~

The parking lot was deserted. Simon jumped from the car and started grabbing the packs. Liz huddled under her coat to ward off the cold. "This is crazy."

Myra couldn't help but smile. "That is what I thought before I came here. Everything will be fine."

"How are we going to move this stuff around without being noticed?" Lizzy heaved a bag full of books to the trail off the road.

"We won't have to move it far. We will stay in one of the cabins outside the Keep this night. My mother will know I am back and send one of my brothers to fetch us."

"How will she know?"

"When your son needs you, do you know it?" Myra asked, not expecting a reply.

"Huh." Lizzy pondered.

"Are you ready for this?" Todd asked Simon.

Simon looked up at Todd like he was nuts. "Is anyone?"

Todd shook his head, ruffled Simon's hair. "You're too smart for your own good."

Myra glanced at the pattern of the trees, searching for a symmetrical spot to place the stones. She found a small clearing which suited her needs before she set her things down in a pile. Todd, Liz and Simon followed her lead.

One by one, she placed the stones in a circle. Slowly, she drew out the moment of their departure for as long as she could. *I'm leaving and I'm never going to see him again.* The words echoed in her mind, creating havoc in her heart.

Unable to put off the inevitable any longer she glanced up. "We're ready." She motioned for Liz and Simon to come inside the stones.

Todd's eyes followed Lizzy as she led Simon into the circle.

Myra waited until Todd's gaze moved to her.

She stood staring at him, patiently waiting. Unable to control it, her heart started to crumble and break.

"Come here," he said.

She rushed to his arms on a cry. Desperate, their lips found each other's, each devouring in a last attempt to hold onto what they knew could never be.

His hands stayed in her hair holding her to him. His kiss was excruciating. She wanted him to beg her to stay, but how could she even if he did.

A silent tear streaked her cheek when his lips left hers. "I will never forget you, Todd Blakely. A part of you will live with me all my days. I have no way to thank you for all you have done."

He wiped her tear away and kissed her forehead. "I'll never forget you." He stiffened his spine and moved aside, putting a small amount of distance between them. He already missed her. She could see it in his eyes.

Her hand slipped from his before she stepped into the circle, where Lizzy stood waiting with Simon. Myra laid her hand on each stone bringing brilliance and light. The inscribed words, written by the Ancients, hummed and radiated heat.

In Gaelic, Myra began:

"Ancient stones, and ancient power, take us back to my home this hour. Take us to my time at last, may only the day's I've been here lapse. Keep us safe and from harm's way, hide us from the light of day. The cabin by the creek, if you please. As I ask it, make it be."

A rush of hot air pushed against the three of them. The stones, once dormant, now shot fire and light above their heads, and swirled into a vortex.

Myra looked up as the ground began to shake, her eyes met and locked to Todd's. Her hand lifted in a silent wave.

His shock registered to her senses. For the first time since they met, she felt his absolute belief in all she had told him, his acceptance of all she had said as truth.

Then he was gone.

The world shimmered in front of the travelers, and the ground disappeared from beneath their feet. A feeling of weightlessness and a falling all at once surrounded them. Colors of all shades shot past them and above their heads. They couldn't tell if they were moving up or down, left or right. The noise was deafening and the wind rushed over them at an alarming speed.

Simon's eyes grew wide. Lizzy held his hand in a tight grip. "This won't last long," Myra yelled over the noise, but she didn't think the others could hear her.

Like a door slamming, everything stopped all at once, the noise, the light, the wind.

A small dusting of snow drifted down from the gray skies above. Their belongings sat in the neat piles they had placed them in only moments before but now they sat on a pile of snow, surrounded by a dark ring where the stones' energy and light had burned into the ground.

"Now what?" Lizzy asked.

Myra snapped out of her thoughts, blinked away her tears, and looked at Simon and Lizzy still holding hands and shaking. Behind them stood a cabin. "We will put our things here, and stay until first light."

"Are we really in Scotland?" Simon asked.

"Aye. Look over there, beyond the trees. Do you see the hue of light?"

"Yeah."

"That is my home, MacCoinnich Keep." A smile chased away her pain. She closed her eyes briefly and sent out a call of 'I'm home' to her mother.

"Come, let us get out of the cold, after we cover up the circle from the stones."

~~~~

Todd sat on the cold, hard ground. His eyes were dry and refused to blink. Jesus, she was gone. She was really gone.

The only thing that remained to remind him she had been there was a black circle where fire had scorched the earth, evidence from the circle of stones that tossed them all from one time to another.

If he hadn't seen it, he wouldn't have believed it possible. Even now, sitting alone in the dark with a mist starting to rain from the cloudy skies, he couldn't wrap his mind around the facts.

From the beginning, he knew there was something about her that was pure. Innocent.

It wasn't until a bitter cold wind bore down on him that he made his way to his car. He looked over to where Lizzy had parked hers, a forestry pass displayed on the dash, informing any official policing the forest that a hiker would return for their car within the time allotted.

Only he knew the driver wasn't a hiker enjoying the great outdoors.

At home, he tossed his keys down and went straight to the liquor cabinet, poured himself a double Scotch, then fell onto his couch. His blurry eyes registered a box next to his fireplace, wrapped up in bright red and green foiled paper, perfect for the holiday.

It was the only evidence in the room that Christmas was less than an hour away.

The card on it was from Myra, it said simply; "Happy Christmas, Todd. Never Forget."

The box was impossibly heavy. It took both hands to carry it back to his sofa where he unwrapped it. Under the wrapping and from the plain cardboard box he drew out a sword.

The ornate carvings were etched deep in the blade and the hilt fit his hand perfectly. He lifted it up and tested its weight.

Never in his life had he held such a weapon. The joy it brought to him was mixed with more sorrow than he expected, more pain than he thought possible.

"Damn. What did I do?"

He took everything off his mantel and placed the sword there perfectly displayed. He lit a fire and wondered if Myra was staring into a fire at that very moment.

"Damn."

~~~~

Myra felt their presence long before she saw them ride up.

Lizzy sat with Simon on a tattered and worn-out cot. The looks on their faces clearly defined their anticipation of what was yet to come.

Even with her heart breaking over leaving Todd, Myra's heart leapt with joy when the silhouettes of her father and brothers rode into view.

She stood on the step outside the door. Fin

145

bounded from his horse, picked her up and swirled her off her feet. "God's blood, 'tis good to see you." His hug was fierce, his voice sincere.

Cian, her younger brother, stepped in and hugged her. "'Tis about time you returned."

Her father's welcome was more stoic. Tears threatened to fall as she ran to his arms.

He held her as if she had returned from the dead. "We missed you so much." Emotion swallowed her whole, and tears leaked from her eyes.

"I missed you all."

Fin stepped past the reunion and noticed Lizzy and Simon standing in the doorway. His elated expression fell, his eyes shot to Myra

"Myra." He cleared his throat. "An introduction if you please."

Myra broke free of her father's arms and turned to Lizzy and Simon who waited patiently for the reunion to end. "Lizzy. Simon. Come meet some of my family."

Lizzy urged her son forward, her eyes glancing toward Fin. He stared both of them down, obviously annoyed by their presence. Myra wanted to question him, but knew she should wait.

"Da, Fin, Cian, this is Tara's sister and nephew, Lizzy and Simon."

Ian sized them up, his face stern. Myra's skin started to crawl. Between Fin and her father, she worried that they would demand Lizzy return at that very moment.

To her relief her father spoke with kindness. "We have heard much about you. Tara will be pleased you're both here." He kissed the back of Lizzy's hand in greeting and motioned for Fin to follow suit.

Lizzy's back was rod straight and tension filled the air.

Myra cleared her throat. "'Tis good you brought extra mounts, father, we have brought back so many wonderful things."

They rode two to a horse. Simon behind Cian, Myra with her father and Lizzy begrudgingly sat in front of Fin. Lizzy didn't complain, but Myra knew she felt her family's disapproval of her presence. The chill from Finlay was coldest. Myra knew she would find out why at the first chance of a private conversation.

~~~~

Damn, if looks could kill. Lizzy knew she stood the risk of ticking off the MacCoinnich's when she forced Myra to bring her back in time, but this was ridiculous. The looks Finlay gave her brought the hair on the nape of her neck to a spike. His arrogance pissed her off more than worried her. From all Myra had told her, Fin would move heaven and earth to see Myra safe. Liz always acted no differently in regards to Tara. So why the cold shoulder?

Out of the corner of her eye, Liz noticed her son trying not to hold on to the waist of the MacCoinnich's youngest son Cian. Simon had never been on a horse before, except for the pony rides at the county fair. Those small animals were led around by a rope and presented little chance for the rider to fall. These massive horses could do a hell of a lot of harm if they took off and left their passengers in the dirt.

She was about to call out a warning for her son to hold on when Fin whispered in her ear,

"Leave him. The horses will do no more than walk on the way home."

She realized he had read her thoughts and found the invasion of her mind disturbing. "He could fall."

"He won't. If you treat him like a child in front of Cian, he will lose the respect of someone close to his age."

"I would rather him lose respect than fall and get hurt."

Fin rolled his eyes. "A loss of respect is more damaging than a bruise or cut. I don't expect someone from your time to understand."

My time? He made it sound so dirty. Her spine stiffened, putting more distance between them. She ignored his chuckle and watched Simon out of the corner of her eye. Despite her best judgment, she said nothing to her son and traveled the rest of the way in silence.

~~~~

The horses picked their way through the light dusting of snow. The massive doors leading into the courtyard of the keep gaped open in welcome.

As they moved closer, her father hurried his mount in front and quickly helped her to her feet. Myra ran into her mother's waiting arms. Tears prickled again when her eyes met Tara's. She knew Lizzy's sister would have questions, could tell simply by looking at her that she felt some of her pain.

Myra sent Tara a pensive smile and gave a quick shake of her head. They could talk later.

Fin and Cian's horses focused her attention to Lizzy and Tara's reunion. Myra smiled over at Amber and motioned toward Tara who now started to notice that her sister was being helped off Fin's horse.

"Lizzy?"

Duncan walked Tara down the steps before she broke away and ran to her sister's arms. "My God, Lizzy!"

Myra choked on their emotional reunion. Despite the strange expression passing Fin's face, she knew she did the right thing by bringing Lizzy and Simon home with her.

Tara broke away from her sister only to grasp a silent Simon and hold him tight.

"How? Why?" Tara asked her broken questions.

Lizzy stared at her sister, tears streamed down her face. "I made Myra promise to bring us. I had to see you safe with my own eyes." Lizzy peeked over Tara's shoulder to Fin. Myra felt his scorn.

"It is just a visit, Tara. Only a short visit." From the sound of Lizzy's voice, she felt Finlay's condemnation as well.

Fin lifted a brow then turned and walked away.

"You're here now. That's what matters."

They hugged again.

"Merry Christmas, Lizzy."

~~~~

They moved into the main hall and found comfortable places to sit. Wine and ale flowed with many hugs and kisses from all of them.

Myra couldn't help but wonder what Todd was doing at that very moment. Was he happy she was gone? Or surprised that she'd told the truth about coming from the past? There'd be no denying it now that he'd seen her leave with his own eyes. She pushed her thoughts aside and attempted to focus on the joy of her family.

"Did you have a premonition, Myra? A sign to say it was safe to return?" her mother asked.

"No, mother." Myra's eyes met the floor.

"Did Grainna find you?"

"We never saw Grainna." Myra swallowed a long drink and prayed her family didn't pry too much.

"So there was no threat from her?" Her mother's eyes searched for answers almost more than her words.

"How did you know it was safe for your return?" her father asked.

Myra avoided the question, asked her own. "Was she here?"

"Aye. But Tara found a way to send her back," Duncan explained.

"When?"

"Just a few days ago."

"'Tis a good thing I've returned when I did then." She closed the chain of questions off and told them all again how good it was to be home.

Tara, who had refused to let her sister's hand go asked, "How long will you stay, Lizzy?"

"A week. If that's okay?" Lizzy glanced over to Ian.

Perfect. Myra wanted to pat her on the back. Her father needed to make the decision. If left up to Fin, Lizzy would have been sent home already.

"The question is how to get you back?" Fin spoke up. Several heads lifted at his words.

"One of you can take us." Liz met his disapproving stare with one of her own.

"It isn't that easy, Lady Elizabeth."

"It's Liz," she corrected.

Fin stood and walked to the fire. "Here you are Lady Elizabeth, widow and mother of Simon."

Liz dropped her sister's hand and took to her feet. "I'm not a widow."

"We know that. But that will be the story you tell."

"Excuse me?"

Myra watched the exchange in silence, all the while glancing at Tara. Both women knew Lizzy enough to understand she was about to lose her composure.

"You heard me." Fin turned away as if to say the topic was closed.

"Listen to me..." Liz raised her voice and reached out to make him face her.

He caught her hand. "You listen. In this time, you are nothing without the protection of this family. And since you saw fit to force my sister to bring you here, you will abide by the boundaries we give you. Your very presence will raise questions, most of which will bring a lie to your lips in order to keep who we are hidden from those who seek to destroy us. Furthermore, I will not allow Simon the ridicule which would come to him because of your thoughtlessness."

Chest to chest, Lizzy and Finlay held their jaws firm. A slight twitch to Lizzy's fingers displayed her anger.

"Lizzy, Fin speaks the truth. While you're here, we have to keep where you are from a secret. For all our sakes," Myra calmly stated, hoping to ease the tension in the room.

"Fine." Lizzy's eyes never left Fin's.

151

Fin's brow rose, silently saying, 'I win.'

Chapter Twelve

The family had gone to bed. Only Fin and Myra remained. Staring into the fire, Myra felt lost in her thoughts, while Fin sat across from her, his attempts to read her mind and emotions obvious. She had learned to block Fin out of her mind when they were children. It frustrated him then, and she knew it frustrated him now.

"Why did you come back when you did?" he asked.

"I needed to."

"Needed to? Why? Was there a threat?"

Her eyes skirted from the fire to him and back again. "Someone was watching us. I'm not sure how much of a threat they were. If the time here kept with the time in the future, then it couldn't have been Grainna who watched."

"If not Grainna, then who?"

"I do not know."

"So it may not be safe for Elizabeth to return." Fin decided.

Myra shook her head. "I didn't say that."

"But you said *us*. Someone was watching us. If it wasn't safe for both of you, then it isn't safe for her alone."

Myra closed her eyes knowing she couldn't keep Fin from the truth for long. "Lizzy wasn't the *us*."

Fin stopped pacing, looked back at her. "Then who?"

She stood, straightened her skirt. "'Tis late, Fin, I've had a very long day."

"Why won't you talk to me?"

"I'm tired. Let us talk on this another day."

Fin stopped her from leaving. "If you didn't have a sign or premonition, and you weren't sure Grainna wasn't there, in fact you believed she was here, then why did you come back? If Grainna was here you would have walked directly into harm's way."

"Nay, Fin. I wouldn't have."

"What are you saying? She will kill the virgin she uses to break her curse, you know this."

"Yes. I know." *Stop asking questions.*

He crossed to her, shook her shoulders, demanding she look at him. "Why? Why would you risk your life to return when you did?"

"Dammit, Fin, Grainna has no use for me *now*." Her words came in a scalding rush. Tears sprung to her eyes.

Fin's mouth snapped shut. He stepped back and asked through clenched teeth. "Who?"

"Does it matter? We both knew it was an option. One I am sure everyone will be thinking I took before long." She turned from him and looked away. "I don't want this to cloud our Christmas, Fin. Please keep it between us. For now."

"Are you with child?" He choked out.

"No."

He let out a long breath. "Then no one needs to know what happened. We can go on as normal."

"Normal?" She looked above her to the candles ablaze on the chandelier above her head. She waved her hand sending the wind above both their heads to put out the flames. "Nothing is normal.

154

Nothing."

~~~~

The phone rang, waking him up. Todd hadn't fallen asleep until the sun started to rise.

"Yeah." Todd answered the phone trying to lift his head out of the fog.

"Don't tell me you're sleeping. Man what is up with you lately?"

He picked up his clock, tossed it back onto his nightstand. "What do you want, Jake?"

"You are sleeping. I thought I was lazy."

"Jake!"

"Okay, okay, listen I have the kids this afternoon and I was thinking..."

Jake's thinking usually involved him. "Cut to the chase."

"What are you doing for Christmas dinner?"

"Microwave and a beer. Why?"

"Well the kids haven't seen Uncle Todd in a while. I thought it would be nice if you came over."

His head was starting to pound. "And?"

"Come on, Todd, you know I don't cook. Denny's just isn't right on Christmas."

Damn. He was looking forward to a full day of brooding. He agreed to help his friend and was about to hang up the phone when Jake stopped him. "By the way, one of those missing women showed up last night."

"Missing women?" Todd wasn't sure what he was talking about.

"Yeah, I got the call yesterday. I thought you and I could check it out, maybe score a few points with the Sergeant, work our way up the ranks."

"What the hell are you talking about?"

"Gwen Adams, the old lady from the

Renaissance Faire."

Todd's eyes flew open as Jake's words registered. "Is she alive?"

"Yeah, she's alive, in the hospital outside of San Luis Obispo. Not saying much from what I've been told."

"Any idea where she's been all this time?"

"See, I knew you'd want to know more. How about we go on up tomorrow and find out?"

Todd hung up, scratched the stubble on his chin spoke to himself, "Let's see if the evil witch is all Myra said she was."

~~~~

Christmas, medieval style, blending with the twenty-first century was a joy to watch. Myra brought many things to share with her family. Everyone held a miracle in their hands.

"Here, Fin. I know the bathroom Tara has been on you to finish has given you trouble." She handed him a book. "'Tis a book on plumbing that should help."

Fin smiled, gave his thanks and leafed through the pages.

Lizzy handed a box to Tara. "I thought you might like this. Cassy took it at the Faire."

"Did you tell her about me?" Tara took the box.

"Yeah. She thinks I'm crazy, but I told her."

"That's all you can do."

"Open your gift."

Tara slowly lifted the lid of the box. Inside was a framed picture of her and Duncan the day they were handfasted in the twenty-first century.

"Oh, Lizzy. Thank you so much." Tara hugged her sister with tears in her eyes.

"Cian, 'tis for you." Myra handed him a box.

"What is it?" he asked, pulling the wafer thin device from the box.

Simon bounded out of his chair. "Dude, it's an iPod."

"What is that?"

Simon rolled his eyes and turned it on. "Myra what did you load in here?"

"I asked the merchant to add whatever the boys of your time listened to." She smiled when Simon put one of the earpieces to his head and the other to her brother's. Before long, they were both bobbing their heads and smiling.

"Hey, how are you going to charge it?" Simon asked.

Myra put her hand on the device and pulled in the energy around them, then channeled it into the machine. "Man, you have to show me how you do that. Think of the money saved on batteries, mom." Simon's excitement had them all laughing.

Amber held her diary and the assortment of ink pens as if it were gold. No more quill and inkblots on parchment paper. It was the perfect gift for her eleven-year-old sister.

Lora looked over the books on healing herbs and medicine made from them.

For Ian, Myra had thought of many things, but what she brought him was what she had seen Todd enjoy. Several bottles of Scotch sat in front of him. He poured a portion for himself and his eldest sons, all of whom approved.

"Your time has many wonderful things," Lora said to Lizzy.

"It does. I think Myra has brought one of everything. She had us up and down every aisle at every department store."

Tara laughed. "God, I haven't thought of shopping in months."

"What we couldn't find there we searched for in other stores like it. Buildings the size of our village."

"You jest," Ian said waving his hand in the air. "Why would anyone need such large buildings to store goods?"

Myra leaned over and picked up the bag of chocolates they were all enjoying. "Take these simple candies. There are maybe ten different flavors just by this name on the bag. Those flavors have different color wrappers. Why they even had pictures of stockings and snowpersons—"

"Snowmen," Lizzy and Tara corrected together.

"Aye, snowmen decorating the bag."

"Why so many?" Fin asked.

Lizzy smirked. "Because the companies that make them want to make money."

"Remember I told you that Christmas was too commercialized?" Tara asked.

Several of them nodded.

"People in the future buy too much, eat too much and have forgotten about the important things. Like family." Tara reached over and held Duncan's hand.

Myra swallowed as her gaze slipped to the floor. It wasn't that she begrudged Tara and Duncan their happiness, but her heart felt empty. She couldn't help but wonder if she would ever feel whole again.

~~~~

Watching her baby sister with her husband filled her heart with love. Liz always knew Tara would find a deep and meaningful relationship, but never imagined it would be with a medieval knight.

Everything looked like a fairy tale. From the long dress she wore, to the slippers on her feet. Liz couldn't have felt more out of place if she tried. Yet Tara blended in quite well. Even her words had changed. A little of the MacCoinnich accent floated off her tongue and had Liz looking at her twice.

Dear Lord, she could hardly understand the servants. When one arrived in her room to help her dress, all Liz could do was stare wide-eyed, afraid to talk after Fin's little speech about keeping her identity a secret. She didn't have to bother. Apparently they sent Tara's maid who was used to their strange speech.

In fact, all the MacCoinnichs spoke differently than the others at the Keep. The family worked hard learning the verbiage of the future. That way when they had to blend in, they could.

She stole a peek at Fin dressed in a kilt. *What does he wear under that thing anyway?* She shook the thought from her head. The red plaid hung just below his knees. His boots went half way up his muscular calf.

Why do all the assholes have to be so good looking? Boy, was he an asshole. Not to Simon, however. No, Simon had talked with Fin several times in the morning hours about the machines of the twenty-first century. Even now, with both of them huddled over the book on plumbing, they acted as though they had known each other longer than a few hours. Having fixed her toilets more than once, Liz knew she could help him with the bathroom project. It was much more entertaining however, to watch the jerk struggle.

As the day went on, Myra became more and more silent. Her blank face stared at the fire or off into space. A pleasant smile surfaced when someone spoke directly to her, but it was forced. When she excused herself from the room, Liz waited a few minutes before following her with Tara and Amber close behind.

The three of them quietly walked into Myra's room, where they found her curled up in a ball, weeping. Slowly they sat on the bed and each placed a hand on her to tell her they were there.

"I miss him, Lizzy."

"I know," she said wiping a tear from her eye. "I'm sure he misses you, too."

"Why does it hurt so much?"

"Loving someone is a powerful emotion. Losing that is just as strong."

A sob broke free and Myra clasped her hand. "When will this empty pain go away?"

Liz looked at Tara and Amber who both sat quietly. "I don't know."

Then Myra cried, cried until the tears dried up. Only when she had fallen asleep did the sisters leave the room.

~~~~

The hospital walls sported greeting cards and cheap garland. Someone tacked tinsel on the ceiling and half-eaten boxes of candy and cookies were everywhere.

Todd and Jake arrived at the hospital in plain clothes. They were out of their jurisdiction, but that didn't stop them from flashing a badge when they hit the wall of a nurse who wasn't willing to point out where Gwen Adams was.

She was sleeping when they entered her room. The only noise came from the roommate's television.

Todd lifted the picture he had of Ms. Adams and compared it to the woman in the bed. Even asleep, she appeared younger. Odd, he thought most elderly people looked older without makeup. So this was the woman Myra feared with her life.

Suddenly, Ms. Adams eyes darted open and straight to his. Her instant scowl quickly changed to a knowing smile. "Officers," she said in greeting.

Jake looked at his partner than to her. "How do you know we're cops?"

She didn't answer. Instead, with her eyes never looking away from Todd's, she said, "Sit, please."

"Where have you been, Ms. Adams?" Jake asked the minute they were comfortable.

"Well, we old people are quite forgetful at times."

"You don't remember where you've been for half a year?"

"Bits and pieces. I'm sorry to have caused so much trouble." Moaning, she extended her hand asking for her water. "Please?"

Her eyes shifted to Todd's again. *She's creepy, Myra. I'll give you that.*

"I fell you see, that I remember. Then nothing for quite awhile. Clearly someone took care of me, since I am not hurt or deathly ill."

"Are you saying you had some type of amnesia?" Jake wrote something down. Todd knew he was comparing notes to Myra's case.

"I suppose you could say that. I remember horses and people dressed in elaborate costumes, but again I may be remembering the Faire players. You do know I manage a Renaissance Faire?"

Todd bit his tongue. Yeah, she could be thinking of the Ren Faire, or she could have been sent back by Myra's family. Either way she was someone he would have to watch. This old biddy was the reason Myra had to leave when she did. For that, he hated her.

~~~~

Grainna stared into the eyes and mind of Todd Blakely. The stupid fool had no idea how easily his thoughts and words oozed from his head and into hers.

He knew the MacCoinnich's daughter and wished for her to return. As she peered deeper, he winced and glanced her way. His hand went to his head as if it ached. Then his thoughts shut off. Grainna's teeth ground together. Frustrated, she dug deeper, but to no avail. He knew much, this man who watched while the other questioned. Knew of her power and sought to discredit her.

She hated his type, full of himself and the power behind his badge. He looked down on her and wanted to dismiss her.

Look at me as if I'm nothing. Under the sheets, she twisted her fingers and chanted in her head.

"So..." Todd started talking, and then coughed on his words. "Do you remember..." He shook his head and coughed again. His hand went to his throat, and his eyes shot over to the woman in the bed. *You question my power and brought this on yourself.* She knew he struggled to breathe and tried her best not to smile.

Grainna drew her brows together. "Are you okay? Here take some water, young man," she

162

handed him her water.

She allowed one quick breath. Once he drank the water, she released her fingers and let her grin slip.

His partner tossed him a concerned look, patted him on the back.

They asked a few more questions, which Grainna avoided. Todd's eyes narrowed.

They stepped out of the room a few minutes later and talked by the door.

"What happened back there? Did you pick up smoking when I wasn't looking?"

"No."

"You sick?"

"No." His voice held a slight tremor.

From inside the room, Grainna laughed.

~~~~

"It's always a man." Lizzy sat across from Tara with her feet up on the table. "Can't live with 'em, can't shoot 'em."

"Was he good to her?"

"Yeah. He was. There aren't many men who will take in a stranger like he did."

"They would for sex."

"I don't think it was like that. Don't get me wrong, I know they had sex, but I truly think Myra meant something to him. He would sit next to her and stroke her hair. What guy does that?"

"Not many."

"I don't think Todd really believed Myra was from this century. Jiminy Christmas, this place is something." Liz tossed her hands to the air and looked around the walls of the Keep. Stone walls with tapestries the size of rooms. Knights in the courtyard below. Shit, she was having a hard time believing it, and Lizzy was sitting smack-dab in the middle of it.

"Or this?" Tara tossed her hand to a candle and lit its wick.

"*I* can't get past that!" Her mouth dropped open. "Do you really think I could learn?"

"Just keep practicing like I showed you. It will come. I couldn't do it the first few times either." Getting back on the subject Tara asked, "So tell me more about Todd."

"I told you, he's a cop. Cute. Really cute, his hair is a little long, but after seeing all the men here I guess not so much. By the way, Duncan is to die for."

Tara swatted her sister's arm. "He's mine."

"I'm just saying...nice."

"Fin has a similar look." Tara cast her a glance.

"Fin's an ass."

"He is not."

"Puleeese. What a chauvinist, telling me how I'm to act and what I'm to say. I tell ya, Tara, I don't know how you deal with it."

"There is plenty of chivalry to go around. Aye, I admit some chauvinism, but the price is little when you compare the two. The men here feel a need to protect the women and the children with honor and respect. In turn, the women cater to their men. I have seen very few men who don't deserve the catering the women give. Of course, I live like a queen, and my husband denies me nothing. I wouldn't have it any other way, Lizzy. Duncan is the best thing that ever happened to me. Fin's been there for me as well. When he marries, his wife will be treated with respect and love."

Liz wanted to correct her sister but instead added, "Then I hope he finds her soon, so she can teach him a thing or two about women."

"I don't think Fin spends much time *talking* to the women."

"Meaning?" Liz asked.

"His reputation isn't all that squeaky clean."

Liz looked down at her skirts. "They never are, Tara. They never are." *Just how soiled was it?*

"You might try and get along with him, Lizzy. He's the one who will take you back."

Liz looked up at her sister and asked, "Why not you?"

"I can't. Not with the baby. I don't know the effect of time travel on him or her. Besides, the Druid wedding vows Duncan and I exchanged are so binding, we truly can't be away from each other for long. We can actually speak to one another in our heads."

"No shit? Like telepathy?"

"Crazy isn't it? The second we tied our hands together, my thoughts merged with his, and we spoke to one another without moving our lips."

Shaking her head, Lizzy said, "I don't think I'd like having someone in my thoughts all the time. What if you're mad at him?"

"Well, there are ways of tuning him out, but our emotions are very strong. When Grainna captured me, he found me because of our connection, that and what I told you about Amber."

"Amber's an empath?" Liz asked.

Tara nodded. "Finding me had more to do with our blood sister chant than her ability to feel my emotions."

Liz shook her head. "You really believe that stupid blood sister pledge we did back in Jr. High connected you to Amber and Myra?"

"Do you have a better explanation?"

"It sounds like a bad 'B' movie." If she weren't living it, Liz wouldn't believe any of it.

"Call it what you want. When Myra went to the future, I knew she would be back. Amber's emotions on the subject were even stronger. When Grainna kidnapped me, I was able to send telepathic messages to Amber. That mental link led Duncan straight to me."

"If Duncan can talk to you in his head, how come he didn't know what was happening?"

Tara's gaze grew distant for a brief moment. A glimmer of pain, probably brought on by the memories of her abdication, shown in her eyes.

"When Duncan is too far away, we can't hear each other. If it weren't for the connection to Amber, he may not have found me. If I were to travel to the future without him, there is no telling if I would survive the trip. According to Lora, the binding vows we pledged to each other give us the advantage of each other's thoughts and emotions, but it also leaves us with a gaping hole if something happens to either of us. Most Druids who marry like we did die within days of each other."

Liz's gaze shot to the men on field. A chill settled deep in her stomach.

"So you see," Tara interrupted Lizzy's thoughts. "Duncan and I can't be separated."

Liz realized she'd asked the impossible. "Of course, I'm sorry I asked."

"Myra can't be asked to go again. Besides,

Laird Ian wouldn't allow it."

"I guess not."

Several men, including Fin and Duncan, practiced their fighting skills with their swords in the courtyard. Loud clangs and clashes with the occasional grunt mixed in the air. Their shirtless bodies wet with the work of their exercise, muscles bulged with the weight of their weapons. Lizzy licked her dry lips, trying not to look when the kilts rose too high.

"History makes these times out to be full of war and death. Is it?" Liz watched Fin swing a double-edged sword over his head.

"Yes and no. Lora told me battles are fought all the time, that the men are always ready to defend the Keep. In the last five years however, things have been relatively quiet. She thinks the Ancients are keeping away the carnage so the MacCoinnichs have time and manpower to defeat Grainna."

"Sounds far-fetched to me."

"You wouldn't say that if you had come face to face with her."

"Come on, Tara, one woman against a whole army of men? And an old woman at that."

"Yeah, a five hundred year old woman. Immortal and full of rage and hatred over everything and everyone."

"Why don't the Ancients take her out once and for all?"

"I don't think they can." Tara shifted in her chair. "I've never had a vision like Lora, but I do have a gut feeling this family will be her demise."

Tara's chin lifted when she talked.

"You banished her from here."

"Yeah, but not for good. She could be anywhere still working on getting her old powers back." Tara reached over and took her hand. "You have to be careful when you go home."

A chill went up Lizzy's arm. "Don't worry about me. I always land on my feet. You know that."

"It's not where you're landing that concerns me. It's where she landed that has me thinking."

~~~~

Time flew by too damn fast for all of them. The stones stood in the mist while the travelers said their goodbyes.

"I love you," Tara cried with her final hug to Lizzy.

"Have a wonderful life, Tara. Not a day will go by that I don't think of you."

Simon handed Cian his Gameboy. "Here, I can get another one."

Myra stood back and watched as Fin readied their belongings to leave. He dressed in clothes she and Lizzy had brought back with them, twenty-first century clothes that would allow Fin to fit in. The jeans reminded her of Todd. Would he be waiting in the woods for them? Would he be sorry she didn't return? Her staying was for the best. If she went, she might never return to her family again. Either way the outcome would leave her empty.

Amber walked over, linked their fingers together. "All is going to be fine."

Myra smiled at her sister. "I know."

Amber gave her a knowing smile.

The four sisters held hands for a brief moment and chanted a rhyme. They asked the Ancients for the knowledge of the others' safety.

With final goodbyes said, Myra stood back and watched them go.

When the stones hummed and lit the ring, the vortex swallowed the travelers whole. Myra couldn't help but feel disappointed that the Ancients willed Lizzy and her son to return.

"I'm going to miss her," Tara sobbed in Duncan's arms.

"We all will," Lora stated.

Myra caught Amber out of the corner of her eye and found her behavior odd. Amber picked up a cat at her feet, smiled and walked back to where the horses stood waiting to take the family back to the Keep.

Chapter Thirteen

A constant pounding on Todd's door woke him up. He jumped out of bed, pulled on his shorts and yelled at whomever it was to hold their damn horses.

The door hit the wall with a crash. All Todd saw before a fist connected with his jaw was the blurry face of a bearded man. The punch threw him back three feet, another punch hit his right eye and had him landing on the floor.

"Get up!" the man yelled in a Scottish accent.

Todd was on his feet in a split second with his hands in front of him, ready for the assault.

Liz rushed into the house at a full run. "What the hell are you doing?" Todd's lip was split and bleeding, his eye already swelling. She placed herself between them and turned. "Stop it."

"Get out of the way, lass. This doesn't concern you."

"The hell it doesn't, Fin MacCoinnich. I brought you here, and I will not be a part of any fighting."

"Then move aside." Fin's eyes never left Todd's.

Todd looked at Myra's brother, wanting nothing better than to give him a taste of his own blood. It's a hell of a thing waking up with someone else's fist in your mouth. He realized then that this was Fin's twisted way of protecting his sister.

Todd wiped the blood with the back of his hand, looked at it then said, "Cheap shot, MacCoinnich."

Fin straightened his spine, lowered his hands slightly. "The next one will be even."

"What is wrong with you?" Liz pushed Fin's chest, which didn't move even an inch. "You said you wanted to thank him, not beat him up."

"I lied."

Todd snickered. Like sister like brother. He lowered his fists as the tension passed.

"I'd like some coffee before we go another round." Todd walked beyond the two of them and into his kitchen.

Todd splashed water on his face and winced at the sting behind Fin's punch.

Now what?

He started a pot of coffee, went back into the laundry room, and tossed on a t-shirt and jeans. By the time he ran a comb through his hair, he was able to fill a half a cup of coffee before Lizzy's heated words rose over the percolating pot.

"Why don't you just take your damn stones and go?"

Good idea, he thought.

"I'll go when I'm ready, love, and not a moment before."

Todd wiped his hand across his mouth and moved back toward the room.

"Well you had just better get good and ready, because you're not staying with me! And after this, I don't think Todd's going to want your company."

"She has a point," Todd said when he sauntered into the room.

Fin stood, only to be pulled back down by Liz.

"Knock it off."

"We're not done," he spat out.

"We are for now. What did you plan on doing? Drag me back to the sixteenth century to make an honest woman of Myra?"

Fin glared at him. "The thought did cross my mind."

"Is that what Myra told you to do?"

"Nay, Myra only weeps day in and day out. She would never demand the hand of the man who ruined her."

That stung. He lowered his stance. "What your sister and I shared was mutual, MacCoinnich, she knew what she was doing."

"That is where you are wrong. She was too innocent to be sent here alone. Now she will spend her life paying for it. Unless she is forced to this time to pay for her mistake."

Shouldn't they have thought of that before sending Myra? "Didn't your precious Ancients tell your family to send her here?"

"Aye. To keep her from Grainna."

Todd sat his cup on the table and looked Fin straight in the eye. "Then it would be best you keep her away, because Grainna is back."

~~~~

It was one of the hardest days in Simon's life. He wanted desperately to tell his best friend Tanner all about his trip. Of course, he couldn't do that, or he might end up in some type of crazy house with a bunch of weirdoes.

Instead, he told him he went to Scotland and stayed in a sixteenth century castle, leaving out the part about it being *in* the sixteenth century.

Ohhh, and the part about starting a fire

without a match ate at him, too. Again, the thought of some padded cell came to mind, and Simon kept his secrets to himself.

Mr. Price went on and on about the importance of Algebra and the need to study in order to get a good grade on the upcoming test. Simon rolled his eyes before shutting them.

He fingered the blade Cian had given to him, hidden in his jacket. That too could land him in some type of cell for bringing it to school. He touched it instead of showing it and tried to listen to his boring teacher.

His mind opened when he started to relax, and all at once, he heard the thoughts of his teacher. *Damn kids aren't listening to a thing. They're still on vacation. I might as well be talking to the moon.*

Simon sat up and shook his head. As soon as the thoughts went in, they left. All he heard was the singsong voice of Price talking about solving for X.

Cian told him to expect a few surprises now that he was open to them. He didn't say they would come so soon.

The bus let him off a block from his apartment. He pulled out his key knowing his mom wasn't going to be home for another hour. Only this year, she started leaving him home for that hour without a babysitter. Every time he let himself into their place, he felt a little more grown-up.

He put the key in the lock and turned the handle. To his surprise it didn't click, indicating the door wasn't locked. *Maybe Mom left Fin here.*

"Mom, Fin, I'm home." He dumped his backpack on the couch.

A noise from his mom's room had him heading in that direction. He peeked around the corner calling for her even louder.

The room was in shambles, blankets torn from the bed, the mattress tossed off to the side. Every drawer lay opened and tossed to the floor. His mom's clothes were thrown everywhere.

The hair on the back of his neck started to crawl, and for the first time since he was five, he thought of the bogyman.

His breath came in gasps as he slowly stepped back and out of the room. Once clear of the door, he pivoted and ran straight into the chest of a man he didn't know.

A hand stopped him from screaming out. "Now, Simon, we wouldn't want that."

Simon froze in place, eyes wide with panic. The last thing he remembered before darkness engulfed him was the stranger holding one of the sacred stones and bringing it down on his head.

~~~~

"She was just laying there? In a hospital bed?"

"Yeah." Todd answered Liz's question. "Creepy."

"How so?"

"It's hard to describe. She looked through you, at the inside." Todd remembered his coughing fit and shook off a wave of cold that threatened to settle in like a bad winter storm.

"What else happened?" Fin watched when Todd's face came up.

"Nothing. I choked on something and had to leave."

"Choked? What were you eating?" Liz asked.

"I wasn't eating anything. I just started

coughing. Couldn't catch my breath."

"Grainna." Fin crossed to the mantel, lifted the sword. "It was she who caught your breath, just like she did to Duncan's and Tara's before they sent her back."

"Why would she bother with me?" Todd didn't like how Fin tested the weight of the sword or how he looked at him while he held it.

"She probably read you and knows you took away her chance of breaking her curse with Myra."

"If that's true, than why not just let me choke to death?"

"Because that's not how she operates. She likes to play with her prey, and make them suffer at her hand. Her specialty is killing lovers in front of each other."

"Sick." Liz turned pale. "With Myra gone she has no use for Todd and nothing to gain by his death, right?"

"Since he is not a Druid, she can gain nothing from him, but she can from you." Fin put the weapon back where he found it.

"I'm no virgin, Finlay."

"But you are Druid, and she has found some strength and powers in shedding Druid blood." Fin's eyes grew distant before shaking his head and continuing. "She would like nothing better than to take your life or that of any one of us."

Todd noticed Liz shiver.

"I've got to get home. Simon should be..." She looked up, and her face lost all color. "Simon!"

Panicked, Liz jumped to her feet and ran for the door.

Fin and Todd followed. "Wait."

"Oh, God. I've got to get home. Simon is there

all alone."

Todd watched as Fin stepped between her and the car. "Wait. We don't know if he is in danger."

"Call him." Todd suggested.

Liz took a deep breath. "Yeah, good idea." She started back to the house to make the call.

Todd took the opportunity to talk to Fin alone. "Someone was watching us, Myra and I, before she left. We thought it was best she stay here to keep Liz and Simon away from any danger."

"Do you think it was Grainna?"

"No. Whoever it was, was much younger, able to leap a fence, and run like hell."

"Then one of her men. Chances are he knew about Liz and Simon."

Todd and Fin exchanged looks. "I'll get my gun."

Todd dashed inside, grabbed his nine-millimeter and his back-up Glock with extra clips. He saw Liz run back outside. On impulse, he pulled his sword off the mantel.

"We'll take my car," he yelled when he opened the door. Liz jumped in the back seat and Todd tossed Fin his blade. "I'd probably just hurt myself with it anyway."

The white-knuckle drive to Liz's apartment was silent. Todd took little notice of traffic laws even without a siren and lights.

Liz jolted out of the car the second it was in park.

"Liz, stop," Todd yelled. "Stay behind us."

They approached the door with caution. Todd's heartbeat did a rapid tattoo when he noticed the door was slightly open. *This doesn't look good.* It felt even worse. He motioned for Fin to stay low, and Liz to stay out.

Todd put his fingers in the air and counted down from three. He hit the door hard, crashing it behind him in his wake. Quickly, Todd swiveled in a circle and kept behind the couch for safety.

Fin rushed in behind him, ready for battle with his own weapon.

The search of the small apartment was quick.

It was also empty.

Liz ran to Simon's backpack, clutching it to her chest, her eyes wide with panic.

Fin caught Todd's eyes and stared at the floor. There, almost directly under his feet, was what appeared to be blood drying on the carpet.

Carefully, Todd sat next to Liz and tossed one of the pillows over the spot to keep it from her sight.

"Where is he? Where is my son?" Tears welled behind her eyes as she rocked back and forth. "What has she done to him?"

Todd pulled in his years of police work and tried to give her hope. "She needs something from him, or she wouldn't have taken him."

Liz looked at Fin for answers. "Will she hurt him?" They all knew the answer to that, and Fin's expression only confirmed it. "Oh, God!"

"Look for a note." Todd stood and started searching the room.

With something to do, they all started searching. Fin noticed the stones were missing.

When he told the others, Liz asked, "Can she control them?"

"I do not know. They call to a higher power, and she may find them useless."

Fin needed to work on his game face, Todd

thought. He lied almost as poorly as Myra.

"They could be anywhere. Any time." Liz ran her shaky fingers through her hair. "Oh, God."

Fin took her hands and forced her to look at him, "Listen to me. You and Simon have a special bond. Every mother and child of our kind does."

"Our kind?" Liz pulled her hands from his. "I'm done with this Druid crap. I just want my son back."

"Then listen to me." He grabbed her hands again, and forced himself into her view. "Close your eyes and listen to me."

"Why?"

"Your bond will help us find him, Elizabeth, so stop the tears and concentrate."

His tone was angry and direct, perfect to snap Liz out of her rising hysteria. "Slow your breathing, think of the air going in and out. Good. Now, think only of Simon. Call out to him. Keep breathing slowly."

One breath followed another. Todd stood back and watched the two of them holding hands. Fin closed his eyes as well and spoke to her in calming tones. His words soothed her and focused her.

"Where are you Simon? I'm looking for you. Simon."

Around them, mystical light started to swirl, and the air lifted their hair. A soft glow caught on the particles of dust the wind picked up, covering them in a blanket of sparkling lights.

She called to him, over and over.

Her lips parted. "I think I hear him," she whispered. "Please, Simon. Where are you?"

~~~~

Simon lay in the backseat of a large sedan. His

feet and hands were bound, his mouth covered in tape.

His kidnappers drove in silence. The man, tall, blond, and not past forty drove, while the old woman watched the passing terrain.

Her piercing glare drove into him the second his eyes fluttered open. They stayed only seconds before returning to the view from her window.

Scared, more than he had ever been in his whole life, Simon curled into a ball and shook. He knew who the woman was, and with that knowledge, a sense of impending doom settled over him.

Choking on a whimper, he started to cry, but his nose clogged up, and he found it difficult to breathe.

When he closed his eyes and tried to get control, it was then he felt the old woman's presence in his mind, looking. *Get out!* He shouted the words in his head over and over.

Slowly Grainna's presence faded on the inside, but he felt her glare from the front seat. Keeping his eyes shut, he ignored her as best he could. It wasn't easy.

Then he heard his mom crying out to him. Her voice cried over the rumble of the car and the noise off the road. *Mom,* he called out in a desperate plea. *Help me.*

~~~~

Liz almost fell to her knees when she heard his voice. Fin kept her upright. "Ask him where he is."

Liz squeezed his hands and spoke in her mind. "Winding road. Trees out the window," she said aloud for Fin. "He's so scared."

179

"Have they used the stones?" Fin calmly asked.

Shhhh...Simon, have they used the stones?

No...they didn't work.

Did they say where they're going? Liz felt her connection fading, heard only Myra's name and woods before it was completely shut off.

"Simon, Simon!" But he was gone.

"What did he say, Elizabeth?"

"I didn't hear him well. I heard him say Myra and woods. What do you think it means?"

Fin rubbed his hand along his short beard. "Grainna is trying to go back. If the stones didn't work she is looking for energy to bring them power."

"Would there be energy where they were last used?" Todd asked.

"Aye. Some."

"Then she's headed to the forest."

~~~~

Orange and red hues on the horizon spread out in front of them, capturing a few clouds darting across the sunset. They would have enjoyed the sight in any other situation.

Fin coached them both on keeping their thoughts to themselves when they made their approach to where they believed Grainna to be. "She can read people clearly, to the point where she knows your next move. Sing a song in your head and keep her confused."

Adrenalin shot through his system with an eerie familiarity. Todd parked off the road, close to where he had parked just over a week prior.

They walked the familiar path with what little light the day held. Ahead of them, voices caught on the wind.

"Turn them on." The demand came from the man who held Simon by his shirt and yelled in his face.

"I don't know how."

Grainna cut the cords that bound Simon's hands and pushed him to his knees. "Touch it."

With a shaking hand and trembling lip, Simon held his hand out to the stone. Nothing happened. No pulse, no heat. Nothing.

Grainna screamed in frustration and raised her hand to strike the child.

"Touch him and you're dead." Todd's gun leveled at her head, he clicked off the safety. Satisfaction came with the surprise on her face.

Grainna lowered her hand and slowly let a smile creep to her lips. "Officer Blakely, so nice of you to join us." She moved to the side and let them all get a full view of the boy cowering under her feet. "Your gun doesn't worry me, or did they forget to tell you of my immortality?"

"They told me, but I'm thinking you might not like the hole it puts in you or the pain it causes."

"You stupid little man." Grainna twisted her fingers, and the air left Todd's lungs. His vision started to swim, and his gun wavered.

Fin said, "Let the child go, Grainna." He stood next to Todd, with his arm gripping Liz around the waist to keep her from running to Simon.

"Now why would I do that?"

"Because he can't help you," said Fin.

"And you can?"

"I can activate the stones."

Grainna looked from Fin to Todd. Her fingers stopped rubbing together, and air rushed into

181

Todd's greedy lungs. Gasping, he lowered his gun.

The blond with Grainna pulled Simon to his feet and used him as a human shield. Grainna nodded her approval. "Mr. Steel here will hold young Simon until all the stones are working."

"Mom?" Simon cried out.

"Leave him alone." Lizzy's wail put a smile on Grainna's face.

She cackled. There was no other way to describe Grainna's laugh. Todd realized Myra hadn't exaggerated when she described this witch.

"Hurry, Finlay, I'm growing tired."

"I need to be in the circle," he challenged and stood taller, releasing Liz.

"We will try it without you."

Steel held Simon with a force that made the boy cry out. The knife he held pressed against Simon's neck kept everyone tense. Liz slowly moved closer to her son.

Grainna sputtered a curse and had Liz on her knees gasping for air.

"Leave her be. Or I will not touch them."

"Hurry, Finlay. I have one here." She motioned to Simon. "And you have one there. Unless you wait and that one dies."

"No!" Simon yelled and struggled against the man who held him. "Mom!"

Fin moved quickly, placing a hand to the rocks. They sputtered to life. Unlike when Todd watched Myra use them, now they appeared weaker, failing.

Liz gasped for breath as each stone was lit. Todd motioned for her to stay down with a slight movement of his hand. She stayed on her knees and watched as Todd moved closer to the circle with a vigilant eye on Grainna.

In turn, the witch watched Fin light the last stone and demanded, "Send us back."

Todd circled behind them and knew when Fin caught his movement, an unspoken agreement passed between the two men.

Fin chanted the rhyme, his words clear and loud keeping the attention of Steel and Grainna.

When the wind started to shift and the fire surrounded the ring, Todd noticed Liz inhale deeply and jump to her feet. Everything around him moved quickly, giving him no time to think and only seconds to react. Todd lunged, tackling Grainna to the earth when the world outside the circle started to shift.

Fin and Liz bolted into the circle at the same time. Liz grasped Simon around his waist and fell to the ground.

Everything outside the circle dripped from Todd's sight.

Chapter Fourteen

The vortex surrounded them. With no earth under them and no gravity to pull them, they sat in a state of weightlessness.

Todd felt Grainna beneath him, her frail body struggling to be free.

He found himself coughing and losing his breath. The world around him changed. Colors swirled in different shades, more vibrant than he had ever imagined.

Maybe it was the loss of oxygen to his brain, or the realization he was traveling through time, but he could have sworn he heard Myra's voice telling him to hang on.

As quickly as the wind hit, it stopped. Air rushed into him as he kicked out to put distance between him and the object who stole his breath.

He managed to collect enough air, crouched in a defensive position, and looked around to see what was coming.

Liz covered Simon with her body. Fin stood, with sword ready to strike at her side.

Steel hovered over Grainna, eyes confused and searching.

Todd yelled for the others to run, at the same time aiming his gun at the enemy. Without warning, he fired. Against all training, he let the round go without thinking of the consequences. Without regard for the enemy it took.

Once the shot was fired, he took off after the

others. He looked over his shoulder briefly only to see Steel dragging Grainna away.

Fin heard Todd's order. He covered Liz and her son under his protective arms. In flight, he grabbed two stones and ran.

The moist earth quieted their escape. Only the sound of panting breaths broke the silence as they ran.

Because Todd had no way of knowing where he was, he followed Fin blindly, all the while thankful for every breath he took. Grainna's power over him had been merciless. He would never again underestimate her.

The sky darkened the outline of the Keep looming above them. Fin bellowed an order for the doors to open as they approached the massive gates.

Slowly, the heavy frame of wood opened and accepted the son of the Laird and his company.

"Gregor, help Lady Elizabeth and Simon inside, quickly. Raise the gates and post extra guards."

Todd took in Gregor's clothes. A tunic and leggings and a double-sided sword clasped to his back and another one attached to his waist. Gregor eyed Todd's clothing with trepidation, and unspoken questions.

Jesus, I'm not in Kansas anymore.

Not that he thought for a minute they were still in California, but the Keep and the man at the gate sealed it for him.

"Aye, My Lord."

Gregor wasted no time following the orders sent out by Finlay.

~~~~

Myra slept in a chair by the fire in her room when the commotion from below woke her from her restless dreams.

It was Fin's loud voice that made her move.

She stood at the top of the stairs and watched the scene unfolding in front of her.

Lizzy clutched Simon in her arms. The boy cried, his bruised and bloodied face streaming with tears. Both were dressed in blue jeans and shirts. Fin ushered them to the stairs and headed to where their rooms had been during their stay.

The world tilted out of focus when her eyes landed on the lone man at the bottom of the stairs. Joy leapt in her heart at the sight of him. Her eyes burned into the back of his head until he slowly turned in her direction.

His jaw dropped, his gaze swept over her from head to toe and his face lit up. With a twinkle in his eye, he bounded the stairs two at a time.

His name barely passed her lips before Todd folded her into his embrace. His kiss was demanding, deep with longing. She hardly believed he was there, full of life, pressed against her.

Stunned, her body molded to his, exactly where it should be. Her hands lifted to his face, held it in place for fear he would leave. She broke their kiss long enough to ask, "Are you really here?"

He seemed confused. "I don't know." His answer delighted her.

He didn't stop kissing her until the sound of a throat being cleared caught their attention.

At the bottom of the stairs, Ian scowled up at the two of them. His hands perched on his hips told them both he wasn't happy with what he saw.

"Unless you plan on marrying my daughter this very evening, I suggest you step aside."

They both sprung back.

Myra clasped her fingers together, uncertain how she should act.

Todd helped her by taking her hand and walking her down the stairs.

"Todd Blakely," he announced while extending his hand to her father.

Ian extended his hand in a firm grip. Myra took a small breath, thankful her father didn't call him out right then and there.

Ian's look never wavered or gave a clue to his emotions. "*Laird* Ian MacCoinnich." He emphasized his title.

Lora stepped from the shadows breaking some of the tension rising in the room.

"Welcome to our home, Mr. Blakely," Lora offered.

"You must be, Mrs. MacCoinnich."

"*Lady* MacCoinnich," Ian corrected, his deadly stare unwavering.

One of the servants took that moment to announce dinner was about to be served.

"Maybe we should finish the introductions once you are more suitably dressed," Ian told him.

Lora removed her hand from her husband's arm and moved in. "Sir Blakely, come with me. I am certain Fin has something for you to wear. We wouldn't want too many questions that we can't answer."

Ian nodded his approval and watched Lora hurry Todd up the stairs. He stopped Myra when she started to follow.

"Do I have to remind you that such displays

outside of marriage will not be tolerated?" He wasted no time getting to the point.

"No, father."

"So he is the man who..." He saved her the embarrassment of finishing his sentence.

"He is."

Ian turned so fast she had to move quickly. "And I am to accept him into my home?"

"Just as he accepted me into his."

"Ha! What father would allow that?" He opened the decanter of Scotch and poured some into a glass.

"The father that sent me away knew the risks, and the consequences." She pointed out to him.

"Why is he here?"

"I do not know. He ran in after Fin, Lizzy and Simon."

"Something must have gone wrong." He finished his drink with one swallow. "Find your brother and send him to me."

~~~~

Myra's mother shuffled him into a room by candle light. "I'll be back in a moment," she said before ducking out the door.

The sparsely furnished room, with towering walls and a fireplace on one end, surprisingly looked exactly as he'd pictured Myra's home to be. He hadn't expected her parents to be so young. He should have, he chided himself. During these times, people were married and having children before the average twenty-first century kid received their High School diploma. Still, their youth surprised him.

Todd scanned the room and lit three wall sconces to add light to the dim space. "Jesus. I'm really here."

A timid knock sounded at his door. He spun around, uncertain what to do.

"Yes?" He called out.

"'Tis Amber, Myra's sister. May I come in?"

"Ah, yeah."

A mass of dark hair popped through followed by the youngest MacCoinnich. Todd knew instantly how Myra must have looked as a child. Amber held a bundle of clothing and quickly placed them on the bed. "My mother asked that I bring these. She asked that ye, ah, I mean you, come down once you've changed." A warm smile followed her words. Her attempt to make him comfortable didn't go unnoticed.

"Thank you."

Her long skirts made wispy sounds as the fabric moved along the floor. She stopped in front of the fireplace. "The room's cold. Would ye-you like a fire?"

"Ah, well..." the girl didn't give him time to say a thing. She simply opened her hands and flames leapt between the logs. Amber turned and charmed him with another smile.

"I don't suppose there's any way I can learn to do that?"

She giggled before walking up to him and patting his hand like a parent would a child. "Welcome to Scotland," she said before leaving him alone with his thoughts.

Todd removed his clothes and tucked them away in a chest at the foot of the bed. He kept his leg holster and back up revolver in place and shrugged the long sleeved shirt before attempting to put on the snug pants he'd seen only in stage plays or history books. "Oh, hell. I feel like Peter Pan," he mumbled to himself.

He took his time composing himself before working his way downstairs. Todd found Myra and her mother by the fireplace in the main hall. Myra caught her lip between her teeth, and her eyes sparkled with joy.

Todd asked, "Where is everyone?"

"My father, Fin and a few others went to search for the remaining stones."

"They've been quite a while." Lora added.

Behind him, Lizzy descended the stairs, her arm around Simon, both transformed by the clothing they wore.

Todd didn't need an introduction to the couple who followed them. Tara McAllister, now MacCoinnich, stood by her husband and looked exactly like the photo he'd studied in an attempt to find her.

"Todd Blakely, this is my oldest brother Duncan and his wife Tara." Myra made the introductions.

"We've heard a lot about you, Mr. Blakely," Tara managed.

"Aye, a lot," was all Duncan said. He did shake Todd's hand, but his death-grip reminded him of his place.

The door opened and Fin and Ian strode inside.

Lora hurried to her husband's side. "Did ye find them?"

"Only one, love."

"What does that mean?" Simon asked.

It means we're screwed, kid. Todd kept his thoughts to himself, refusing to think beyond the day.

"It means we're stuck here, doesn't it?" Lizzy asked on a sigh.

Fin nodded. "Aye. All of you."

Silence filled the room until Amber bounced down the stairs. At her side was another MacCoinnich son, the family resemblance, striking. Todd did a little mental math and realized there was an end to Myra's family. His eyes shifted around the room. The men stared at him, while the women watched Myra.

Amber broke the tension. "'Tis time to eat. I'm sure Lizzy and Simon are hungry."

"I'm starving," Simon said as he followed the girl into another room.

They gathered again around the table, serving themselves after dismissing the kitchen help for the night.

Simon sat close to his mother with Fin flanking him on his other side. Ian sat at the head of the table with Lora and Myra close at hand. Todd sat strategically on the far end of the table.

Todd wasn't easily intimidated, but Ian MacCoinnich's deadly stare caught him off guard. Even the encouraging smiles from Myra didn't block the chill coming off her father. Stiff spines came from Duncan and even the teenager, Cian.

Fin tolerated him with more patience than the others. Nothing like engaging in a little battle to bring a couple of guys together.

"We need to find her weakness."

"Or a power to keep her from controlling our breathing."

"Maybe you can send her back again," Myra added.

"And let her take the stones with her? I don't think so." Ian's voice of authority stopped that flow of conversation. "Grainna is dangerous to all time now. There is no way of knowing if she can work with the stones and the power they hold."

"I thought the stones were controlled by the Ancients," Todd said.

Myra nodded. "Ultimately they are, but Grainna is very powerful. There's no telling what she can do. They are dangerous in the wrong hands, and her hands are most definitely the wrong ones."

"What about the guy who was with her?"

Fin spoke up, "He looked familiar, but I couldn't see him well in the dark. Simon, did you hear his name?"

"She didn't talk much, at least not out loud. I heard her call him Mr. Steel, but I never heard a first name."

Tara perked up and asked, "Blond hair? Same build as Duncan?"

"Yeah, he had blond hair, but he was a little shorter."

"Duncan, remember the other knight who challenged you at the Renaissance Faire?" Tara took a deep breath and turned to Fin. "Could that have been him?"

Fin nodded. "Aye, Tara, I think you're right. He was the only man who matched us on the field. I remember him talking with Grainna once or twice during the Faire."

"So, he is practiced in horsemanship and fighting in our time?" Ian asked.

"Aye." Duncan and Fin both said together.

"Did he have a gun, Simon?" Todd sat back

and gave up trying to eat.

"I didn't see one."

"Do you mean a matchlock gun?"

Todd reached down to his leg where his backup was clamped onto his ankle. After removing the clip and checking the chamber to make sure it wasn't live, he handed the gun to Ian.

"No, not a matchlock. These are much more powerful with mechanism to kick out an empty shell and reload with one squeeze of the trigger. These keep your enemy at a safer distance." Todd watched Ian's frame relax as he studied the weapon. He took his silence as an invitation to elaborate. "Matchlocks will eventually lead up to this design."

"How can something so small be deadly?"

"The speed and power propelling the large caliper bullet make up a deadly combination. Of course the closer you are to the perpetrator, the more likely you are to hit them."

"All men in your time have such weapons?"

"I wouldn't say *all*. Hunters, law enforcement officers, and some homeowners own them, but very few walk around with them strapped to their hip. Except of course, most criminals seem to have them."

"It would be best to assume the man with Grainna does as well," Ian stated flatly.

"I don't think so," Todd argued. "If he did, he would have held the gun on Simon, not a knife."

Liz shuddered with the memory fresh in everyone's mind.

Ian handed the gun to Duncan. "Maybe, but we take no chances. Until this man and Grainna are found, none of the women or children are to leave the Keep. This includes you Cian."

"But..."

"Nay, Cian. You are needed here and your training is not complete. I will not have you in battle and risk you being captured then used as a pawn by Grainna." Ian's decree gave little room for argument and his tone was final. "Duncan, you and Fin are to show Todd our ways, in horses and weapons. I trust you are willing to defend this family."

It wasn't a question really, more of a statement to which Todd gave immediate agreement.

"Then you will go with us when we search. You and your weapons."

"What good is a gun if Grainna is immortal?" Myra asked with evidence of worry etched in her face.

The conversation stopped.

"How do you know that she is immortal?" asked Todd. He couldn't help but wonder if anyone at the table knew for certain such an unbelievable fact.

"It is written in the legend," Myra told Todd.

"It is also written that she is powerless, and we know that isn't true," Duncan reminded them.

"Maybe there is some type of loophole. Some way to destroy her." Tara offered.

Todd's head scrambled with all the possibilities. For now, he sank into his seat and watched as the family pushed food around on their plates and mulled over the facts as they knew them.

Simon, who had remained quiet most of the night, finally spoke up when he asked his mother,

"We're not going home, are we?"

Todd sent Simon a sympathetic look. *We don't go home.*

Liz's gaze went past her son and settled on Fin silently asking for answers.

"Simon. Remember how you said you didn't like your school?" Fin asked.

"Well, yeah, but..."

"But what? Cian can work with you to teach you what men need to know here."

His withdrawn eyes widened.

"Aye, and I can help with your Druid gifts as well. Like we did last week," said Cian.

"Does this mean I'm going to miss my midterm in algebra?" he asked his mom.

"I think so."

"Cool."

Todd earned a disapproving grunt from Liz when he told him, "You'll never use algebra anyway."

Tara chuckled and offered Todd a smile.

"I'm tired," Simon announced as he pushed his chair away from the table.

Liz jumped to her feet. "Come with me. You can sleep in my room tonight."

"Elizabeth?"

Todd wasn't used to hearing Liz's full name used. From how quickly Liz swiveled toward Fin, it was obviously something she didn't like.

"He will be safe with Cian."

Liz's jaw tightened. "Simon, why don't you change, I'll be up in a minute."

Simon nearly bounced out of the room. Several family members stood to leave.

Todd waited and watched. Once Simon was

out of earshot, Liz grit her teeth and glared at Fin. "I want him with me."

"He's safe with Cian," Fin repeated

"And he isn't with me?"

"I didn't say that!"

"You implied it."

"You cannot be with him every second, Elizabeth."

"Who says so? You?"

"It isn't possible or healthy."

Liz clenched her fist. Anger and fear washed over her features. Her whispered words solidified her feelings. "I almost lost him, Fin. I won't let that happen again."

"I know. I won't let it happen, either."

"None of us will, lass," Ian spoke up softly.

"I don't know what I would have done if we hadn't reached him in time, and she left with him or hurt him."

Fin lowered his voice, touched her hand lying on the table. "We rescued him. He is safe and in the other room. She will not get to him here. I promise you."

"I'm holding you to that."

After a moment of silence, Ian stood. "Blakely."

Todd met his eyes.

"A private word."

Taking a deep breath, Todd stood and followed Myra's father from the room.

~~~~

Ian MacCoinnich was one hell of man, Todd thought as he followed him into the massive room. It wasn't a surprise that Myra remained a virgin for as long as she had. With a protector like her father and brothers, it was a wonder she ever had that first kiss in the barn.

Todd took pride in his ability to read people and their worth with few words. So far, Ian proved to be a man he wanted to be on the same side with. His absolute authority over his family and his men was awe-inspiring and exactly as Todd imagined Lairds in the sixteenth century should have been. *Shit*, he needed to stop thinking like that. It's the way they were.

Ian said nothing as he poured generous portions of Scotch in two glasses and handed one to him. One thing Todd knew, the impending conversation with Myra's father would be the one where Ian would determine Todd's worth. A quick comparison of meeting the parents in the twenty-first century didn't hold a candle to this encounter. A spark of humor mixed with the tightly woven anxiety sitting on his chest. A slight grin tempted the corners of his mouth.

As Ian flicked a hand toward the hearth and the coals caught fire, Todd thought of it as the Druid way of flexing one's muscles.

It worked.

Minutes ticked by while the men drank and stared into the flames. At first, Ian clearly wanted to intimidate him. Yet as Todd relaxed into his seat, he glanced and noticed Ian's jaw lose its twitch and his breathing evened out.

What a bitch of a day.

Todd let the Scotch trickle a path of fire down his throat, thankful for its numbing effect.

"I didn't want to send her to your time." Ian broke the silence. "But when faced with her death in ours, we had little choice."

"I imagine I would do the same if I had a child." Todd stared into his cup.

"The bruise on your eye, how did you come by it?"

He had almost forgotten about Fin's fist greeting him that very morning. It seemed so long ago. "Fin."

Ian's lips curved slightly.

"Would you like to blacken the other?"

"To serve what purpose?"

"Oh, I don't know—make you feel better?"

Ian grunted, drank his Scotch. "It might be difficult for you to hit a target with that gun of yours if your vision is blurry."

"Later, then?"

Ian laughed. "Maybe."

They finished their drinks in silence, each coming to terms with the other.

Todd put his glass down and stood to leave, "Are we finished here?"

Ian held him up for a few more minutes. "Sir Blakely..."

"It's Todd."

"Nay, while you are here and looking at my daughter the way you do, you are Sir Blakely. I will not have Myra's virtue questioned or your intentions." He paused as if waiting for Todd to explain his intentions.

Truth was, Todd wasn't sure what his intentions were. He was damn happy to be in the same century with Myra again, but beyond that, he hadn't given it more thought.

Instead of talking of the future, Todd explained where he was at that very minute. "I am not ashamed of my relationship with your daughter, and neither is she from what I can tell."

"But it will not continue here in this time, the way it did in yours."

Todd wanted to argue, but thought twice before he opened his mouth. Instead, he nodded his understanding and let himself out.

Myra jumped to her feet when Todd walked into the room.

"Tomorrow will be a busy day." Ian gave his orders for them both to seek their beds without using the words.

"I will show Todd to his chambers," Myra stated.

Ian paused and looked at the two of them, pivoted and left the room.

Chapter Fifteen

Finally alone, Myra turned to Todd and offered him a smile. She looked different. It wasn't just because the dress she wore swept the floor when she moved, or how her hair was piled up and folded between materials. It reminded him of a style he'd seen in movies, ones he'd reluctantly watched. No, here she seemed older. No, not older—more confident.

She looked confident because she was on familiar turf. He hadn't seen this part of her at his home. There she was always uncertain and apprehensive. This was her time, her place, and it showed, from the way she addressed the servants, to how she spoke to her family. This was where Myra MacCoinnich belonged, not in some two bedroom bungalow in Orange County, California, but here, in a castle straight out of a fairytale.

In a castle befitting a Lady.

The tables had turned, and he now felt out of place, unsure of how he should act. Lady Myra MacCoinnich was way out of his league.

"How are you doing?" Myra nodded to the stairs her father had just used. "I pray he didn't threaten you, did he?"

"Your father is only watching out for you."

"And this?" She touched the bruise on his face. "Is this Fin's work?"

"Big brothers have a right to defend their sisters." It was in the *Codebook of Guy*.

"But still..."

"It's fine. Doesn't hurt at all," he lied.

"I missed you."

He thought of the nights he didn't sleep after she left. "I missed you, too."

She moved closer. He pulled away. The hurt expression crossing over her face made him feel like crap. "I think we should get some sleep." His eyes traveled up the stairs then back to her. The last thing he needed was to add homeless to his list of problems.

A small noise from above reminded them they were being watched. She frowned, looked behind them, then walked him to his room.

~~~~

Duncan and Fin began Todd's training between trips out of the Keep to investigate Grainna's whereabouts. Snow dusted the ground, making their task harder. The tracks that once led into the forest were indiscernible, now. Grainna and Steel were nowhere to be seen.

"It's as if she's disappeared into thin air." Todd scrubbed his hand over his face as he walked to the bailey to train with the brothers. "Have all the cottages surrounding the Keep been searched, now?"

Although the brothers never treated him with disrespect, Todd still felt the weight of their disapproval. Forced into the situation as it was, they had little choice but to accept him.

"Aye. We've checked and rechecked over the past week to make certain Grainna didn't occupy them."

"There's nothing to do. The villagers were told to report any strangers, especially ones matching the description we gave 'em." Fin added.

Todd took a practice swing with the broadsword. He'd been relieved most of their training happened in private, away from the other knights. At first, he could hardly hold a sword in one hand, let alone use the thing. Within the first week, he wielded it with some skill, knowing he'd be dead in ten minutes in a true fight.

He grinned to himself as he swirled it over his head, because despite only a little more than a week's training, he managed to wield it nonetheless.

His introduction to the other knights had been formal and vague. Apparently the MacCoinnich's men were well versed in the art of looking past the family's secrets.

Todd caught Myra's glance out of the corner of his eye. Her cheeks flamed red and his leggings, tight around his thighs, stretched further.

Myra brought her hand up to her neck and fanned her fingers along the long column of her throat. He could almost taste the salt tinged flesh as if he were pressing his lips to her neck.

Duncan growled behind him, forcing Todd's thoughts to the sword in his hand. He turned in time to block Duncan's sword in mid-air. Todd ducked, kicked his feet out, and managed to topple his opponent. Duncan was on his feet in seconds forcing Todd to react again.

He knew Myra's brother saw their brief exchange. Not that a mere look should warrant such force, but it was something he was growing used to dealing with. The only intimacy he'd shared with Myra in over two weeks was no more than a brush of her hand over his.

No one left them alone. If it wasn't Ian, it was Duncan or Fin coming between them.

His dreams were flooded with images of the two of them together. So much so, that deep in the night when his body woke him up he had to stop himself from going to her.

From being with her.

What could he offer her? He wasn't a knight. He had no land or money, no means to support her. And why the hell was he thinking like that?

Damn, he needed to get his head back on straight.

~~~~

Myra suffered, but not silently. She plagued Tara and Lizzy daily about her feelings.

"I can't stand it," she told them both. "He's all sweaty and short of breath, working out there, and I can't think beyond how I want the same for us both."

Tara didn't even try to hold back her laugh. "You better not even think like that. Your dad would have both your heads if he found you together."

"Why? It isn't like he doesn't know what occurred between us."

"It isn't the same," Liz told her.

"Ma walked in on you and Duncan," Myra reminded Tara.

"It isn't the same with a daughter." Tara held up her hands. "I know, I know, it isn't fair, but those are the facts."

"Well, they stink!"

Tara and Liz nodded their agreement as they sat back and watched the men train in the courtyard.

Tara held her belly, where her unborn child grew. Liz watched Simon trying to keep up with Cian, and held her breath every time he picked up a sharp object. Although Myra understood Lizzy's concern, she was simply too focused on her own misery to worry about someone else's. She licked her dry lips when her breath caught at the sight of Todd blocking a sword with the shield he held.

~~~~

Todd pulled a long drink from a cup set out by one of the serving maids when Fin granted a break from his training.

"So, what do you think?" Fin knocked Todd on the back, which had him dripping water on his chin.

The tip of his tongue held a smartass reply, but instead he gave him an honest answer. "You're kicking my ass."

"Aye. That I am. And enjoying every minute of it," Fin replied.

"Don't count on that lasting, MacCoinnich."

"You have a lot to learn, Blakely."

They both smiled at each other and acknowledged the truth.

"What do you have going with Liz?" Todd did his best not to look at the women who made a sport out of watching them.

"Why do you ask that?"

"Come on, the two of you spar like arch-enemies. Which only means that you are or..."

"Or what?"

"Or you have it bad."

Fin glanced at the women, and smiled.

Lizzy looked away.

"Nay, I don't have it bad." Fin professed.

Todd didn't believe him for a minute.

~~~~

While the men trained with swords and fists, the women decided to sharpen their Druid gifts to help defeat the enemy.

Alone in Myra's chambers, the sisters gathered on the bed. Tara removed one of the books she'd asked Myra to bring back with her titled, *Modern Witch Craft from Ancient Times.*

"I don't understand the purpose."

"It's just a hunch, really," Tara started to explain. "So little is known about the Druid people in our time."

"Because we are quiet about our heritage," Amber told her.

"Quiet enough for Lizzy and I to be oblivious to it. What if others from Druid ancestors found ways of channeling their gifts?"

"As in witchcraft?"

"Exactly."

"Witches aren't real, Tara," Liz crossed her legs under the massive skirt.

"How can you say that after all you've seen? Grainna is definitely a witch."

"And Druid," Myra added.

"Remember our corny chant back when we were kids?"

"Blood sisters."

"Well, I've already told you how Amber, who we know is an empath, chanted along with me to find me."

Lizzy sat forward, listening. "Go on."

"Even before all that happened, the day Myra and I mixed our blood, I saw the scissors, the ones we used to prick our fingers with, glow. Somehow, even then I knew something about the chant worked. When Myra left, I knew she'd be back. I felt it deep inside."

"I did, too," Amber chimed in.

"How is all this going to help us get rid of Grainna?" Myra asked.

"I'm not sure, but I don't think a sword will take her down."

Amber sat up. "Nay, I don't think so either."

"And you think 'sister power' can? Come on, Tara, you really have watched too much TV," Lizzy chided.

Myra considered the twenty-first century television and understood Lizzy's humor.

"What do we have to lose? Reading a couple books and practicing a few chants, spells, or whatever you want to call them, can't hurt. If it doesn't work...oh, well. If it does...who knows, it just might save a life like it did with Duncan and me."

Myra studied the book over Tara's shoulder. Amber snuggled into her side.

"Witchcraft, gifts, powers of premonition. I'm a lost cause." Liz tossed her hands in the air before Myra could contradict her. "Yeah, I know what I've seen with my own eyes. But I haven't even managed a spark from these fingertips."

"You haven't tried," Myra reminded her.

"Yes, I have. I just can't do it. Even Simon's tapping into his gifts."

"He was so cute when he lit the candle last week."

Myra agreed with Tara.

"He's even starting to talk to me in his head."

"Really?"

Liz shrugged. "He called me into his room the other night. I thought he was yelling, but when I realized no one heard him but me, I thought I'd go check on him."

"Did he do it on purpose?"

"I think so. Ever since Grainna kidnapped him, he's been a little more needy."

"I've never heard of a parent and son connection. My father and mother, and Tara and Duncan connect, but only because of their vows. Can you speak with him? Or is it one way?" Myra wasn't sure what to make of it.

"Both, sometimes. We connected because of the trauma of Grainna's attack. At least that's what Fin thinks. I tend to believe him."

"Having someone poking around in your mind isn't always a good thing, Lizzy. I love Duncan, but sometimes having him in my head can be a real pain in the ass."

Lizzy laughed. "I don't think Simon has clued in to any real 'private' thoughts."

"What thoughts?" Amber remained silent until that moment. Myra realized they weren't being very careful around someone so young.

"Nothing," she changed the subject. "What does that book say?"

Going along with her suggestion, Tara pointed to the page in the book. "It talks here about casting a circle for protection."

"The stones are placed in a circle," Amber reminded them.

"A circle of fire kept Grainna imprisoned right before I sent her back."

Myra wiggled up off the bed. "Should we try it?"

Tara added to the overall excitement. "Let's use the candles."

Myra and Tara took candles from around the room and set them in the middle of the floor. "Now what?"

"We should sit in the middle, then light them."

Amber enthusiastically hopped off the bed and sat next to her sister.

Liz had to be pried off the bed.

"Come on, Lizzy. What do we have to lose?" said Tara.

"This is lame."

"Just get over here."

Once seated in a circle, Amber lit the wicks and Tara read from the book.

"Our circle is cast, we come in peace." She flipped the pages and shook her head.

"What is it?" Myra asked.

"These words don't apply to us."

"So we make up our own."

"Does it have to rhyme?" Liz rolled her eyes.

"These do."

Myra tossed her hair over her shoulder and grasped the hands of Amber and Liz who sat on each side of her. Tara followed her lead and began to speak. "Our circle is cast not once but twice—"

"Twice?" Liz questioned.

"Well, we're once and the candles are twice."

"Lame. Stupid and lame."

Undaunted, Tara continued, "We sit inside and seek advice. We look for promise, for hope and love, the gifts we've been given from God above."

The flames drew higher around them, taking Myra by surprise. The others gasped.

"Close your eyes," Amber told them all, her

voice exceeding her tender years. "Help us connect and see as one."

At her request, Myra felt her hand warm. She opened her eyes and noticed their hands sparked. Liz jolted back, but Tara held firm and wouldn't let her go.

Images flew into Myra's mind. She saw Simon calling his mom. She felt Tara's emotion as she held her pregnant belly. She watched everything through Lizzy's eyes as Duncan laughed and held Tara. All the feelings welled up inside her. Joy, frustration, anticipation, and fear. Everyone's fragmented thoughts threatened a headache of extreme magnitude.

"Let's try clearing our thoughts, all these visions are giving me a headache," Liz took the words right out of Myra's thoughts.

Myra opened her eyes and glanced at the others. So did Lizzy. "Ahhh, Myra?" Lizzy cleared her throat. "Are you doing that?"

One by one, the others peeked to see what Lizzy meant.

Below them, some two feet below them, was the ground they had all been sitting on mere minutes before.

"It's not me."

"Great. Well, it's safe to say the circle thing has some validity to it."

Myra peered over her shoulder and noticed her skirts hung to the floor but her legs felt like they were on solid ground.

"How the hell is this happening?" Tara slid a look to Amber, whispered an apology for her language, which was met with a shrug.

Undaunted, Amber closed her eyes and kept

going. "Let us get back to what we were doing. 'Tis not like we are hovering above the Keep, risking a fall to our deaths."

"That's a cheery thought."

"She's right. Let's keep going."

"I think we should all try and focus on one person, and see if our thoughts become one," Tara suggested, "How about Todd?"

"Nay!" Myra glanced at Amber. "I don't think that would be wise."

"Oh, yeah, how about Fin?"

"How about Simon?" Lizzy suggested.

"Aye. Simon is safe." Amber's laugh brought a smile to Myra's face. Her little sister was truly wise beyond her years. Myra glanced at Lizzy and Tara.

"Come now, I have eyes. I may be young, but I'm not dense." Amber's head shook in a mock of Simon's *I'm not stupid* expression.

Liz shook her head, "I'll have to remember that."

Myra closed her eyes and felt their energy focus on Simon. There wasn't any other way to describe it.

Amber started to giggle.

Myra saw the image of Simon in a bath when he couldn't have been more than two. He splashed with a red plastic toy and squealed every time it went under water.

"I remember that," Tara said. "Is that Elmo?"

"Yes. He was so adorable. Remember how he threw that toy at Dad?"

"I do."

"Dad never laughed, not once." Lizzy's somber emotion welled within Myra. The pain of an unaccepting father broke her heart.

Quickly, the baby pictures changed and the nightmare of Simon's abduction flashed into Myra's mind. Fear, desperation, and hate welled within her.

She heard Grainna's voice rake over her soul. The anxiety of a mother unable to help her child filled her with dread.

"Oh, God." Tara gasped in panic. From the thickness of emotion, she knew every one of them swelled with a frantic need to flee.

Myra's pulse quickened when a blond man took a knife to Simon's neck.

A quiet sob escaped Liz. "Oh, no."

"Enough." Myra swiftly opened her eyes. "Enough. 'Tis done."

"I'm so sorry, Lizzy." Tara had tears in her eyes.

"It's okay, he's safe now."

"I didn't want to bring back all that pain."

They floated, unmoving for a moment.

"It worked."

Myra squared her shoulders. "It did."

"Should we try it again?"

"Not now," Lizzy appeared weary to the bone. "Not today."

Myra attempted to lighten the mood. "Any idea how we get down?" she asked.

A knock on the door resulted in Amber removing her hands from the others, and with it whatever levitated them disappeared.

With a thud, and more than one bruised butt, each of them fell to the floor.

"Mom? Are you in there?" Simon yelled and knocked again.

"Just a second."

Lizzy scrambled to blow out the candles. "Quick, put them away," she ordered.

"Hey?" Simon let himself in the room. "Did you need me or something?"

Liz glanced behind her, at Myra and the others in the room. "Why do you ask?"

"I heard you calling me. It sounded important."

"I didn't call you, Simon."

"Yeah you did." He pointed to his head. "In here."

~~~~

Tossing in his sleep, Todd woke with an excruciating erection and a fast-beating heart. "Damn, not again."

Frustrated, and unable to get back to sleep, he tossed his blankets off and pulled on his pants.

The fire in the hearth had dwindled to nothing more than coals and the room chilled at the edges. He found it amazing how quickly he adapted to life in these times.

He reflected on how Myra acted with every new experience in his world, how awestruck she had been with a simple hamburger. He remembered how big her eyes got when he drove her in his Mustang and her laughter when the waves from the ocean crashed over her toes.

"Damn." He tugged on a shirt and left the room in search of a drink.

Like a teenager sneaking booze from the liquor cabinet, Todd felt a pang of guilt over splashing some of Ian's stash into a glass. Lucky for him, the feeling didn't last long. It was his damn daughter who caused his anguish.

And Ian's damn rules.

The flicker of light caught him by surprise when he left Ian's study. Everyone was asleep, or so he thought.

Myra sat and toiled with a small plate of food in her lap. Her long and shapeless nightdress pillowed over her legs, which she curled up under her. Only the pink of her toes peeked out. Her beautiful toes.

The door creaked when he closed it. Myra jumped at the sound.

"I didn't mean to startle you."

Her face slid into a grin when she realized it was him. "I thought I was the only one awake."

Todd lifted his glass. "Couldn't sleep. You?"

"Nay. I'm a bit restless these days."

Todd fidgeted for a while and kept glancing toward the stairs, expecting someone from the family to interrupt them, as they always did.

"Do I make you nervous?" Myra asked in a low voice.

"Is it that obvious?"

"It is." Nodding toward the stairs, she said, "I'm sorry for my family's pressure on you."

"No pressure. Unless they catch us together. Then I would think that *pressure* would be an understatement."

"They can't fault us for talking," she told him.

He took the hint and sat across from her a safe distance away.

"How is your training?"

"Tiring. I have an understanding of why men in this time are solid muscle."

"You are fit, even for your time."

He sipped his drink. "Lifting weights isn't the

same as working with your weapons. And riding the horses is a chore all in its own."

"I'm sorry."

"For what?"

"You wouldn't be here if it wasn't for me." Myra sat her plate of food on the table.

"Grainna forced that hand, Myra. Not you."

"True, but if we had never met, you wouldn't be involved."

He sat his drink on the table, raised his voice. "Is that what you think I want? To never have met you?" When she didn't answer right away he added. "Do you wish you had never met me?"

"Nay!" she pleaded. "Every sleepless night I think of you. Of us. Never have I regretted anything."

"Sleepless nights?"

"Aye, every one."

Todd could see the lost sleep in her expression. The dark circles under her eyes and the dreamy way she gazed at him elevated his heart rate to a thundering speed. As he stared longer and watched her lip curl between her teeth, he lost it.

Without words, he stood and crossed over to where she sat.

Chapter Sixteen

Picking up her hand, Todd helped her to her feet. His fingers lifted back the length of her hair while one lazy finger swept over her cheek. Her gut clenched with his simple loving touch.

"I can't sleep. Everyday I work harder trying to find the point where fatigue will dull me to dreams, but nothing works. You are there when I close my eyes. These lips..." He smoothed his fingers over them as he spoke. "They torment me." He gently urged her head back, exposing her long neck. "Your skin calls to me." He dropped his mouth to her beating pulse, tearing a gasp from her.

Fingers clasped around him, pulling him closer. Her nightgown trailed off her shoulder where Todd sent a blaze of heat in the wake of his tongue.

Her head rolled back and her eyes closed. Heat shot to her stomach and lower. Any concern about where they were or being caught escaped her mind.

Slowly, her hands drifted down his back and skimmed over his tight bottom. His reaction was instant. His lips found hers with crushing need, bringing with it hunger for more.

Familiar hands stroked her sides, his tongue danced with hers in a rough exploration of every crevasse, every valley.

Hands grasped her hips, urging her against

the stiff pressure of his erection. He caught her cries of pleasure with his mouth. Tension gathered with every suggestive movement of his hips against hers. Tasting him, feeling him, having him was a need beyond any hunger she had ever felt.

He stopped her hands when they tugged at his shirt, and held them close to his heart.

Slowly, he ended their kiss.

She searched his eyes and asked, "Why did you stop?"

He looked to the stairs. "You know why." He curved a hand around her face.

Her father's words echoed in her mind, *Unless you plan on marrying this evening, I suggest you step aside.*

The threat of a forced marriage stopped him, she thought. Her father would have them married if he caught them like this. The thought didn't disturb her, but it obviously distressed Todd. Could she live with a marriage of force and not of love?

Myra stepped back and broke their contact.

"You're upset." Todd concluded. "Your father would..."

"I know what my father would do." She pulled her pride together and stood a little taller.

"He would have my head if I put you in a questionable situation."

"Is that what I am to you? A questionable situation?"

Todd stepped back. "You're more than that."

"Am I?"

"You know you are." His anger matched hers.

"How do I know? Because you want me, desire me?"

"That and more."

Myra waited for him to explain, but he didn't. "Let me know when you are ready to tell me what *more* is, Todd. In the meantime, I'll be sure to not place you in a 'questionable situation.' I wouldn't want you to be forced into anything."

She marched past him to the stairs, but he caught her before she took the first one. "No one forces me to do anything I don't want to do."

"Really?" she pulled out of his grasp. "Look around, Todd. It appears to me you have been forced to stay here."

"Do you think I didn't know what would happen when I jumped into the stones? That I didn't know I might never see my life as it was before again. I knew exactly what I was doing, Myra, and I did it anyway." He took a step back. "I chose to do it anyway."

Her hands covered her arms in a struggle to keep warm. "Why?"

"Because of you, dammit! I couldn't stop thinking about you." He turned away. "Get some sleep. Tomorrow will be another long day."

~~~~

She would need an army, and an army she would have.

Far outside the reaches of the MacCoinnich family, Grainna paced the grounds of a forgotten home. It in no way resembled the Keep, but neither was it a hut. Its grounds overgrown with vegetation, its walls crumbled in disrepair. Even the roof leaked. The overgrowth made for great camouflage and surprise when people passed by.

Their recruitment for her army came slowly. Only one or two at a time could go undetected from the groups of people who passed by. Much like a lion stalking prey, those who lagged behind their pack Grainna picked off, men and women alike.

The minds of the people she abducted were easily manipulated, much like those in the twenty-first century. For those who had stronger convictions, she bent them to her will by means of force.

Grainna wasted little time negotiating. If they were too difficult, she simply killed them.

Over two months had gone by, and in that time she found only two people with Druid blood running in their veins, bastard blood amounting to very little power.

She considered keeping them alive and using their skills to her advantage, but her hunger for youth was too strong. Ending their pathetic lives in a ritual she had perfected over time returned some of her strength and youth, but none of her powers. The youth was fleeting. Yes, her body surged when their life-force drifted into her, but the temporary vitality faded quickly.

This only added to her desire to regain it all. The blood of a Druid virgin would remove her curse in one quick act. It would be permanent.

The rain fell in sheets, causing her bones to ache. She watched Michael push the man he tried to train to the ground.

"Useless," she cursed. Most of the men were only numbers. A few could hold their own, and in time, she would have more.

She turned and added herbs to the tea simmering on the fire. These herbs kept her minions' minds bound to her.

~~~~

Winter lost its grip and the rain took the place of the snow. Torrents of rain and storms crossed the land. The weather was normal to the MacCoinnichs who had lived here all their lives, but the cold and damp took some getting used to for those who'd lived their lives in Southern California.

Liz glanced out her window toward the barn where she knew Fin was preparing to leave the Keep. She noticed when Simon snuck out and followed him. He'd been whining for days to get out and stretch his legs. Hell, they were all pent up and had been for months.

Simon's voice interrupted her thoughts. *Simon to Mom, Simon to Mom, come in Mom.* He paused, waiting for her mental reply to his call. She laughed at his monotone internal voice and couldn't help but picture a futuristic 'B' movie where the characters closed their eyes, rubbed their temples and spoke telepathically to anyone they chose.

What do you need? She attempted to ask back. Liz felt certain that not all her words were heard.

I'm in the barn. Can you come in here? I have a question.

Liz concentrated hard, attempting to ask what he needed, but Simon had mastered blocking her out when he didn't want her in. Donning a cloak, she left her room and made her way out to her son's side.

The aromatic scent of the stable and the fresh smell of rain mixed when she entered the barn and shook off the collection of rain water she'd acquired in the short walk.

Fin stood beside his horse, adjusting his

saddle. Simon's teeth glistened behind his smile. He was up to something. "And you wanted a cell phone," she told Simon as she walked over and ruffled his hair.

"Lot of good it does, if I can only talk to my mom. No offense."

Fin cast Simon a surprised look, but kept quiet.

"Sorry, sport. I guess it's just you and me for awhile." Liz nodded to Fin. "What's up?"

"Fin told me I needed to ask you first, but I'm sure you're going to say no."

"Say no to what?" She eyed Fin, but he didn't elaborate.

"Fin's going into the village, and since I'm only going to make you crazy hanging around here, I thought it would be good for me to go with him."

Fin hunched his shoulders, lifted a brow. "Don't look at me. I told him to ask you."

"So I can be the bad guy?"

"I don't know about that."

She shook her head. "Right."

"Fin will watch out for me, won't you?" Her son sent a hopeful look to him.

"I'm staying out of this." Fin raised his hands.

Simon touched Liz's arm. "We won't be gone long."

Liz measured them both with a stare. Fin expected her to say no, she knew it. He didn't want to lose that look of awe from her son. Well, maybe it was time to turn the tables. "All right."

"Really?" Simon nearly pounced on her.

"What?" Fin turned almost as quickly as her son did.

"With one condition."

"Anything," Simon said, grinning ear to ear.

Fin peered through slanted lids.

Liz sent him a sly smile. "I'm going, too."

Relieved, Simon yelled, "Great."

Fin said, "No."

"Excuse me?" Liz took a step closer to him.

"I said no. It isn't safe."

"But you were willing to take my son. Why not me?"

Fin squirmed under her stare. "Simon will be a man before long. It would do him good to spread his wings."

"So it's a sexist thing. Okay for boys but not for girls?"

"Something like that."

Liz matched him stare for stare. Without taking her eyes away from his, she said to Simon, "Can you give us a few minutes, sport. Fin and I need to talk."

Once he left, she bit out, "You're full of shit, you know that?"

"If that's what you choose to believe."

"It isn't what I choose. It's crap! All of it. I won't have my son living life thinking women are the weaker sex just because we don't have that thing dangling between our legs."

"Is that so?" He made his advance slowly, one step at a time until the heat of his body met hers.

Liz held her ground, refusing to be intimidated.

"It isn't our sex that makes us stronger, Elizabeth, it is us. The sooner you see that the better off for everyone."

Her eyes twitched, a slightly nervous tick she had when she was unbalanced and damn if Fin didn't take notice of it. He cast her a cocky grin, evidence he knew he was getting under her skin.

Drawing her shoulders back, she took a deep breath. "I could have you on the floor in seconds, MacCoinnich, so don't tempt me."

"In your dreams, lass," he challenged, his frame nearly touching hers.

Without thought, Liz brought her knee up. But she didn't have the edge of surprise, and Fin dodged her blow with ease.

Her anger went to her hands, reaching for him in another aggressive move. He pinned her flailing hands in his grip leaving her useless and incapable of moving. His body pressed up against hers preventing her from doing anything.

Anger for anger. Stare for stare. Their breath mixed as they glared at each other.

His triumphant stance wavered. Her breath hitched when his grin slowly faded. They stood too close. Little fluttering waves of pent up desire blossomed and took root. She needed to back off before either of them did something they would regret.

But she was too late.

"God's teeth," he murmured right as his mouth reached for hers.

Bittersweet was his taste. Spice and honey mixed with vinegar. He probed her mouth, she gasped in surprise. He took advantage and slipped his tongue inside.

Where the hell had this seduction come from? Why couldn't she tear herself away? Even now her body betrayed her mind when she melted into him.

Fin let loose her hands. Once unbound, she thrust them through the panel of his shirt, needing to feel the smooth texture of his skin under her fingertips. Her fingers fanned up and clutched his shirt.

A bomb wouldn't have broken them apart, seconds passed, minutes, both of them engulfed in a passion which had simmered just below the surface for months.

When a small voice, sounding shocked and concerned, penetrated the silence, they separated. "So are we going or what?" Simon's pre-teen attitude came across loud and clear.

Liz swiveled away to stare at Simon. Out of the corner of her eye, she saw Fin watching her every move. She needed to catch her breath.

Simon stood with his hands on his hips. "Well?"

"Get your coat." Fin told him.

Simon didn't waste any time before he ran off to the house.

"But..."

"No *buts*. You win," Fin said, then went over to the tack room and grabbed a saddle for another horse. "You're riding with me," he told her.

~~~~

"He what?" Tara pulled the brush through her hair a little too quickly after hearing what Lizzy had said.

"I said, he kissed me."

"Oh, my God. When?"

"Yesterday, before we went to the village." Liz flopped on the bed her sister shared with her husband and covered her eyes with her arm. "What the hell was I thinking?"

"Did you try and stop him?"

"If by stopping him, you mean jumping him

and damn near ripping his clothes off, then yeah. I don't know what got into me. I kissed him back. We don't even like each other."

Tara laughed, turned back to the mirror, and finished brushing out her long hair.

"Why are you laughing?"

"Puleeeese...You and Fin, Fin and you, everyone saw it coming. I can't believe you didn't."

"What do you mean 'everyone'?"

"Everyone. Myra asked if you had said anything to me. So has Duncan."

"That's not everyone."

"Duncan told me Ian mentioned you and Fin would be well suited, if you could stop fighting long enough to figure it out."

Liz stared at the ceiling. "Simon saw us." A line formed between her brows. "A few minutes longer and he would have to seek therapy when he's older."

"You're not the first mom a kid's caught kissing a man, Lizzy. Give yourself a break. Simon likes Fin."

"I've always kept my private life away from him, not that it's been too difficult. The men were few and far between over the years. Simon hasn't so much as met any man I've dated, let alone caught me kissing one."

Tara wobbled to her feet, slowly, carrying the weight of her pregnancy, now in its seventh month. "Did you do that to protect him? Or you?"

"What do you mean me?"

"You've never let anyone get close, Lizzy."

"Some of them got pretty close."

Tara hit her sister with a pillow, "I'm not talking about sex. I mean here." She tapped her chest. "In order to get close to you, they would have to know Simon. My guess is you probably didn't let many of them meet him. I think that's why you fight so much with Fin. He's getting close, and he already knows your son. And you."

"You're wrong. It's not like that."

"Oh, yeah? What's it like then?"

"It's only physical," she said defensively. "I can't let it happen again."

Tara put the brush down and glared at her. "Why?"

"Fin's a player. So was Simon's dad, you remember." Tara nodded before Lizzy continued. "I won't get mixed up with his type again. Besides, I'm going home the first chance I get."

Tara flinched, making her feel like shit for being so blunt.

"You know you can stay here. Why work so hard to leave?"

"This isn't my time, my place. I know you want us to stay, but it isn't right freeloading off the MacCoinnichs like we are. In all my hard times, I never so much as asked for food stamps. How am I supposed to live off someone else without paying my way?" Liz flipped over on the bed and eyed her sister. "You know I'd do anything for you, but staying in the sixteenth century is asking a little too much."

"I know, but I have to try."

"And I have to say 'no'."

~~~~

"Are you going to tell me what's bothering you? Or are you just going to kick my ass all day long?" Todd raised his sword to block Fin's move.

Sweat poured off Fin's brow and had been for

over an hour. He was working off some serious aggression, and Todd received the worse end of it.

Fin stepped back, circled around, and lunged again. "Women."

Todd countered when Fin left himself open. "By women, you mean Lizzy?"

"Aye."

A few more passes and clashes of steel later, Todd said, "Suck's doesn't it?" He wiped the sweat from his brow. "Seeing them all day long. Hearing them. Smelling them. And not being able to do a damn thing about it?"

"You refer to my sister?"

Todd picked his words carefully. Knowing a brother might not like to think of his sister the way he thought of Myra. "Lizzy is someone's sister."

Fin and Todd both lowered their swords when the objects of their affections walked by on an upper terrace. "Damn," they both said in unison.

~~~~

A mountain is only a mountain, until pressure starts to build from below. Fire churns, heat and smoke rise causing that mountain to become a volcano. Todd saw his current situation in a similar way.

On its journey from mountain to volcano, earthquakes rattle the nerves of people around it. Sometimes, right before it erupts with the force of a nuclear blast, small amounts of ash come out and litter the land with its warning.

Although the table was relatively quiet, the sounds of utensils hitting plates filled the lack of conversation. Todd glanced over to Myra who sent him a timid smile. God she was beautiful. The dip in the fabric of her dress gave him a glimpse of her creamy white skin. The thought brought a wave of longing over him. He cursed his erection, tore his gaze away from Myra and stabbed at the dead bird on his plate.

"Todd and I will be going to the village tomorrow." Fin's announcement brought all eyes to him.

Todd held his breath. Although he'd agreed to go with Fin, he wasn't sure he could keep the reasons for going from Myra. He didn't want to hurt her, but Fin insisted that they find a couple of women to ease their pain.

Todd knew he wasn't going to go through with Fin's plan, but he couldn't exactly blow off his request. Telling Fin, 'Gee, I think I'll just wait until I can find a way to be with Myra,' didn't seem like a healthy choice of words. The thought of the broadsword swooping down on his neck popped in his mind.

"What is it you need there?" Ian asked.

Fin exchanged a glance with Todd. "Repairs from the winter's storms need to be addressed." His excuse wasn't entirely without merit.

"Maybe you would like some company," Lora suggested.

"Nay."

"No," Todd put in.

Myra tilted her head to Lizzy, who stared at Fin.

"I think you should take Simon and Cian," Liz told Fin. "Wouldn't you like that?" she asked the young boys.

"We go alone, Elizabeth."

"Why is that, Finlay?"

227

Damn, Liz wasn't fooled. Todd knew without any doubt that she'd already pegged their ulterior motives. He glanced at Myra, but she appeared lost. Innocent.

Guilt and remorse hit him hard.

"Because I said." Fin's voice started to rise.

"Really, Fin. I don't see what the problem is." Myra glanced at Todd. "I'm sure Simon and Cian can help with repairs."

Todd shot his eyes to the plate in front of him.

"We don't know if it's safe to be leaving in big groups." Todd followed his comment by placing a forkful of food in his mouth.

"Fin took Simon and Liz out the other day. It will be no less safe tomorrow," Myra argued with Todd.

Ian slammed his massive fist to the table. Everyone jumped. "Enough of this." Ian tossed his hands to the dogs who had moved far away from the table when the arguing had begun. "Even the dogs are sick of this conversation. If the men want to go alone, they go."

"That's it? What the men say sticks, and we can say nothing?" Liz sputtered.

"You can say what you want, lass. But it will make no difference." Ian was firm and met her stare.

Liz pushed away from the table and threw her napkin on her plate. "Great! That's just great." She stood and left the table.

Todd watched her go and dared his eyes to meet Myra's. They narrowed with sorrow before falling to her hands.

Shit!

~~~~

"You do know why they're going right?" Liz poured the wine the maid brought to her room.

"Women." Myra accepted the glass.

"Damn right women. Women that aren't us." She tossed back half a glass in one gulp.

"I thought you didn't like Fin."

"I don't—not like you mean anyway." She coughed. "But are you going to sit back and let him lead Todd to who knows who? Have him introduce your guy to the hotties in town?"

"I don't think Todd will go through with it."

"You can bet your ass he would. Men suck that way. Anything in a willing skirt and off they go."

"I'm a willing skirt, and he hasn't jumped on me." Myra put her glass down.

"He would if your father wasn't just outside your door."

"I don't know, Lizzy. He hasn't even attempted."

"He values his head. Can't blame him for that."

"If he wants someone else, maybe I should let him go?"

Liz rolled her eyes. "He doesn't want someone else. Damn, listen to you. He wants you, and it's high time you remind him of that." Liz gestured with her glass, "He's just outside that door."

Torn, Myra didn't know what to do. "I couldn't go to him. What if someone heard us?"

Liz appeared lost in thought before she asked, "How about a spell?"

"A what?"

"Just a little silence spell." They had been working on many things over the past months, using Tara's book as guidance. Lizzy had taken to studying the books on witchcraft. In fact, Lizzy seemed obsessed with mastering everything Druid. Myra remembered her saying that the only way to defeat Grainna was to get inside her mind.

"I remember a spell about keeping silent in both secrets and noise." Her hopeful expression worried Myra on a deep level.

"I don't know."

"Coward."

Myra sat up taller and felt the challenge Liz had given her. "Fine."

Lizzy jumped up and found the books hidden in a secret hole in the wall. She took the one she needed and returned to the bed. She flipped through the pages until she found what she wanted. "Here. It suggests using an object to charm."

"What does that mean?"

"Like a lucky rabbit's foot."

"A foot of a rabbit?" Myra wrinkled her nose at the thought.

Lizzy laughed while she scanned the room. She uncrossed her legs, walked over to the vanity, and removed a cord used to hold her hair back. "This should work."

Myra blushed and shook her head. "I don't believe I'm doing this. 'Tis wonderful."

Lizzy chuckled. "He won't know what hit him."

They used a small cup and filled it with water and a dash of lavender. With great care, they cast their circle. Somehow, the power within the circle of candles bound their thoughts, their energy, their gifts and made them stronger. Uniting them.

Liz slowly added the cord to their moist mixture. She closed her eyes. Myra followed her lead.

"Nature calls Myra to her man, we ask for silence from within. Use this object to keep the quiet, to help her with her desperate plight. If the Ancients will it so, we ask this please so she can go."

At first, there was nothing, not a tingle in the air, not a spark from the flame. Then, the candle that heated the cup grew bright and blue before blowing itself out.

"That was corny," Lizzy said, rolling her eyes.

"Did it work?"

"I'm not sure." Liz removed the cord and wiped off some of the moisture. "Let's test it."

Liz stepped outside the room and into the dark hall. Myra placed the cord on the handle and closed it. Once alone in the room Myra called out to Liz. She did it quietly at first and then louder.

Lizzy poked her head inside and whispered, "You're supposed to yell."

"I did."

They giggled like teenagers when they hustled back in the room.

Chapter Seventeen

He'd agreed to go with Fin, but the look Myra sent him at the dinner table paralyzed him with guilt.

What the hell did he have to be guilty about? It wasn't as if they were married or anything. Since when did a bachelor have to concern himself with the whims of a woman? Isn't that why he'd remained a bachelor for so long, because he didn't want to answer to anyone other than himself? He sighed, knowing this was only partially why he'd never married.

He punched his pillow and tried in vain to turn off his thoughts. He would go to the village tomorrow to meet one of the women Fin knew, and if he didn't get some sleep he wouldn't be able to...damn!

Myra's big doe eyes flashed in his head. Who was he kidding? He wouldn't be able to anyway! When had life gotten so complicated? And where the hell did the conscience come from?

He cursed women. All of them. Then turned to his side and tried to find some rest.

His mind finally started to drift when he heard the latch of his door. Instinctively, he reached for his weapon before he realized it was hidden in a panel on the opposite side of his room. A small dagger on his bedside table was the only thing available. He inched his hand over to it.

~~~~

Her heart pounded so hard Myra thought that alone would wake everyone in the house. She slipped inside the room, undetected by anyone, and placed the cord on the door. Her breath came in a rush.

I made it.

Before she opened her eyes, she heard Todd's sporadic breathing. It was in a pattern that told her he wasn't asleep. When she opened her eyes, Todd was alert, his wide-eyed gaze focused on her. His jaw was slightly ajar, and his expression seemed confused.

With a confidence Myra didn't know she had, she pushed away from the door and walked to his bed. Her heartbeat rose even faster, but now it was for an entirely different reason. What if he sent her away? Could she face him again if he did?

She stopped short of his bed and pulled her lips into a knowing smile. His chest moved faster telling her he wasn't unaffected by her presence. He lifted himself up on his elbows, but didn't say a word.

Slowly, she untied the belt holding her night robe in place, and with one bold move, removed any doubt from Todd's mind what her purpose in being there was.

He shivered.

"You look cold. Maybe I can help." Lizzy told her to use that line. From the way Todd licked his lips, she knew it worked.

Every inch of her skin was clothed in nothing more than the flame from the fire behind. His eyes swept over her.

Myra sauntered to his side, just out of reach and tossed her head back.

233

He gulped.

A wicked smile creased her face. "Thirsty?"

"Oh, yeah," he managed, before he reached out and tugged her to his bed.

His mouth found hers in a probing kiss that took on a life of its own. The months of longing poured into their embrace. His bruising kiss threatened to leave a mark both physical and mental.

Thoroughly, she savored each touch, each taste. Weeks of desperation and dancing around their desires were over. She was finally in his arms again, exploring, touching, feeling his body press against hers. His firm hand wound behind her neck. His fingers, cool against her hot skin held her close, refusing to let go.

Over and over she called his name, responding to every touch with a gasp, a moan. His lips released hers, and he pushed her to his side. His smoldering gaze focused on the taunt pink nipple he grazed with the palm of his hand.

"God, I've missed you." His mouth took possession where his hand had been. Her body arched up while her fingers dug into his back.

"Oh, Todd." She let the sensation of his mouth, teeth and tongue travel through her body sending shockwaves of indescribable pleasure over her. Her body clenched, heated, and wanted more than ever.

Her hands dove to his erection, curled around it and stroked its length. He all but collapsed on top of her at the pleasure she gave. Her hips thrusting with every stroke of her palm against his hard length brought her name from his lips. When she felt the moisture bead at the crown, she smiled under his kiss, knowing how much she pleased him.

Through slit lids, she enjoyed watching as she drove him mad. She chuckled to herself at the power she held and pushed him over so she could look down on him. His eyes opened and watched her as she stroked him. As his body shuddered, she held back, waited then touched him again. He pulled her down in another searing kiss, more desperate than the last.

"I'm going to explode if you continue that," he warned. She released her hold and let her thigh brush against his. He tried to roll her beneath him, but she wouldn't give him that view.

"Not this time," she whispered.

She pushed him on his back and laughed at his shock. Pinning his shoulders down, her lips found his. His muscular chest rippled beneath her hands fanning out over him.

She straddled his hips and slid close, teasing him mercilessly.

Fingers stroked up her thighs and wedged between them. When he slid one finger into her moist heat, her body bucked as he passed over the tight bundle of nerves screaming to be fulfilled. Teasing him bordered on pain for her, until finally he grabbed her hips, positioned himself, and pushed into her.

Her orgasm, instant, fierce and completely unexpected, forced a moan from her as she shuddered with her pleasure.

He almost lost it when her body clenched around him, but he stilled, forcing control over his movements until he felt her relax. Somewhere in the far reaches of his mind, Todd knew they would be found out, but he didn't care. Couldn't consider anything but the woman riding out her pleasure over him. Her long hair cascaded around them, billowing like a sheet of privacy, and enclosed them in a world where only the two of them existed.

Rolling limb over limb until she settled under his weight, he had her where he wanted. Her passion spent for the moment, but he knew he could draw more from her. He demanded she take more.

Slowing their frantic pace and filling her body completely, Todd's lips joined hers, encouraging her and pleasing him when her body started to respond.

Her fingers raked into his flesh. Need built. His thrusts became more urgent and fast, until her gripping orgasm pushed him over the edge. "Myra," he wailed when they crashed into the blinding light.

Panting, as if they had just run the final lap in a twenty-six mile marathon, they collapsed. She murmured his name as the tremors faded to pleasant twinges.

Myra flung her hands to the side, bringing one staggered breath in after the other.

"I'm crushing you."

"Aye," she said, laughing. "I would not have it any other way."

He rolled off, but kept her close. "You're wicked, you know that."

"If I am wicked, then how is it what we just did felt so good?"

He smiled, kissed the tip of her nose. "So very good," he agreed.

"I've missed you, Todd Blakely...and missed this."

He nodded toward the door. "I can't believe that door hasn't come crashing down."

"No one can hear us."

"Oh, honey, you are not quiet." He laughed.

She poked a finger at his chest. "Neither are you. But Lizzy and I found a way around that."

"What do you mean?"

"See the cord hanging on the door?"

"Yeah."

She leaned down, traced his nipple with her tongue. "It keeps all sound inside this room, here, where it belongs."

He bit back a groan when her head moved lower, over his stomach. "Really?" His body was already responding to her touch.

She watched him fall back on the pillows, and abandon all thoughts. "Let's test it." She moved lower, his cry grew louder than hers had ever been when she took him into her mouth.

~~~~

The hours they slept could be counted on one hand, but Todd couldn't remember feeling so alive. No one was the wiser to his and Myra's actions.

Todd quietly filled his plate with a generous portion of food. Next to him, Fin equaled his platter with that of Todd's.

Myra and Liz arrived at the table together, speaking in hushed whispers. Todd stood and pulled out chairs for Myra and Lizzy, when they started to sit. "Good morning, ladies."

"Good morning," Myra called out, sneaking a glance at Todd from beneath her long, dark lashes.

"I trust you slept well?" Ian asked.

"Aye, like a baby."

"Best night's sleep since I got here," Liz added. "It was very quiet last night, don't you think?" she asked to no one in general. She jumped as if someone had kicked her under the table.

Todd attempted to look around the room to avoid staring at Myra.

Ian's eyes narrowed but Todd didn't respond. "So, when are you going into town?" Ian asked Fin.

Fin smiled over at Todd. All Todd could manage was a shrug.

"Well..." Fin sneered. "Later today, I guess."

"Yeah," Todd added. "Fin, maybe it wouldn't be such a bad idea if Simon and Cian accompanied us. They could help with the repairs, and we can get back faster."

Fin stared at Todd, eyes narrowed. "If that is what you want."

Myra smiled, lifted a sausage on her fork and carefully put it in her mouth. "Good sausage."

Todd licked his lips and attempted to keep from choking. Fin's eyes grew wide.

Ian, at the far end of the table, set his jaw in a firm line of disapproval.

~~~~

The glass whipped past Michael's head, so close in fact, if he hadn't ducked, it would have impaled shards of glass all over him.

He heard Grainna ranting from outside the walls. Her tantrums became more and more frequent, leading him to question her sanity more than he already did.

He watched now as she paced the darkened room. The stench of blood coated every corner, every surface. No one was allowed in here except he and Grainna. The sight that was there would have sent the most seasoned warrior away clutching his stomach.

A limp, lifeless form of a woman sprawled on the floor, surrounded by a ring of blood, was becoming a weekly sight. Steel didn't gag at the image. He no longer noticed the dead. Instead, his eyes traveled to Grainna to see if the years of age had been removed.

When they had returned to this time, Grainna's skin sagged like that of an eighty-year-old woman, complete with stringy gray hair and spots covering the wrinkles and lines. Now her age had reversed by twenty years or more. Slight streaks of black peppered her hair, and her skin tightened enough to reveal that she'd been a beauty once, in her youth.

It took many weak Druids to give her what she had gained. Knowing the MacCoinnichs were powerful, and therefore able to give her much with their deaths, it became increasingly difficult for him to restrain her.

Even now, they argued over how soon they would be ready to attack.

"We aren't ready."

"I have watched the men train, some of them show skill."

"Some, but not all. And with so many MacCoinnich's, it will take every one of ours to be at their peak to defeat them."

Grainna pinched the bridge of her nose and closed her eyes. "We will not win this war by massive numbers, but one by one. I say we start picking them off."

"And warn them? With even one of their

deaths, an army will search us out. How confident are you in defeating them all before we are ready?"

He cleared his throat and tread on thin ice with his next words. "Only two of them sent you back the last time. All ten might end your life."

"I'm immortal, or have you forgotten?"

"A lot of good that will do you if your head is removed from your body." Michael knew he had said the right words. Although she didn't fear death, the thought of being kept alive in such a state did spark concern somewhere in her brain.

"We will see them dead. All of them before I am done."

He lowered his head. "Yes, My Queen. We will prevail."

She slid to him and touched his cheek, spreading blood from the body of the woman on the floor to his skin. "Together we can rule this world, and once we have the other stones and the MacCoinnichs' powers, we will rule not only this time but all the others as well. Immortality will be my gift to you."

"Yes, My Queen." He was counting on that.

~~~~

Liz knew Fin followed her. She left the hall and made her way to the gardens outside.

"You know what is going on don't you?"

Liz turned, her hand flew to her throat, in a forged effort to appear surprised. "Why do you sneak up on me like that?"

"I did not sneak. And don't change the subject."

"What subject was that?"

"You know what I'm talking about."

She marched over to the tools. "No I don't. If

you'll excuse me."

"Dammit, woman." He put a hand on her shoulder, intending to turn her around.

Liz grabbed his arm, kicked out her leg and knocked him off balance. To both their surprise, he landed on his back staring up at her. Liz did a little happy dance on the inside, but kept it there thinking it wasn't good to gloat. "Keep your hands to yourself."

"You didn't say that in the stable."

"Momentary lapse of sanity," she explained. "It won't happen again."

Fin wiped his hands on his shirt when he stood. "What is happening between Todd and Myra?"

"Ask them."

"Myra refuses to talk."

"They're adults, Fin. Leave them alone."

"She is my sister."

"And old enough to make her own decisions. Leave her alone."

"My father will handfast them both if he catches them together."

Liz granted him a smile and a wink before leaving his side. God, she loved getting under his skin. It made her feel so giddy inside.

Chapter Eighteen

The subject of wandering off to the village dropped. Todd told Fin he couldn't hurt Myra, which was the truth. When Fin questioned him further, Todd kept his mouth shut.

Whenever time allowed, Myra snuck into his room and slept in his arms. For the first time in months, Todd started to feel like he belonged.

With their stomachs full and the women retiring in the main hall, one by one, the men filed into Ian's study.

Todd graciously took the splash of Scotch Ian handed him and stood by one of the long narrow windows. "So when do you expect this rain to let up?" he asked to anyone who listened. It was quite an adjustment having the world be so damp all the time, but then again, adjustment had been his middle name since he slipped through time.

He often wondered what Jake would say if he saw him now. He'd let his hair grow long, but refused to wear a beard or mustache. A few knights shaved, but they were the minority. Even Cian, who was just past his seventeenth birthday, let what chin hair he could manage, grow.

And the clothes, damn if he didn't long for the jeans. Yes, he'd adjusted all right, as he stood in sixteenth-century attire. The leggings were a hell of a lot better than the kilts. He'd be dammed if he would wear a dress.

"The rain will decrease slightly by the end of

the month, and by summer we should have several dry days," Cian told him.

Duncan tossed another log into the fireplace before he took his seat. "So," he regarded his father. "What is this meeting about?"

Ian looked up at his eldest son and then to Todd. "It's time we start searching for Grainna, and find out what she is doing. It has been quiet for too long."

Todd heaved a sigh of relief.

"You agree?" Ian asked him.

"I think it's long overdue." Todd pushed off the ledge he leaned on and moved closer to the fire. "I would much rather be on the offense than defense."

"It does feel like we are waiting for her to make the first move."

"Do you have any idea where she might be?" Todd asked.

"She could be anywhere, but if history is any clue, she will have found a forgotten shelter of some sort. There are many of them littered over the Highlands."

"Then we send scouts to see what they can find."

"And risk her getting a hold of them? Nay, Fin, we have to think of another way. You both told me she controlled the men surrounding her in the future. She may be doing that again. Consider how easily she handled Lancaster."

Todd noticed Duncan's worried expression as he no doubt recalled the painful memories. Todd had heard the story many times. Grainna had kidnapped Tara with the help of Matthew of Lancaster and they both nearly lost their lives.

CATHERINE BYBEE

Lancaster, to this day, remembered nothing of what occurred. If Grainna was able to control the minds of more experienced knights, there was no telling what evil she could vent.

"Then how do we find her?" Cian asked.

They sat and pondered, as men do, with a drink in their hands and an expression of great thought on their faces.

"Has anyone else noticed how much time the women have been spending studying and practicing their spells?" Todd asked. "Why not put some of their power to use?"

"Ask the women to find her?"

"It's worth a try. I know all of you want the whole Druid power thing to be underplayed, but my guess is Grainna isn't going to hide anything. In the end everyone here might be exposed."

"It's risky," Duncan said.

"Let me ask you this. How much of your last showdown with her was done with swords?"

Duncan shook his head.

"I thought so. If Grainna showed up here right now with an army, swords would be used, I'm sure, but without taking her out, they'll keep coming. As much as I love Fin kicking my ass every day on the field, I won't hesitate to put a bullet in anyone wanting to kill me."

"We will use every resource we have," Ian thought aloud, "even our women."

~~~~

The women were waiting quietly when the men walked slowly into the room. It wasn't as if secrets could be kept when two of the couples could read each others minds.

Tara relayed some of the conversation from

the other room, while Lora did the same.

Myra laughed at her father's expression when he squinted his eyes at her mother and asked, "You know why we are here, don't you?"

Lora nodded. "Guilty."

"Sorry, love," Tara said to her husband. "We were a bit curious when all of you left the dining hall so quickly."

"What I want to know is why it's taken you so long to think of us?" Lizzy asked.

"The role of women is not to have to concern themselves with these things." Fin offered.

"But the fact is, we could use you. All of you." Todd took a chance and sat next to Myra. "What have you ladies been working on?"

Lizzy had asked that they all keep quiet about their spells, worried about how Simon might react to their newfound coven of sorts.

Myra glanced at Lizzy who now sat staring at her son.

"It's okay, Mom. Geez, it's not like I don't already know you guys are practicing spells. If you did that last year, I'd probably have had a problem with it, but hellooo... we've traveled in time, start fires with our minds, and talk to each other in our heads. Spells seem kind of tame if you ask me." Simon rolled his eyes.

Lizzy smiled and ruffled his full head of hair, causing him to pull away in embarrassment.

"Well?" Ian asked.

"One of the books Myra brought back has been very helpful. If I had to guess, I think someone like us wrote it. Since most people in the twenty-first century think Druids are only priests and mystical at that, they never connected the dots. The lady who wrote the book thinks she is a witch and believes that with a coven, or group of witches, most anything is possible." Liz turned an eye to Myra to elaborate.

"Together we are much stronger. Sometimes Liz and I will try something new, and we can't make it work, but the four of us can."

"Like what?"

"The first thing we tried was reading each other's thoughts and memories." Myra told them about seeing Lizzy's visions of Simon as a baby and his abduction by Grainna.

"I heard you calling out for me in your mind." Simon said, recalling the day they first cast the circles.

"Yes."

"That might be our biggest obstacle, seeing in without Grainna noticing. I mean, we all thought of Simon, but he knew we were there, or at least he knew Lizzy was there." Tara added. "I assume you want us to try getting into Grainna's head."

"It would be best if she didn't know we watched."

Myra though about the cord they had charmed to keep noise within a room. "Maybe there is a way." She glanced at Liz, cocked her head to the side in the direction of Todd. "The cord."

"Oh, my God. Yeah, that might work. We can charm our circle."

Most of the others in the room appeared confused, except for maybe Todd.

"Would you two mind explaining?" Lora asked.

"Ah...Myra?" Todd glanced at Ian.

"Oh. Well, we would have to practice it first."

Liz caught on, "We wouldn't want to bore you

with the details."

"I am not bored." Ian told her, his voice firm.

"Well. Myra and I were trying to think of a way to keep our magic more private." Liz squirmed under Ian's watchful eye.

"Aye, and we thought it would help if no one could hear what was happening in the room. Just in case one of the maids was nearby. You understand?"

"So you found a way to block out sound?" Lora held her breath when she asked. Myra knew her mother well enough to know she figured out what other sounds the charm blocked out. Myra noticed Ian's eyes narrow when he arrived at the same conclusion.

"And did it work?" asked Cian, who listened, but remained clueless about all the unspoken conversation going on in the room.

"It worked," Liz told him. "Now if we can hide behind another such spell or charm, maybe we could keep Grainna from seeing us."

"We'll need to practice on someone else first."

"One of you." Tara pointed to the men.

"You mean peek into our heads?" Simon asked.

"Yeah, but we shouldn't tell you who it will be or when."

Todd laughed. "Better than a wire tap."

Liz and Tara laughed. No one else got it.

"Never mind." Todd shook his head.

"Anyway, if it works, then we have our ticket into her head."

"And her plans."

A collective nod went around the room, and before everyone retired, it was decided the sisters would experiment over the next few days to see if their plan would work.

~~~~

Michael scouted for Druids. It became a routine for him to blindly go and seek out people of his own race to fill Grainna's needs.

Her quest for power was as maddening as it was insatiable. The prize of a Druid virgin had yet to be found, but that didn't stop her slow progression to youth.

She would be hard for any of the MacCoinnichs to recognize now. The last woman she sacrificed had given her back ten years, and now she looked like a well-kept woman in her early fifties. Smoother skin, with hair that was turning back into the lush black it had been, returned her beauty.

She moved quicker, yet kept the same slow, evil eyes that watched everyone. Even Michael found himself questioning whether or not Grainna planned his demise. Although she promised him a deliverance of eternal life and power, he wasn't stupid. She was driven by something larger than him, and she would think nothing of ending his life if she wanted to.

For now, she needed him. A virgin would do little good without him there to perform her ritual.

He kept his own plans hidden from her prying mind. His Druid powers were not without merit, and he was capable of keeping Grainna out of his head. He had also studied some of her spells when she wasn't watching and found ways to counter some of them, so as not to become her next victim.

He ventured closer to the MacCoinnich land than she deemed necessary. Nevertheless, his own plan kept his eyes to the massive Keep that housed the family and the remaining stones.

Power, no matter how excessive, meant little to him if he remained trapped in this century. He wanted his life back where it belonged.

Even if he was given immortality, he wanted nothing to do with waiting for time to catch up with him.

He would search out the stones, study the family who owned them, and find a way to steal them all.

Above him, a hawk soared with outstretched wings spanning some five feet. Michael closed his eyes and lifted his thoughts above, calling out to the bird. Its cry pierced the silence when Michael willed the bird to fly toward the Keep, and screamed in protest when his eyes looked through those of the hawk.

Transfixed, Michael saw the earth below as if he actually rode on the back of the bird. The rush of air from the flight caught his breath. Small animals scurried beneath him, the hawk wanted desperately to clench its claws into his prey, for it had been one full day since it had been able to catch and kill its dinner, but Michael overpowered the animal's mind and kept it flying forward.

The bird circled the Keep once it reached its destination. He rested on the peak of a turret, and scanned the people below.

Several knights in armor stood guard, watching from the towers of the Keep. Below, the courtyard was filled with men training for battle. The bird moved closer until Michael could see the faces. He recognized some of the family and the man from the future. His hair was longer and his clothes had changed, but the same determination and fight was apparent in his movements and stance.

The hawk cried out, but no one noticed. No one but the young boy Simon, who eyed the bird for a brief moment then returned his gaze to the field of men.

Michael counted them, and made note of the entrance to the yard. He made the bird take flight and reached the tallest peak, there he saw where the stables were and the path that led to the village beyond.

Pleased with his reconnaissance, he released the bird and opened his eyes. Briefly, his irises took on the shape of the hawk. He closed them and shook his head. Opened again, they were only his, bright, blue and completely human.

He turned his horse around and started back.

~~~~

The rain started to let up and the repairs of many of the village homes were underway.

The women gathered in Lizzy's room and this time Lora joined them.

"Who should we try first?" Amber rubbed her hands together in excitement.

"Not Duncan, our connection is too strong and with you here Lora, Ian might sense what's happening." Tara settled into a chair placed inside the circle for her comfort. The others would sit on the floor.

Liz held the book in one hand and jotted down a few notes in the other. "I think this will work." She closed the book and tossed it on the bed. Unlike the other women in the room, Liz was wearing her jeans and a sweater, which she had taken to doing whenever they were alone. "Is everyone ready?"

Amber and Myra settled on the floor inside the circle of candles, each of them lit two. When it was Liz's turn, she did so with ease.

"You've improved," Tara told her.

"Thanks. Okay, let's see." Liz sprinkled the dry lavender around all of them. "It's time we peek and use our sight, and look within the other's plight. Use our circle to hide our task, keep us silent, is all we ask. If the Ancients will it so, let us look so we will know." Liz took a seat next to the others and grasped the hands of those at her side.

"So who do we pick?"

"Cian. He has a strong sense of sight. If we can get in his head without him knowing it, then we can try Duncan or Ian."

A low rumbling of energy rolled over Myra and settled into her bones. The familiar power sparked where her fingers met those of Amber and Tara.

The picture of Cian slowly merged into one they all saw. "Try not to think of past memories, just envision him. Good. Help us look through his eyes." Lizzy's words focused all of them. A quiet settled around the room. Only their breathing could be heard.

Their vision changed from a picture of Cian, to the lush green of the countryside. He was on the back of a horse riding alongside Simon who was talking and pointing.

"Can anyone hear what is being said?" Myra asked.

"No."

Myra heard her mother gasp and opened her eyes.

"You are all levitating," Lora said with

surprise in her voice.

"It's okay. We come down when were finished," Lizzy offered in explanation. "Concentrate."

The village emerged into view and Cian sped up his horse. He peered over to Simon and said something Myra couldn't hear.

Simon kicked his mount into a full run, darting past him. Cian's head came back, as if in laughter before leaning over his horse and urging him faster.

They raced over the land. Simon bent deeper into his horse when they came upon a fallen log. The horse jumped over it with ease. Simon glanced behind him as Cian matched his speed to catch up.

Neck and neck they drove their horses to the edge of the village, but Simon bested Cian by a small margin.

The boys smiled at the thrill of a good ride, and the horses pranced around anxious to take off again. Cian leaned forward and patted Simon's shoulder.

Myra felt Tara squeeze her hand before she opened her eyes and broke off the connection with Cian.

"I'm goanna kill him." Lizzy shook her head. "I've told him over and over not to run the horses."

"But he did so with such skill," Amber came to his defense.

"Did you see him jump?" Tara asked with pride in her voice.

Myra nodded and smiled. "That was great."

Lora came to her feet, and stared at the still elevated sisters. "How do you get down?"

"Not very gracefully I'm afraid." Tara considered the floor and cringed.

None of them could quite figure out why they hovered, let alone how to ease themselves gently down.

They had tried many different rhymes and made up incantations, but none worked.

"You guys ready?" Liz asked.

They winced as each one of them hit the floor despite the pillows they had put under them.

Tara was better off in the chair, but still she called out, "Damn, that always makes me need to pee."

Myra tossed her hand and the candles went out.

Amber clapped her hands together. "We did it."

"Did anyone hear anything?"

"Nothing," Tara told her while rubbing her backside.

"I did feel a few things, and I could almost smell the smoke of the chimneys close to the village."

Amber agreed. "Do you think he knew we were watching?"

"We'll have to wait until tonight to find out. If I had to guess, I would say no." Liz pulled one of her gowns out of a trunk and started dressing. "You're the empath, Amber, what did you sense?"

"Kinship. Cian likes Simon's company and feels the need to mentor him. My brother didn't like losing the race."

Myra helped Liz lace up her gown. "Your ability to feel other's emotions will be helpful if we're unable to hear what's happening."

"I agree," Myra saw the praise sink into her young sibling. Amber completed their circle, despite her tender age.

They all helped put the room to order.

Liz stuffed the book away, hidden from the casual eye along with her modern clothes.

They spread the candles around the room, merely functional again.

Pleased with the results they left the room, in search of food.

Calling on the powers they provoked together always made them hungry.

Chapter Nineteen

"I think the stones need to be a priority." Duncan said between bites.

"They will be of little help if Grainna regains power," Ian told him.

"But with the stones, can we not simply go back in time and stop her?"

"It is not us who decides the time in which the stones send us." Lora placed a calming hand on her son's arm.

Myra noticed the exchange, knowing that Duncan and Tara were becoming increasingly anxious as the weeks ticked down to the coming birth of their child.

"How do we know? Have we ever tried to make the stones take us to a specific time?" he asked his parents. "We have only done what your visions have told us. Consider how Myra was able to isolate where to be placed on her return, and she wasn't given a vision."

"He's right. My subconscious repeated Tara's words about Magicland when I left, which was where I ended up. It might work to choose the time in which to be sent."

Liz put up her hand. "Wait a minute. Let's assume you can do this. What happens if you try and come back to a day last week? You already exist in that time." Liz glanced at Tara and Todd who gave her a brief nod. "Maybe I've watched too many hours of television... but couldn't that change the course of history? Our history?"

"It hasn't been tried," Ian said. "But I think your concerns are valid."

"We still don't want the stones to stay in Grainna's hands." Duncan sent his wife a brief smile

"Have you ladies tried to get into one of our heads?" Ian asked after wiping his mouth with the back of his hand.

Myra locked eyes with Todd. His questioning gaze had her sending him a quick shake of the head to say they didn't pry into his. "You tell us."

Fin sent a nervous eye to Liz, then on to his brothers who shrugged their shoulders. Simon shook his head no.

"Well then." Lora smiled. "It seems to have worked."

"Really? Who did you spy on?" Fin took a long drink of the ale sitting in front of him.

"Relax, Finlay. It wasn't you," Liz informed him.

"Who then?"

Liz eyed her son. "I thought I told you not to jump or run the horses."

Simon's eyes grew wide. He tossed a bite of bread in his mouth to keep him from having to speak.

"So you looked into Simon's head."

"No, we went into Cian's thoughts, who was riding with Simon. No, make that racing Simon." Myra scowled at her younger brother who didn't seem concerned for his actions.

"He's an excellent horseman. I don't know why any of you worry about him," he told them all while patting Simon on the back. Myra had to agree, but from the look crossing Lizzy's face, she didn't out loud.

"Still..." Liz started.

"Leave it, Elizabeth." Fin dropped his hand on the table, causing the plates to rattle. "Simon is capable. In time he might outride any of us here."

Liz turned in her chair and gave Fin her full attention. "The last time I looked I was his mother. And you have no right to interfere. If I don't want him running the horses at breakneck speed, then he doesn't."

"I say he does."

Her mouth dropped open. "Just who the hell do you think you are? You're not his father, and never—" she yelled.

"As long as you are under the protection—"

Liz put her hand up. "Yeah, yeah. I've heard this before. And I'm done listening to it." Her voice rose to match Fin's. "I think those stones are a priority after all. It's time Simon and I go back home."

"You don't like the rules so you run away. Is that it?" Fin's jaw stood firm.

Myra cringed while watching Liz and her brother stare each other down. Todd's hand gathered hers beneath the table. His hold sent a silent word of comfort.

With hands clutched at her waist, Lizzy spat out. "It's not the rules I want to get away from. It's you!"

Simon shot out of his chair. "Stop it! Stop it, both of you." Tears pooled in his eyes. He ran from the table and up the stairs.

Without another word, Liz sprung out of her chair and took off after her son.

Fin stood to follow; Tara halted him. "Lizzy has been a single mom for many years. No one she has seen socially has ever even met Simon, let alone been given the right to dictate how he should be raised."

Fin listened, but made no effort to move.

"Unless you plan on stepping into a fatherly role, I suggest you back off."

"The lad needs male guidance."

"I couldn't agree more, but it's Lizzy's place to choose who that man will be. If you choose Simon without Lizzy, or Lizzy without Simon, either way you're doomed. And if Lizzy doesn't choose you, you stand no chance."

"Women here stop raising their sons by Simon's age."

"You keep forgetting that she isn't from this time, and if you back her in a corner she will find a way to leave."

"Where would she go?" Myra asked nervous of how Lizzy would survive without them.

Tara glanced at Myra. "Anywhere. It wouldn't matter to her if she had to bunk down in a shack. She won't stay where she feels threatened."

"She would risk her life and that of her son's for her pride?"

"You make that sound like a fault, Fin. Isn't honor and pride what every knight lives by?" When he didn't answer Tara went on. "Besides, Lizzy has always found a way to support herself and Simon. Granted, it's done a little easier in our time, but it isn't impossible now."

Myra spoke when no one else did. "Widows in our time live in relative poverty. If the truth were known about Simon's birth being out of wedlock, they would both be outcasts even amongst the poor."

Fin stormed away in the opposite direction of Liz.

Myra held Todd's hand under the table her worried expression met Tara's. "Would she really leave?"

"Yeah, yeah she would."

~~~~

"Simon, open the door." Liz stood outside his room pleading. His sobs had tapered down to an occasional choking breath. Liz knew he listened, but she didn't want to yell at him to get him to let her in. "I'm going to sit here in the hall until you open up."

Nothing.

"It's cold out here in the hall." She tried a slight laugh to lighten the mood. "And dark." He knew she had a slight fear of the dark.

Beyond the door, she heard a rustling of feet and Simon's grunts as he moved furniture. His footsteps retreated and were followed by a plop of a hundred pound boy flopping on a bed.

Liz slowly turned the handle and found the resistance she had met before gone. The heavy door creaked slightly when she pushed it open. She eased herself into the room and quietly closed the door behind her.

Simon lay on his side facing the wall, she would be talking to his back, but at least she was in the room where they would have some privacy.

She took her time lighting a few candles and stoking the fire set by one of the servants. With the shadows chased away, she took a seat in the room's only chair. "Do you want to tell me why you ran away?"

Simon took a deep breath before he spoke. "I didn't want you fighting over me. Either of you."

"We weren't fighting over you."

"Oh, yeah, you were."

"I know it seems that way, but—"

"You don't want me running the horses and Fin thinks it's fine. He trusts me."

Shit! His words cut close to her heart. "I trust you, Simon. I don't trust the horses."

He turned slightly. "But I'm good with them. They don't want to hurt me."

"You can't know that. Horses are unpredictable."

"Not for me they're not. I know when they are tired or hungry. I don't push them where they don't want to go."

He spoke with absolute conviction. Liz had to keep from smiling at him and giving away her disbelief in his words. "How can you tell if they are tired?" she quizzed.

"Well." He tucked his legs under him and sat up. "Meg pulls to the side when she's tired, and bites her bit more when she's hungry. I've never ridden Durk, but he shifts his eyes right before he takes off. And Auntie Tara's horse shakes her head when she isn't happy with what you ask her to do."

"You're very observant to notice those details."

"It's more than that, Mom. It's like they talk to me. I know that sounds crazy, but it's true. Sometimes I think they understand what I'm thinking. Right before I kick one into a run, they tense up and sometimes they run before I do anything."

Simon's sincerity was difficult to ignore. "I

don't know, Simon."

"Fin believes me." He lowered his eyes to the blankets he sat on and started picking at the balls of lint.

"You told him this?"

"Yeah."

"And he believes you talk to the animals?"

He nodded.

Liz closed her eyes and shook her head.

"See I knew you wouldn't believe me."

"People don't talk to animals."

"Some Druids do. Fin told me. Maybe that's my gift. Remember the falcon at Renaissance Times?"

She did remember, but she was stuck on how many times her son referred to Fin. They had already formed a bond, a bond she should have stopped.

"Don't you think talking to animals could be my gift?" he interrupted her thoughts.

"Maybe. All this magic and power stuff has me a little confused." She stood and moved over to the window. The sun had set and she couldn't see a thing. The cool air that found its way through the cracks helped clear her head.

"Mom?"

"Yeah?"

"I don't want to leave. Even when we find the stones, I don't want to go back."

"Simon, our place isn't here."

"Yes it is. Laird Ian said we could stay forever."

"That doesn't mean we should."

"Why not? It isn't like this house isn't big enough." His big blue eyes melted her heart.

"What about your friends? Remember your skateboard? What about a toilet that flushes?"

He bit his lower lip. "I have new friends and a whole new family. Horses are better than any piece of plywood with wheels. Besides, Fin has almost finished the bathroom. It won't be like our old one but it should work." Singing Fin's praises wasn't something Liz wanted to hear from the mouth of her son.

A knot formed in the back of her throat, she worried for the day she would have to remove her son from this life. This was Tara's life, not hers. The knot thickened when her thoughts drifted to Fin and his future. When Fin went on to marry and have sons of his own, he would push Simon aside. It was only natural.

"Will you at least think about it?"

She gave him a half smile and pushed her rebuttal aside for now. "Yeah, I'll think about it."

He pushed further as any teenage boy did when they thought they could. "And the horses, can I ride them like Cian does?"

Liz's eyes narrowed. "Don't push it, buddy."

"But..."

"No buts. Let me get used to all of this. It isn't like there's an E.R. around the corner when you break your neck. You're all I've got." She headed to the door.

"Hey, mom?"

She turned; he shifted his gaze to the floor, uncomfortable.

"If you and Fin wanted to...you know. Get married or anything, I'd think that was kinda cool."

Her hand flew to her mouth to keep the ache

inside when the magnitude of his words hit her. "Oh, Simon, I don't think that's going to happen."

"Why not? You like him and he likes you."

"It's complicated," she told him.

"Grown-ups make everything complicated," he declared.

She turned away so he wouldn't see the tears.

Chapter Twenty

Michael stumbled upon her during his routine surveillance. He had stopped searching for more Druids, let alone virginal ones, for Grainna to rape them of their powers and youth.

He was busy talking with a merchant when he skimmed over the young woman with little more than a glance.

His fair hair and muscular build caught many eyes from the women he passed, from the innocent to the more knowledgeable. The girl took notice of him when they accidentally bumped into each other.

"Forgive me. I wasn't watching where I walked."

In an instant, he felt her power. A slight prickle of awareness one feels when in the presence of something familiar. His head ached slightly, a sure sign someone looked inside of it. He quickly shut the girl out, but not before she sensed his interest in her. Silly chit, she didn't know what drove his curiosity. *Are you a virgin?*

Michael flashed white teeth, and the dimple he had been born with, and always knew when to use. "'Twas my fault. I was so taken in by yer lovely eyes I let ye run right into me so that I might learn yer name."

She wasn't particularly pretty, and her body didn't have the curves he preferred on a woman, but her eyes were a deep shade of blue that had a piercing effect which caught his attention. She was well-spoken for a village girl, and even if her outfit was made of muslin and wool, it smelled clean.

She hid her grin. The scarlet of her cheeks spoke volumes about her virginal status. "They call me Margaret," she giggled.

"'Tis a pleasure." He captured her hand, brought it to his lips. He didn't think her face could turn a brighter shade unless it was on fire. Margret wasn't used to this kind of attention, even though she wanted it. That innocent desire would give him what he wanted.

Michael kept hold of her hand once he removed it from his lips. He studied their clasped hands, gave a gentle squeeze, then released her.

"I am sure yer husband must be looking for ye."

"I have no husband."

"A fiancé then?" he smiled.

"No man has spoken for me."

"Well then." He took her elbow and led her out of the merchant's store. "Allow me to escort ye home. The hour is growing late and yer beauty might attract the wrong sort."

Margaret's smile showed slightly crooked teeth. "That is not necessary, sir. I have been in this village the whole of my life. I am verra safe here."

He sent her a pout. "Ye wound me, Margaret, for I only want to spend a few more minutes in yer company."

"What is yer name?" she boldly asked.

He offered her his arm and walked her down the relatively deserted street. "Jones. Michael Jones," he lied. Even though he was in the village of Lancaster's domain, he didn't need his real name returning to the neighboring MacCoinnichs.

He toyed with what he should do with the girl. He knew he would pay dearly if Grainna knew he found a virgin and didn't return with her immediately, but it wouldn't serve his purpose for Grainna to regain complete power yet. If anything, his continued concern with Grainna's sporadic behavior made him question if he should show the Druid woman to her at all. Maybe if she knew her salvation was only a breath away, she would concede and give him the eternal life he craved. Either way, he wouldn't force Margaret to go away with him now. Perhaps with some time she would go willingly. Then no alarm would be raised.

"Are ye a knight? Are ye Sir Jones to the Lancasters?"

His lies came easy. "A knight, aye, but not to the Laird of Lancaster. I am only traveling through."

Her eyebrow rose. "Then ye are not staying?"

"That depends."

"On what?"

He placed a hand over hers that rested in his arm. "On if ye are asking me to stay—for a time."

She stumbled. Michael caught her.

"How could I ask such a thing? I do not know ye."

"But ye want to. I think."

She warmed under his touch and his words. "I would entertain the idea of getting to know ye, properly supervised of course."

A virgin, no doubt. "Of course."

She stopped in front of a cottage where smoke rose from the stack. "Perhaps tomorrow ye could come for our midday meal. My mother would enjoy having a knight at her table."

"Until tomorrow." He bowed over her hand and locked her eyes with his when he kissed it again. He heard her pull in a sharp breath and felt the tremor in her hand. He smiled at how easy she was.

How very easy she would be.

~~~~

They waited until the hour grew late and the servants had retired for the evening. Her father placed an extra guard at the gates and another on the highest tower to sound an alarm if needed.

Every family member made his or her way to Liz's room. A few chairs were brought in for extra seating, and despite the size of the room, it was crowded.

Myra and the rest of them were apprehensive about showing the men what they did. Until now, they had this to themselves, a complete no-testosterone zone is how Tara referred to it. Now it would be what Lizzy called a co-ed experience.

Once everyone arrived, Lizzy took the cord and book from her hiding spot, and placed the cord around the handle of the door. Ian glanced at the oversized string, then darted his eyes to his daughter and Todd.

Myra purposely directed her gaze to anywhere but Todd. She really didn't want her father questioning anything right now.

Lizzy hugged the book to her chest, and encouraged everyone to get comfortable.

Tara waddled to the chair, the others sat on cushions.

Myra noticed when Amber smiled at Simon

267

whose eyes grew wider when his mom started talking.

"Okay guys. I know you're going to have questions, but wait until we're done before you ask. If you have a suggestion during, speak out but don't come into the circle."

"Why?" Fin asked.

"The circle is opened and closed by us, breaking it voids what we're doing, not to mention it hurts"

"Hurts?" Duncan stared at his wife. "What hurts?"

"The energy shocks the one breaking the circle, and we fall."

Todd scanned the faces of the women, "What do you mean fall?"

Myra smiled, more confident by the second. "You'll see."

"But since you're here, why don't you and Duncan stand behind Tara." The men exchanged creased brows, but didn't question them.

"Ready?" Amber sounded anxious to start. With the others taking their places, Amber spread the lavender and cast the circle.

Lizzy started. "It's time we peek and use our sight, and look within the other's plight. Use our circle to hide our task, keep us silent, is all we ask. If the Ancients will it so, let us see so we will know." With hands clasped in one another's, the candle flames reached five and six inches in height.

"Since Tara and I are the only ones who have seen Grainna, you both will have to open your minds to retrieve the image."

They closed their eyes, took slow breaths.

Myra felt Tara squeeze her hand harder. Her pulse quickened, and the memory of Simon within Grainna's grasp merged with Myra's mind.

"I see it," Amber said.

"Me too." The image made her nauseous, which was probably a memory of either Lizzy or Tara.

When they started to elevate above the floor more than one gasp came from the men in the room, but none of them said a thing.

"Do you have it?" Lizzy asked.

"Aye," Amber said.

"Aye," Myra agreed.

"You okay, Tara?"

"I'm good."

"All right, let's find the witch." Myra glanced over, saw Lizzy opened her eyes, and stare at the paper where she had written down the spell. "Take our minds across the land, to find the witch and the man. Let us look so we can see, what will be our destiny."

"Clever," Myra told her.

"Only if it works."

It was only them in the room. Even though the family watched in fascination, the women only saw one another. "Which way?"

"The village first. We can all picture it."

As if they were astride a horse galloping at a fast speed their minds soared over the land. A small gust of wind brushed Myra's hair back from the center of the circle. As quickly as the image of the village wiggled into focus, it soared past.

Myra kept her eyes closed and asked, "Who's doing that?"

'Not me' was the collective answer.

269

"Just relax, go with it." The green hills dotted with sheep rushed past them, another village swept into view, not the village outside MacCoinnich's Keep. "Where is that?"

"Lancaster," Myra told Lizzy.

Their minds traveled farther, then turned toward the forest. The imagery came so fast it felt as if an eagle soared above the clouds, complete with dips and turns.

As fast as they raced, they stopped. Myra noticed a blur of a rundown home before their journey suddenly ended.

Grainna peered into a glass sphere in front of a fire. The room had the stench of death in every corner.

Amber gasped when the vision of a blood soaked table emerged.

"Stay calm." Myra held her sister's hand tighter.

"Is that her?"

Tara's hand trembled in hers. "Yes, but..."

"Younger," Liz finished Tara's sentence.

"Yeah, a lot younger."

Duncan finally spoke up. "Can she see you?"

"I don't think so."

"What do you see?" Ian asked.

"She watches. She watches Steel in her sphere."

"She's angry," Amber told them.

"I think you're right, but why?"

Myra felt Tara's mind wander the room in which Grainna stood. "Oh, God."

"What?" a choir of voices asked in the room.

"Don't look, Tara. There is nothing we can do for them." Myra knew the minute Lizzy saw the

270

dead, at least two of them. Liz felt Tara's pulse start to pound too fast. The thought shifted into Myra's head quickly. Worry and fear made her open her eyes.

"We have to end this."

"I'm okay," Tara assured them all. "What else is she seeing in the crystal?"

Myra tried to look, but the image in the cloudy glass became distorted. "Can you feel anything, Amber?"

"Anger. Violence. Peace."

"Why peace?"

"She sees her redemption, but the image angers her."

Suddenly, Grainna swiveled away from her crystal ball and looked around the room.

They grew still, held their breath. She waved her hands over the sphere, which grew dark. Her eyes pierced the orb as she started to chant.

Tara felt the hair on her arms start to stand on end. "We have to get out of there." The chant was familiar.

"Fast."

They opened their eyes removing the image, but not the link. "Okay, Duncan, get ready to catch." Liz told him.

"Catch what?"

"Your wife. Myra?"

Myra acknowledged Lizzy's request. "Thank you for our link and inspection. Close our circle and our connection."

From Myra, a gust of wind blew out the candles, but not before Grainna squealed.

"Did you hear that?"

"Yeah, that's a first."

"Ready?"

"Grab the chair, Duncan."

"Why?"

"Help him, Todd." Myra nodded.

Once the men were in position the ladies let go breaking their link and fell.

Tara braced herself, but instead of falling, the men caught her weight, although somewhat off guard, and placed her gently on the ground. "That was better."

Duncan swirled around on her, stared down with a watchful eye. "Do you mean to say, you have been falling to the floor every time you did this?" He tossed his hand to the women nursing aching backsides.

"It wasn't so bad..."

"Tara Louise MacCoinnich, 'tis our child you carry and I will not have you taking that fall again."

Myra's brows shot up with his full use of Tara's name. Lizzy's eyes widened quickly.

Tara sent Duncan a coy smile. "It isn't so bad."

Duncan's stern face melted when his eyes matched his wife's. His hands grabbed hers. He knelt to her level. "I can't bear the thought of you hurt, lass."

"I never hurt." She passed a quick look to the women in the circle. "Not much anyway."

The other men helped the women to their feet.

"What happened?" Ian asked.

Collectively, the sisters moved around the room, returning candles, cushions and any evidence of what they had been doing. It was poetic to watch, and very well orchestrated.

"Well?" Fin finally asked.

"Grainna noticed us," Lizzy told him.

"Are you sure?"

Amber sat by her mother when she asked.

"Why else did we hear her? And we all sensed the need to get out."

Fin moved to the fire and tossed a log inside. He caught a flame with his hand, played with it while he thought.

"Liz is right. She knew something."

"What did you see?" Fin tossed a ball of fire in his hand like it was a marble.

"They were outside Lancaster. In the forest."

"They?"

"Aye, Grainna and Steel and other people. Many more," Myra said.

"How many more?"

"Two dozen, maybe more."

Fin tossed the ball of flame into the hearth. "Knights?"

"Some," Myra told him. "Others were servants and only numbers, men who obviously haven't been trained for war."

"How could you tell? We moved by them so quickly."

"There were horses, only knights have horses," Myra explained to Lizzy. "Or noblemen, Grainna would have no use for them."

"Amber." Liz sat next to her on the bed. "Did you feel anything else?"

"Fear. Grainna was afraid of something."

"Good." Todd stood next to Myra, touched her arm briefly, then let her go. "Fear will make her sloppy, irrational. Which can be to our benefit."

"Can you map out where she was?" Duncan asked his sister.

"I think so."

"We need to do something quickly, she's killing people, Duncan," Tara pleaded. "Her youth is returning, with it her strength."

Myra leaned into Todd's shoulder; fear surged through her. Tara held her unborn child as if protecting it from evil. Amber stood beside Simon who had moved next to his mom. Ian and Lora stared at each other. An overwhelming sense of dread hovered deep in the room.

Would they all survive? Would her strong family be whole when this was complete?

Chapter Twenty-One

The night before the men were to ride out to find and destroy Grainna, Myra slipped into Todd's room. He sat next to the fireplace, his feet resting on a table in front of him. After placing the rope on the door, she went to his side. Settling at his feet, she placed her head in his lap. His hand stoked her hair.

"Are you worried about tomorrow?"

"No, not really. All this waiting around for her to strike is a lot harder to handle."

"It does feel better to be doing something."

"Yes." The slow gentle strokes of his hand had her snuggling deeper. "Are you going to be okay here?"

"We'll be safe. My father's men will protect us at all costs. 'Tis you and my family I worry for. Are you sure you are ready?"

Todd's deep breath caused her to look up and into his eyes. "This may not be my time, but fighting the good fight doesn't change from century to century. I might not be able to spit fire from my fingertips like all of you, but I can still kick some serious ass."

Myra laughed despite herself. Her smile quickly faded as her concern for his welfare sent doubt through every inch of her body.

"Don't do that," Todd scolded.

"Do what?"

"Look at me like I'm never coming back." He

275

closed her face within his hands and kissed her soundly. She went pliant in his arms, wanting him closer still. When he broke their kiss and sat back, his thumb traced her lips. "I'm a fool," he said more to himself than her.

"Why?"

"I let you fall in love with me."

"Let me?" she laughed.

He searched her eyes. "When I was a child, my mother sat home after my father went to work and said a prayer for his safe return every night. She didn't realize the worried expression that crossed over her every time a police car drove by. Or how she jumped when the phone rang. It was like she knew the call would come someday to tell her my father was dead."

His painful memories translated into a heartfelt sob in her throat.

Todd went on, "When the call came, I held her while she crumbled to the floor, but I wasn't enough. I didn't have what she needed to pick up the pieces after my father's death. When she died, only months after we buried my father, I swore I would never put a woman through that anguish. Here I am, doing exactly that with you."

Tears glistened in Myra's eyes. "Your parents must have loved each other deeply."

"They did."

"They had a happy life, then?"

"Yeah, the best."

"Do you think they would have wanted it any other way?" Todd started to answer but Myra held up a hand for him to stop. "Your father had a reason to come home every night, Todd. He was probably more careful with every step he took because of the love he had for your mother and for you."

"Probably."

"We have little choice as to whom we fall in love with. And you're right. I do love you. When I left your time, I knew I'd never find another to take your place. I was destined to live my life with only the memories of our few weeks together. Fate brought us together again. I have a hard time believing fate would be cruel enough to take you away from me now. If she did, however, I'd always look back on these times and remember our love." Myra snuggled into his palm as he caressed her cheek.

His finger circled her neck, holding her in place as he drew her in for another taste, another kiss. Only this time his touch was tender, deeper than any they had shared before. Myra leaned into him, her breasts brushed up against his chest searching for more contact. Todd backed away. "I don't deserve you."

"Make love to me, Todd."

He shook his head. "No."

She sat back, shocked at his refusal. His playful smile had her eyes narrow and lips draw into a pout. "Why?"

Instead of answering, he stood, urging her to her feet. Without words, he marched across the room, took the cord off the door, and opened it.

"What are you doing?" Myra poked her head out into the long hall and ducked back into the room. "Someone will see us."

"Let them."

His eyes twinkled as he pulled her along with him on the short path to her parents' chambers.

Myra's heart pounded in her chest. Part of her knew exactly what Todd was doing. The other part, the one that wanted to hide in a corner, was frightened, worried about her father's reaction. A thrill shot up her spine and threatened to escape in a completely adolescent giggle.

When Todd pounded on the door, it sounded like a cannon in the silence of the hall. Hiding behind Todd, Myra tried to ignore the doors down the hall opening and the heated stares from her siblings.

On Todd's second knock, Ian flung open the door in alarm. Myra's hand gripped Todd's as the fierce look on her father's face rounded on them. Todd tossed the 'silence cord' in Ian's direction.

He caught it with a glare.

"I'm going to marry your daughter."

Myra's eyes grew big as saucers.

A muscle ticked in her father's jaw.

"Are you asking, lad?"

Oh, God.

Todd turned to her, smiled. "Marry me."

A short laugh burst out. "He wants you to ask him," she explained.

"I don't want to marry him. I want to marry you." But he was joking. His hand moved around her waist and pulled her close. "Marry me, Myra. Give me a reason to come home every night."

"Oh, Todd." All nerves and fear swept away when she boldly kissed him in front of her entire family.

Ian's growl broke their kiss. "Let it be known that this man…" Ian grabbed Todd's hand from Myra's shoulder. "Has spoken for this woman." Myra felt her father remove her hand from Todd's hip and place it in Todd's. "They are now considered handfasted until a man of..." Ian's words trailed away when Todd kissed her again. "...a little attention, if you please."

Todd pulled away, smiled.

"Until a man of the church can be brought forth to marry the two of you."

Smiling, Todd picked her up and carried her back to his room. Myra grinned at Tara as they passed her room and caught a glimpse of her father's smirk before Todd kicked the door closed behind them.

~~~~

Todd brought her to the bed, pressed her against the mattress, and stretched out on top of her. His glorious weight secured her place in life. Figuratively, literally. His hand traveled down the side of her waist, fingers brushed against her hardened nipples, and she arched into him, wanting nothing less than complete possession of him. Tender kisses brought her breathing to short heated gasps.

He brushed her hair back, causing her to open her eyes. Emotion clouded his stare.

"I love you, Myra. I have no idea how I'm going to provide for you here in your time. I just know I can't live without you. I want to give you the world."

"You are my world," she whispered. "Once, when I slept alone in your house, I silently chanted and vowed to love you three times as much as you loved me."

He kissed her nose. "Then I need to love you even more to make up for your vow."

A single stroke of his hand up her thigh and

under her gown reminded Myra of where she was. The fact that her moan could be heard down the silent hall had her holding back. That simple act made his touch seem more intense, more explosive.

Stripping away her gown was like opening a long awaited present. The anticipation was more than Todd had ever known. She was his, forever, completely. The idea of walking down the hall and claiming her hit him as primal, medieval in every sense of the word. He knew long ago he would never return to Anaheim. His life as Officer Todd Blakely held nothing compared to his life as Sir Blakely, husband of Myra Blakely. If he rode to his death tomorrow, he would hold no regrets for his actions. The MacCoinnichs were decent and honest people fighting the good fight. Cliché? Maybe, but that was how he felt.

He held a piece of heaven in his arms. Under him, her stifled moans filled the room. Once he had her naked, he rounded over her exposed breast and tugged it between his teeth. He should have had the good sense to be embarrassed when she wailed under his touch, but he didn't. Instead, he longed to make her scream her release, to prove to everyone within earshot that she was his.

Lifting his shirt over his head, he felt her light touch weave through the hair on his chest. Simple strokes met his skin as her hands trailed lower, fighting with the clasp of his pants.

His hands found the soft inner skin of her thigh. From there he traveled until he found her moist heat. One swipe of his thumb over her sex and she bucked under him. Her hands stalled in the pursuit of delivering him from his clothing.

Lost in pleasure, he slipped a finger inside of her. Slow suggestive motions mimicked his intensions.

Her head fell to the side. Todd trailed his lips over her body, purposely brushing his bristled chin against the most sensitive skin.

"What... what are you doing?"

Myra sat up, looked down on him, her expression matched her innocence.

"Shhh." He pushed her back down to the bed. "Trust me." He sent a heated breath over her core. Her eyes closed. He kissed along her skin, making his presence known in the most intimate of ways. Her knees started to close bringing a smile to his face. Something about being the only man who had ever, or would ever, know her in this way washed over him. His mouth pressed firm over her, tasting her. She collapsed at the first pass of his tongue. Soon he had her writhing under his skilled touch. Her moans deafened him. He drove faster until her body stilled and hovered, then called out her release.

Not giving her time to think, he shed the rest of his clothing and plunged into her moist depths. The act they had done before, but this time held more meaning, more emotion. She was his in every sense of the word.

His mouth returned to hers, and with every thrust, he took what was his. Her body quivered around his, and in one final gasp, he emptied into her.

~~~~

It was the first time Myra saw Todd dressed for battle. His horse stood tall next to her brothers' and her father's. His sword, the one she had given him in the twenty-first century, was sheathed and resting on his hip. He had a crossbow strapped across his back where he could reach it with ease. Beneath his tunic, she knew he carried his modern weapons. His guns.

They had made love twice the night before. When he reached for her a third time, she feigned a tired state. In fact, she simply wanted him rested and ready to face the challenges of this day.

Although she knew there was a chance he might not return from the fight, Myra focused on the advantages Todd held on his side. He would battle the evil of Grainna alongside her father, Duncan and Fin.

In nearly every step of her day thus far, she prayed, for her husband and family's safe return.

All the women who were left behind would be with them still in spirit. They would watch and warn them of dangers they did not see and do everything within their power, individually and collectively, to bring them home alive.

Myra and Todd repeated their handfasting vows before all of the family and knights under her father's rule at first light. The binding ceremony was brief.

Myra stood and watched her husband from afar. She promised herself not to cry, not to show him the fear growing deep inside the pit of her chest, threatening to swallow her whole. Yet as she walked through the courtyard and passed her family, they said their goodbyes, and the tears came. Not simply for her, but for all of them.

Duncan stood next to Tara, his hands on her swollen belly. "We will be back, lass."

Tara shook her head; her voice wavered with pain. "I know. I know. I'm not having this baby without you."

"I didn't survive Grainna once to die at her hand now."

"You better not, dammit. Or I'll make your world hell in our next life," she grimaced.

Myra caught Lizzy's eye. Fin was speaking to Simon, who would pop his head up and look his mother's way every once in a while and nod.

Lizzy walked to her son. Fin's hand rested on his shoulder. Myra noticed tears in Simon's eyes. He wiped at his eyes, desperately trying to rid his face of the wetness.

Pain rolled off Simon in waves that even Myra felt. She swallowed the knot that threatened to block her lungs.

"Hey, sport?" Lizzy grinned as she spoke, but Myra wasn't fooled.

"Hey, mom." Simon stared at his feet as he shuffled them on the ground.

Fin watched Lizzy approach. Myra hoped they would make peace before their battle.

"Why the long face? You don't have to worry about Fin. He's too ornery to let a woman get the best of him." Lizzy's words brought a lift to Simon's lips.

Fin chuckled. "Your mom's right. Remember what I said, I'll be back in less than a week."

Simon gave him a fierce hug then ran to Tara.

Lizzy's gaze followed her son. When she turned back to Fin, he was watching her intently. Myra noticed Lizzy shifting her feet under his stare.

"Well, you should get going. You don't want them leaving without you," Lizzy said.

She stumbled over what to say. He lifted his

pack and moved toward his horse.

"Fin," she called to him.

"Aye?" He turned.

At first Myra didn't think Lizzy was going to say a thing. Then her smile faded. "Don't die."

His eyes widened at her words. Myra's throat tightened when Lizzy turned to walk away.

Myra turned away and noticed her father holding Amber and kissing the top of her head.

"Take care of your mother."

"I will, father."

"Cian," he said to his son. "Take care of everything."

Cian stood tall, understanding his father's meaning behind the words.

"What about me?" Lora asked.

Ian's lips didn't move, but her mother's face softened in a way that told Myra he said something tender with his mind. She envied their link, their bond that gave them the ability to talk to each other that way.

"You." He grabbed her waist, bent her back. "Take care of you, so I have a reason to return." It was his last words to her every time he went off in battle.

When he lifted his head from kissing his wife, he looked over and saw Myra staring.

"Come here," he bid.

She ran all but two steps and fell into his embrace.

"I'll bring him home to you," he promised. Although she knew there were no guarantees, the child in her wanted to cling to his words and cast away any worry she held.

"Be safe," she said before stepping from his

arms.

This time when she glanced up, the only one watching was Todd. His battle wear newly placed, his skills ready to meet an enemy, but could he best Grainna? Myra shook the thought from her head and walked to stand before him, tears streamed down her face. She cursed them, wishing for the strength her mother held, or that of Lizzy.

"Don't cry. I'm coming back." Todd wiped the tears off her cheeks and held her face within his hands.

She didn't trust herself to speak, instead she moved into his arms and lifted her mouth to his. He pressed firm against her frame, one hand cradled her head while the other rested intimately at the small of her back. One kiss reminded her of every moment they'd shared, every kiss they gave.

Myra tore her lips from his only to move them to his ear. "Come back to me."

"I will."

She smiled into his eyes, ignoring the stares of several of her father's men who watched. "I almost forgot." She pulled back and reached into the pocket of her dress. She removed a pendent attached to a chain. Its Celtic lines and circles were etched in gold and sparkled in the glint of the sun. "Lizzy called it my lucky rabbit's foot. I don't know what she meant, but she said you would understand."

Todd bent his head while she put it on him. He held the charm in his hand. "Thank you."

He kissed her again.

"I love you," she whispered.

He sighed at her confession. "I love you, too."

Myra knew his words solidified their bond. As

new tears swelled, she heard her father mount his horse.

"'Tis time we go," Ian called.

They saddled up and prepared to leave.

"Close the gates behind us, Gregor," Ian bellowed. "To all who stand here now, ye are to follow the guidance set out by my son, Cian. Ye are to protect our women and children at all costs."

He signaled to the gatekeeper who opened the massive doors that led them out of the safety of the Keep. Ian's falcon sat perched on his arm.

Once they cleared the stones of the yard, they kicked their horses into a gallop. The bird took flight and followed in the air above.

Liz let out a long-suffering sigh when the gates closed. "I need a drink!"

"So do I," Tara put her hand to her back.

"Yeah...right."

It would take the men three days to get to where Grainna was staying, and the waiting would be hell.

~~~~

Michael noticed the hound cringed under the hand that slid over its coat. The eyes of the dog matched those of all the fighting men in the courtyard, and most of the women.

Grainna's reign over her people was held in place with fear. They worked endlessly on repairs of the home she had made out of the ruins.

She sat as regal as a queen looking over her subjects, with her back rod straight and her dark hair piled high on her head. Even the costume she wore befitted royalty. The woman who previously wore it had the unfortunate luck of traveling through her land. The two knights who had escorted the lady were now posted as guard over Grainna's court.

It was eerie how she changed almost daily since they had come here. Her eyes weren't dark, they were black. Unlike eyes of a mere human, her pupils almost never constricted. Instead, they stood open, in constant surveillance.

Michael took the last few steps and stood at her side.

The dog curled into a ball, whining at his mistress as he approached. Michael felt sorry for the hound that couldn't leave until she released him.

"I trust you had a fruitful journey." Grainna folded her hands in her lap.

"Perhaps, but as you see I come alone."

She lifted her chin, but said nothing.

"There is one promising woman in a village near Lancaster."

"And she is not with you... why?"

Michael nodded to the people surrounding them.

"I think we should continue this conversation in private."

"I," she spoke in the deadliest of tones, "decide when we will speak in private."

He cocked his head, gave a slight bow. "If you insist. Her name is Margaret. She is like us, and possibly intact. I won't know for certain until I bring her to you."

Pain hit his head hard. He did his best not to flinch at her intrusion into his head. She peered to see if he spoke the truth and he prayed his abilities kept her unaware of every thought he possessed.

"Then bring her, woo her. Marry the bitch if you must, but bring her to me."

She had dangled the carrot, his gift of immortality, in front of him long enough. He wanted payment before he delivered.

"Our war with the MacCoinnichs is coming," he said. "Now would be a good time to guarantee my survival."

As her head slowly moved in his direction, and her deadly stare met his, Michael held his breath and did his best to think only of serving her.

Her glare turned into a smirk. "Yes. Yes you have waited long enough. I warn you...it is not for the weak of heart. Immortality has its own set of, let us say, side effects."

"If it is the curse you speak of, I already know."

"Not only that, but the task of living long past everyone you know, anyone you will meet."

"I don't crave human companionship, Grainna. Besides." He placed a hand on hers. "We will have each other. Even now your beauty shines through. I would take your bed if you allowed such a thing."

"It pleases me to hear such a conviction, as that is exactly what my ritual requires from you."

His stomach rolled and bile rose in his throat. Forcing a smile to his lips could quite possibly have been the hardest thing for him to do.

Michael stared into the eyes of what equated to the devil. He swallowed the bile that threatened at the thought of fucking her. He would have to prepare for the event, give him time to protect himself from her evil if she turned on him, or attempted to control him as she had the others. "Tonight then." He picked up her hand and kissed the back of her cold hard flesh.

"Tonight is so long from now. Meet me in my rooms in half an hour. After, you can return to your Margaret's village and retrieve her."

"As you wish." He would have to hurry. He left her side, rushed to his room, and purged every morsel from his stomach.

~~~~

The men camped deep in the forest, far off any path or road in which they might meet up with renegade warriors or mercenaries wanting battle, or gold. They needed their strength for the impending fight.

Duncan sat smiling into the flames of the small fire they had made to cook the fresh meat they had hunted.

"What's so amusing?" Todd asked after noticing Duncan's expression.

"The women. They are drinking and carrying on like drunken men. Not Tara of course, but she tells me that Lizzy is ripped. What does that mean?"

Todd's head tipped back and a hollow laugh escaped. "Drunk. Lizzy's drunk." He elbowed Fin. "Nice to know what effect you have on women, MacCoinnich."

"Don't speak too soon, Blakely, Myra is as well." Duncan stopped, obviously listening to something Tara said. He slapped his hand to his thigh and laughed hysterically. The three men scowled wondering what it was he knew. Even Ian had to guess what was happening, because Lora was keeping him out of her thoughts.

~~~~

Tara thrust a plate of food in front of the

women. "You guys had better start eating, or you're going to regret it in the morning."

Lora hiccupped, bringing Myra and Liz back into a fit of laughter.

"Tara is right, this is really inappropriate," Lora said.

"I for one am t-tired of always doing what is appropriate," Myra stuttered.

"Hah!" Liz moved to the wall where she kept the cord. "You're the poster child for sixteenth century propriety." She tossed the cord in Myra's lap. "You won't need this anymore."

Myra's jaw dropped, eyes rounding to her mother.

Lora attempted to hide a laugh behind her hand.

"You knew?"

Lora laughed harder.

"Ma?"

"I am not brainless."

"But if you knew then so did father."

"You were always a bright child." Lora picked up her glass, finished her wine. "Do you think your father waited to bed me until we had exchanged vows?"

"Why, Lora, you big hussy," Tara teased.

Myra stared at her mother. Where was the woman who had given her every rule of right and wrong for her twenty-one years? Her confessions liberated everything she had done since she had met Todd. Relieved her of any guilt she had felt for deceiving her parents.

After having Todd confess his love for her, she only had to wait for his safe return so they could begin their lives together. The thought sobered her. The beat of her heart stuttered at the thought of him not returning safely.

Lora filled her glass, reached around her in support. "Have faith."

"They're going to be fine." Tara reached for her hand, her smile waning.

Liz had stopped laughing, the jovial mood of the room changed, there was no denying why. "So Lora, is Ian as serious in bed as he is out of it?"

A gasp went up, but her shocking question pushed them back to where they were minutes before.

~~~~

Candles lit the room, not in the romantic way a lover would prepare for his mate, but in the way of rituals and rites.

Michael's knock on the door, timid and unsure, brought a smile to her lips. She bid him to enter but kept her back to him when he closed it and turned the key.

She heard his uneven breathing. If she could, she would slip into his mind. But he kept her out and that angered her. Then again, if he knew her thoughts, he wouldn't come anywhere near her.

Before long, she would remind him who was the leader here. Who held all control.

"Pour us a drink, Michael." Grainna used his given name to set him at ease.

He crossed to the serving table in the room. The red wine in the decanter was warm. He poured it into the goblets, handed one to her. She turned and let him watch as she placed it to her lips.

He lifted his own glass, steadying his trembling hand. He wondered how he would sustain an erection to do as she asked.

He took a deep swallow, and watched her do the same. "Relax, Michael."

As if on command, he felt some of the anxiety leave his head. He held his goblet and wondered if she had put something into the drink.

Grainna moved to him, put the flat of her hand on his chest and let it slide down, brushing over his body. Her face seemed to soften, while his body responded to her touch.

"What preparation do we need for the ritual?"

"Most is already done. Finish your drink."

He brought the wine to his lips once again, this time finishing its contents. His head instantly swam. Yes, she had drugged him. He found the back of a chair for balance and closed his eyes. "What was in that?"

"Something to make the transition easier, trust me."

He opened his unfocused eyes. "How do you expect me to screw you if my mind is in a fog?"

"It isn't your mind that has to work." She laughed. To prove her point, she reached out, and groped the bulge between his thighs. It instantly hardened.

"Why is sex part of the change?"

"Joining our bodies, before our blood, gives you the gift."

"If that's all there is, why haven't you given it to me before now?"

She moved away from him, waved her hand around the room, extinguishing half of the candles. The change in light dilated his eyes and had him squinting to see. "Vanity," she told him.

He blinked several times. When his eyes

focused again, she was naked. Peering closer he noticed the soft peaks of her breasts and firm expanse of her stomach. Grainna appeared no older than twenty-five. Head aching, he knew she slipped into his mind. Knew she placed a young image for him to see, to react. His concern about how he would perform the task of taking her was forgotten.

Michael licked his lips as his eyes swept over her body. His gaze traveled lower drawn by her hand stroking her own thigh. He sucked in a breath and moved toward her.

"How do you want it?" His smoky words vibrated in the room.

"Fast and hard."

He removed his clothes at her request and backed her onto the bed.

Chapter Twenty-Two

Lora stood holding Tara's hand. They both had their eyes closed in deep concentration. All Myra and Lizzy could do was watch and wait.

The men had ridden so far that by themselves, they couldn't talk to their spouses, but together their power doubled, allowing them the freedom they had both become accustomed to.

"Where are they?" Myra tapped her foot, pressed forward with her questions. "Are they safe?"

"Shhh..." Lora ordered.

Myra silenced her tongue, and watched a smile crest Tara's features. They were safe, she knew by the unseen calm that entered the room.

Liz slumped in her chair and waited for Tara and Lora to start talking.

"They are camped outside Lancaster. Todd was sent into the village to find out what he could about Grainna and Steel."

"Alone?" Myra gasped.

"Your father and brothers would have been recognized, their presence would have required an explanation to the Laird of Lancaster."

"Did he find anything?"

Tara stole a glance at Lora, their smiles turned, concern wrapped over their expressions. "A woman, young, virginal, left the village without the permission of her parents yesterday, aided by a man matching the description of Steel."

Glancing out the window, Myra noticed the setting sun. *'Tis over.* "Then it may already be too late."

"We need to get into her head, see what's happening." Lizzy moved out of the chair in a rather uncharacteristic haste and started gathering candles.

"Lizzy, call Simon and have him bring Amber and Cian," Myra suggested.

Within minutes, they all gathered and the sisters cast a circle.

"Ma, you should come into the circle with us this time. In case we need to contact the men."

"Are you sure?"

Hunching her shoulders Myra said, "We've not tried it, but I don't think we have a choice."

"We won't know until we try, Lora," Liz told her.

Myra took her mother's hand and gave it a squeeze before sitting on the cushions and pillows placed upon the floor.

Liz started the familiar chant, but before the words were out a low hum floated over the room. The air thinned making all of them breathe faster.

Myra sat in the circle, clutching hands with Tara and her mother and staring at the vision of gold, yellows and white hues hovering between them.

"The Ancients," Lora mumbled under her breath.

A woman, with features of porcelain and glass hovered before them. Her image softened by the glow of the candles, her voice sang like that of hundreds in a choir. "You are the chosen," she began. "Chosen to fight this war. It will take all of you." The woman floated beyond the circle to Simon and Cian who watched. "All of you to defeat the plague that will come over this land and time."

"Are you one of the Ancients?" Liz asked, her tone fearless.

"I am."

"Do you have a name?" Amber asked in a small voice.

The vision wafted her way. Her iridescent hand reached out and stroked Amber's cheek. Amber sighed and leaned into her touch. "I am but one of the daughters of Calderon. You may call me Elise." "Why don't you take her out?"

Myra sucked in a deep breath, cautious of Lizzy's tone.

Elise turned toward Lizzy. "Ahh...Elizabeth. Our law is ancient, beyond what you can imagine. To go against it makes us no better than her."

"If Grainna isn't playing by the same rules, what does it matter?"

Elise smiled. "If we could aide you more we would. It is forbidden. Our vows are sacred, binding."

Tara found her voice. "Tell us how to bring her down. Can she be killed?"

"In your time there are rumors of how immortals are defeated."

"They're staked or beheaded," Simon said from the sidelines. "At least the vampires are."

"But that would require the men to get close to her. How can they and survive?" Lora, who Myra knew had never questioned the Ancients before, did so now.

The daughter of Calderon didn't seem in a hurry to answer. She waited.

Tara's voice lifted. "What about fire?"

Elise hovered about the circle meeting the eyes of everyone there. "Tomorrow your battle will begin. Do not be fooled by what you see." Elise moved out of the circle and over to Simon. "Do not fear what you do not understand. You are chosen." She turned back to the women.

"Will we survive? All of us?" It was the question desperately sought, but all were afraid to ask. Except for Lizzy who Myra thought would question God himself.

"It isn't for me to know or to tell if I did. Our race is dying, it is left to you for our survival. Use your gifts, all of them. Your greatest gift is not what you are born with, but what you give."

The woman began to fade. "What is my gift?" Lizzy asked the fading image. The candles reached a height of over a foot before the image disappeared altogether. Lizzy's question went unanswered.

"What now?" Myra asked when no one spoke.

Tara placed her hand, palm up to Lora. "We tell the men what has happened."

~~~~

She laughed joyously behind him. Her arms circled his waist and held on tight. Her soft little body pressed up against his reminded him of her presence.

He had slept with the devil, and if there was any piece of his soul intact before the act, it was gone now. He had chanted her spells, drank the blood of the dead, and experienced what Grainna called the gut wrenching change.

He felt the warmth of his body replaced with a calming cold, only heated by the memory of

Grainna pressed next to him. Even the lithe little form with her legs straddling the horse, her core pressed up against him did nothing to entice. He could think only of giving Grainna the woman as a gift.

He no longer sought to deceive her. He no longer kept her out of his mind. He was possessed with the striking image of who Grainna would be once they sacrificed Margaret.

Michael slowed his horse.

"Are we almost there?" Margaret asked, eyes wide and searching the darkness for some sign of light.

"Soon." He lifted his flask and handed it to her to drink. "Here."

She tilted the tainted wine to her lips, handed it back to him. "Is there truly a priest who can marry us tonight?"

Steel smiled, pretended to drink, and pressed it back into her hands. She drank again. "Well?"

He watched her shake her head, the wine was having its desired effect.

"Tonight you will be mine." He feathered a kiss over her lips. "Tonight you will be my wife."

Her body trembled, her thighs pushed together. And when she offered her lips to him again, he knew the drug worked. She would be panting and naked within the hour, and anything but virginal.

As orchestrated, the yard to the encampment was empty, except for a man in a robe. Steel had to keep Margaret from falling off the horse when he stopped.

"Is he the priest?"

"Yes," he told her, knowing that even without

the lie, she would be no problem in her current state. The curse specified a willing virgin, so they left no stone unturned.

"Oh, good," she giggled.

"Do you want to go inside, Sir?"

Steel waved his hand. "No need for that." He looked down at Margaret. "The girl is anxious, marry us now."

"Very well." The voice behind the robe recited his practiced lines.

When the 'I do's' and 'I will's' had been repeated, Margaret threw herself up and into his arms, her body ground against his. The aphrodisiac he had given her was better than any pharmaceutical put out in his century.

Stumbling into the room, Margaret clung to him. He kissed her with open eyes as he glanced around the room. A shadow moved in the corner. He knew Grainna watched.

"I do this for you," he said to the silhouette.

Margaret smiled thinking he spoke to her.

He busied his hands and mouth, enticing the virgin to open like a flower and accept all that he would do.

Grainna's hands itched, her blood purred beneath the surface of her skin. The bed sat atop an altar, waiting only for the virgin blood to be shed upon it. Then and only then, would the blood mix and the spell she would chant bring her back to who she once was. Grainna whispered her chants in the darkness of the room.

A chill settled in, several candles were caught by a draft. Their light extinguished.

The woman Steel disrobed shivered. Grainna looked up, lifted her hands and had them glowing again. The fire blazed.

Steel wasted no time. He stripped Margaret of her dress, tearing his own clothes in his haste. He hovered, poised and ready. The virgin's legs fell open. He whispered something in a foreign language, and the room instantly iced. Both women's eyes grew wide, and when he plunged, one woman screamed out in pain, while the other screamed in ecstasy.

All the light in the room extinguished in a flash.

~~~~

By the time the sisters tapped into Grainna's mind, it was over. The girl, sprawled on the bed, lay dead. Steel bent over Grainna, his hand on her back. He spoke to her, but Myra couldn't hear his words.

Steel kept looking around the room, obviously spooked by something.

"The curse is broken." Amber's shaky voice said what they all knew.

They watched as Grainna sat up from her crouched position and walked to the only mirror in the room. Slowly her head rose, her gaze swept over her reflection.

A startled gasp came from the women. Grainna stood strong and tall, her hair jet black, her skin a creamy white, her body perfectly shaped. Her eyes pierced her own reflection with lashes that swept the flawless features of her face.

She was stunning. Any woman would find fault in her own appearance if they compared themselves to her.

"There is nothing we can do." Myra opened her eyes. *Her curse is broken. Oh, Todd.*

"Cian, Simon, catch Tara when we let go."

Amber's shaky voice rang out. "We close our circle for this night, thank you for the Ancients' sight."

Once on the ground floor, they planned their next move.

"I knew this was going to happen," Lizzy declared.

"Did you have a vision?"

She grunted. "No, just a gut instinct."

"Yeah, I knew it, too." Tara rubbed her backside. The continual jolt to the floor, even with the men catching her couldn't be helping her discomfort.

"What do we do now?"

"The Ancients said we are chosen to fight the war against evil."

"She said the war was just beginning," Simon reminded them.

"I didn't like the sound of that myself." Lizzy sat next to her son. "Is Grainna really so powerful? I mean, there are what...eleven of us, and only one of her. Our odds are better."

"Two, she has that man with her."

"Still, our numbers are greater."

"But Todd is not Druid," Myra pleaded. "He has no powers to wield."

"Todd was a cop and a good one from what I could tell." Lizzy shot her a reassuring grin.

"Grainna has regained her powers. The powers of every Druid she has killed over her many years. It is us who are outnumbered." Lora's empty stare tossed what hope they had gained out the window.

"We should call the men back."

"I agree."

"Nay!" Lora broke her blank look, demanded the attention of everyone in the room. "Our fight begins tomorrow. Whether we go to her or she comes to us, it begins. Running is not the answer."

"Lora's right." Tara stood, started to pace. Her pregnant belly led the way. "We don't want her here. I say we turn in early so we're fresh and focused in the morning. Lora? Let's contact the men. Let them know what's happened."

Lora paused, creased her eyes and asked, "Are you okay?"

Tara rubbed her stomach. "I'm tired. Junior here hasn't given me much rest this last week."

"Let's wrap this up then and get you to bed." Lizzy moved away from her son.

Lora took Tara's hand, within minutes Tara was led to her room.

"Stay with her tonight," Myra heard Lora tell Amber. "Her time is coming."

Amber nodded, smiled at her mother, and then left the room.

Chapter Twenty-Three

Morning arrived and the fog lifted over the land, a hint of a Scotland spring slipping into summer was in the air. The horses breathed massive amounts of air as their lungs struggled against the pace their masters drove them to.

None of them had slept after the news that Grainna had regained her youth, her powers.

The world passed Todd by at an alarming speed. Not the speed of his Mustang at eighty miles per hour, but a single horse galloping over the lush hills of a land he only knew existed on a map until months ago.

His thoughts, as he plunged toward God only knew what, were of Myra. She waited for his return from this feeble attempt at ridding the world of an evil he didn't know about until Myra fell out of the sky.

Now, beside his recent father-in-law and two brothers-in-law, he rode to a destiny he couldn't help but think would be his end.

Never before in all his years on the force did he feel dread and uncertainty cover his soul, his heart. Was that because with Myra he suddenly had something to live for? Or was it a premonition of what his fate was going to be? Were they destined to be a fleeting pass of souls amounting to nothing more then a few nights of passion?

He glanced at Duncan. His wife waited at home with a baby only days away from being born, his face set in a determined look of a man destined to fight.

Fin, always jovial and full of life, sat poised and stern on his horse. Occasionally he would glance to one side or the other and pass a grin. Cocky. Careless.

Todd recognized the look. He sported one before he cared if he survived the battle. Then he would catch Fin when he didn't think anyone noticed. That expression was altogether different.

Ian perhaps had the most weight on his back, the most to lose of all of them. A father, a husband, a Laird of an entire land, he might not have been the King of Scotland but the outcome of this battle weighed on him as if he were fighting for an entire country.

Todd was the low man on the totem pole and he knew it. He knew these men had him hand over fist when it came to fighting medieval style, but he rode alongside them, hoping, praying he would come out of this alive.

Ian held up his gloved hand. They halted their horses at his command.

Ian hopped off his mount, reached to the ground and picked up a handful of soil. Todd watched him toss the rock-encrusted dirt. Instead of landing several feet away, the dirt stopped midair, scattered in a vertical sheet, and dropped in a line on the ground at their feet.

A barrier, invisible and completely undetectable, separated them from where Grainna had built her fortress.

"What the hell?" Fin exclaimed.

Ian glanced at the sky where his falcon soared, beyond the obstacle Grainna had set. He called to the bird and brought him back.

"Now what?"

~~~~

"What do they see?" Simon asked from outside the circle.

"There is an invisible wall keeping them from going further."

Lora sat in the circle with the women, hands clutched. Ian spoke to her.

They attempted to get into the mind and eyes of Grainna earlier in the morning, but her renewed power proved too great. Even Steel held more power than they expected. Their attempts with him proved futile.

"How the hell is this going to work?" Liz released her breath in disgust.

Cian signaled to Simon. "You need to attempt a connection. The Ancients told us we need to use all our powers to win."

Simon shook his head. "They are so far away. How can I?"

"You have to try!"

Lizzy opened her eyes. "What are you two talking about?"

"Nothing!" Simon sent a shy glance at Cian. "I mean, I don't..."

"How will you know if you don't try?" Cian pleaded.

Simon's eyes passed between his mother and his friend. "I need to come into the circle."

"What?"

"The circle. Open it and let me in."

"Simon." Lizzy sighed. "This is not the time."

"Elizabeth." Myra jolted at her younger brother's tone. Cian spoke like Fin. "Simon can help. He has the ability to see through the eyes of animals. If the falcon is crossing her barrier, then we can use Simon's gift. Let him in and close the circle."

It wasn't a request. His voice of conviction didn't go unnoticed by any of them. He didn't expect his words to be ignored.

They all witnessed the moment Cian became a man, or at the very least, the kind of man he would become. An overwhelming sense of pride swelled in Myra's chest.

Once inside, Simon held hands with the others, his face serious. His hands trembled. "Think of the falcon," Simon instructed them.

They closed their eyes.

~~~~

They all watched the falcon. Todd waited for Ian to report back from the women.

His father-in-law gasped in disbelief.

"What is it?"

"Simon is trying to call to the bird."

"Simon?" Fin asked.

"Aye."

The falcon circled, obviously distressed. Its eyes darted between Ian and Fin. Then, without warning, it dived, landed purposely on Finlay's shoulder.

Fin flinched, immediately turning his head away, the razor sharp beak only inches from his eyes, its talons clenching to hold its balance.

As quickly as it perched it left, taking to the sky, and circled the men before disappearing behind the invisible wall.

"What the hell?"

"Sonofabitch."

~~~~

"Do you sense the animal?" Cian asked Simon, but the women answered yes.

Simon saw through the eyes of the bird. The ground was terribly far down. He stretched his fingers in the palms' of his mother and Amber, and felt the pinch of talons touching his skin. His sight grew sharper than it had ever been before. He could see the smallest of animals scurrying below. Although the falcon noticed them, he didn't push his desire to hunt, instead he followed Simon's will.

He found a perch in a tree overlooking the yard where men gathered and horses were readied.

Grainna stood in the center of the yard, her sphere of glass stood on a podium, unobstructed, with the sun catching its beauty and casting a shower of iridescent light in a perfect circle.

One of the horses, troubled by the rider who was attempting to mount him, skipped close to the podium. Grainna threw up her hand, knocking the rider off the horse. "Get that beast back!"

She studied the glass. Simon swooped down but stayed out of sight. Inside the sphere, he saw Fin and the others. Ian's hand lay against the barrier, his back pushed into it, attempting to move the unmovable.

"She is watching the men, through her crystal ball," Simon told the others in the room.

"Can you see how she is holding them back?"

"No, but I think it has something to do with the sun on the crystal ball. She keeps yelling at the men to stay back."

"You can hear her?"

"Yeah, hey, Myra, didn't you say that your dad

307

could shoot lightning out of his fingers or thoughts?" Simon moved the falcon to a higher perch, and stifled the cry of the animal.

"He can."

"If her crystal ball is gone, than maybe Grainna won't be able to see them. That's gotta help, right?"

"It couldn't hurt."

"Lora, tell Ian to aim the lightning about..." Simon studied the ground beneath the falcon, "about twenty feet beyond the wall and toward the sun." He hoped his calculation was right.

Simon pivoted the falcon's neck. The falcon's perch made it easy for Simon to see both Fin and the others as well as Grainna. He glanced at Ian who nodded when Lora repeated his instructions.

Ian opened his arms. "We're going to get a little wet."

A smile crested Simon's face despite the butterflies circling his stomach.

Thunder rumbled above him. The falcon and the horses started to spook. Simon wanted to reach out to the animals and settle them, but when he tried, he felt his grip on the falcon loosen. He stayed firmly planted inside the winged weapon and watched.

Todd, who leaned against the invisible force field, slipped and fell.

Simon heard a scream inside Grainna's court. He swiveled and witnessed Grainna wave her hands franticly, and those inside the courtyard flee to the edges. "Grainna's hold is breaking, tell Ian to increase the clouds."

The lightning rent the air with a loud crack. Simon jumped and the falcon cried.

Simon saw the powerful light miss its mark. "More toward the sun, three feet."

"Three feet to the sun," Lora said aloud.

The bolt was closer but still missed. The courtyard was in a panic. Grainna swirled around, searching.

Large droplets of water started falling from the sky.

"Half a foot more," Simon yelled above the noise of the storm surrounding the falcon.

The thunder roared; the crack of lightning stretched over the sky. Sensing what was happening a fraction too late, Grainna turned to her sphere in an attempt to move it out of harm's way. Instead, she witnessed it shatter into a thousand pieces.

"Yeah! Woo-hoo!" Simon screamed, bringing his hands in the air, clutched to the others.

The falcon screeched, with Simon's cry.

Grainna turned instantly in his direction.

"Oh, crap!"

"Simon!" His mother scolded.

"I need cover." Simon ignored his mom, told the beast to move. He felt his own pulse pumping with the adrenalin of the bird. Another bolt of lightning distracted those on the ground, but Grainna's eyes followed Simon inside the falcon. She bellowed for Steel.

Once the falcon safely landed back on Ian's outstretched arm, Simon opened his eyes.

Liz focused on her son and gasped in alarm. His eyes had changed shape like those of a falcon, piercing and keen. The grey color swirled with a mix of blue. The effect was startling. Inhuman.

It took several blinks before they returned to

normal.

"How?" Liz asked in awe.

"Well..."

"We don't have time for explanations. Simon, what did you see?" Lora redirected them.

~~~~

Steel watched through the eyes of a hawk, Grainna at his side, twisting her hands and pacing. "The brothers come from the west."

"The others?"

"I don't see them."

"Find them!" She stormed out of the room. The first soldiers she came across she ordered to intercept Fin and Duncan. They scrambled out of her way to do as she commanded. Seconds later, they rode out of the yard in the direction she pointed.

She opened her arms to the sky, a roar of thunder was so loud it shook the bricks of the walls.

Oh, yes, her powers were back, and the sweet seduction of that power poured in her veins. She sneered from the eaves of the yard, bellowing orders to the remaining men who prepared for battle. As much as she would love to end the lives of every MacCoinnich by her very own hands, her premonitions told her of defeat if she insisted on it today.

Today she would weaken their numbers, those who survived would return to their precious Keep and their women, and she would follow. There she would take her revenge on the family, one at a time, sucking the power and life out of them all.

The falcon Grainna had seen earlier caught her gaze. Its eyes watched her every move. She lifted her hand bringing with it fire.

~~~~

"The men have split up. Fin and Duncan have their swords drawn and are..."

"Are what, Simon. What are they doing?"

Aunt Tara's frantic question reminded him of how vulnerable they all felt so far away. He thought of his Aunt and her unborn child. Of the responsibility of relaying what happened before his eyes inside the falcon. "They are... kicking butt."

He heard his mother laugh.

"Duncan, eew."

"What?" the women cried.

"He sliced through the first guy."

Simon glanced toward Fin, his sword clashed with that of another man, quickly pushing him from his horse. Behind him, another took aim with a crossbow. Simon's heart leapt in his chest. He wanted to call a warning but knew his cry wouldn't be heard above the storm that Ian had called.

"What's happening?" Auntie Tara's voice grew frantic. "Tell me, Simon, I don't want to ask Duncan. I'm afraid of distracting him."

Below him, Duncan's hand went to the air and a ball of flame caught the man with the crossbow and threw him into a fiery death.

Another man came behind Duncan, who met his foe with his sword. Simon didn't have time to relay what happened.

"Oh, God!" Tara cried.

They all looked up. Tara's face was covered in sweat, her eyes were wide and her breath hitched.

She doubled over, grasped her belly and they all fell to the floor.

Chapter Twenty-Four

Lizzy, with the help of Cian, moved Tara to the bed. Simon stared wide-eyed while another wave of spasms took over Tara's body.

"How long have you been in labor?" Lizzy pushed back the covers on the bed and placed several pillows to support her sisters back.

"I don't know. I've had a backache for the last few days."

Lora shooed the boys from the room, who were happy to leave. Myra and her mother helped Tara out of her dress, while Amber went to fetch one of the maids to bring more pillows and water.

"This can't be happening now," Tara protested. "How are we going to help them?" Her eyes were wide with panic.

"Worrying now will do you no good." Myra grasped her mother's hand when she spoke. Her quick and forceful squeeze told her she worried, too.

"Duncan promised me he would be here for our child's birth."

"And if he could, he would." Lizzy passed a concerned look to Lora when Tara's abdomen clenched in yet another contraction. This one less than ten minutes from the last.

~~~~

"What do you mean, you can't hear them?" Todd whispered to Ian who sat like him, back against the wall of Grainna's fortress.

"They've been cut off."

"Grainna?" Todd asked.

"Could be."

Todd thought of their options, sheathed his sword, and reached for his gun. "I'll go in first, bullets should slow them down. Cover me."

Ian eyed him. Todd knew he wasn't used to taking orders.

With a nod, Ian conceded.

They inched their way to the edge of the courtyard. Half a dozen armored men gathered. Todd placed his fingers in the air and silently counted down from three.

He came in low, taking careful aim and fired off two rounds before the enemy realized they were under attack.

Ian sent a ball of fire at a man fleeing the yard. Horses reared with the noise of the gun, and in a panic pulled free of their tethers and bolted.

Several men in the yard fled along with the animals. One larger and more skilled than the others pulled his sword, charged at Ian, and caught him from behind.

A warning from Todd kept the blade from making a deadly strike. Ian tumbled to the ground and rounded on his heels. The man lunged on him fast and hard, knocked him to the ground again.

Ian hit the earth dazed. Todd saw the man lift his sword, prepared to plunge it home. Todd put two bullets in him before he could.

Ian moved out of the way of the falling body, kicked his way to his feet. Back to back, Ian and Todd circled the yard.

Two more stood with swords at the ready. Todd took aim, the gun jammed. His enemy sneered and advanced. Todd had no time to reach for his back up weapon. Sword in hand, he prayed Finlay's torture over the last months would keep him alive.

Behind him, Ian clashed blades with his attacker. Todd listened to the fight, but kept his eyes on the man in front of him. His eyes glossed over, and his look turned fierce.

The first time his sword met that of his opponent, Todd knew he was in a fight for his life. Not that he didn't before now, only this man thrusting his blade, pulling back and heaving again, didn't show any sign of letting up. Keeping his stance, Todd pushed against his foe, matching his attack and wearing him down.

Unlike Fin, he couldn't predict his enemy's movements. The enemy lunged twice, then brought his sword down from above his head, clashing his blade into Todd's. The sword's weight started to pull at his shoulder. His strength started to fade. A deep burning ache began low in his back, working its way to his shoulders.

He thought of Myra, ducked his opponents blow, circled around, and dodged a direct hit.

Behind him, Ian's grunts and his attacker's filled the yard. From the gut-wrenching sound, Todd knew someone was mortally wounded. He refused to look and see who went down. Lucky for him, his foe's eyes glanced behind him. Todd took the opportunity and thrust his blade through the man's chest.

Surprise filled the man's expression before his eyes went blank. Fearing Ian lay dying behind him, Todd swiveled and peered into his father-in-law's smiling face. His opponent lay dead at his feet.

~~~~

Duncan dodged the bow. A ball of fire thrust through his fingers at the two sending arrows into his path. Their shock at his display of magic gave him the advantage. One man ducked under the ball of flame, the other met it in a cry of anguish.

Behind him, Fin crossed swords between the horses. The screeching cry of the falcon above caught his attention. His enemy attacked.

Fin took a blade in the shoulder. Blood spouted. Rage bubbled over, and the ground rumbled with Fin's fury.

The horse of the man fighting Fin reared and tossed the rider to the ground. Fin jumped from his mount and dove upon his enemy with deadly force.

Duncan and Fin watched as the remaining opponents fled for their lives.

"Look," Fin pointed to the sky. The falcon circled. "Can you hear Tara?"

Fear crept up Duncan's spine. "Nay, nothing. Simon no longer appears to be controlling the falcon."

"What do you think happened?"

Duncan's jaw set tight. He couldn't be sure. He simply knew he needed to return to the Keep as if the devil himself was at his heels.

Their father and Todd met them at the crumbling gates. Their enemies lay dead or running over the hills. Only chickens and piles of burning hay remained.

Side by side, they went to find the witch.

~~~~

"They're coming," Steel reported to Grainna.

"Let them," she said with confidence. She gathered her skirt and walked up the crumbling stairway to the highest peak.

"We have no way of getting past them up here," Steel warned.

She ignored his words and continued. Once out in the open, exposed to the sky, Grainna forced the clouds to part and the sun to shine down on her.

Fin, Duncan, Todd and Ian's eyes all stared up to see her.

Her black dress cast a dark shadow upon them. Did they tremble with fear? She attempted to probe into their minds, but couldn't break through their guards. Her hair whipped wildly around her body when she started to laugh.

Officer Blakely shifted his feet, but didn't look away. He would be the easiest to remove from their numbers.

"You think you have won," she called above the biting wind.

"When the world is rid of you, then we have won," Duncan yelled back. With both hands, he pushed a three-foot ball of flame up and in her direction.

Fool. She batted the flames away as if they were nothing more than a fly. The ball of fire fell on the building where she stood. Her laugh crackled over the burning home.

Grainna twisted her fingers, expecting them all to fall without air in their lungs.

Blakely grasped for his throat, but instead of struggling for air his hand reached into his pocket where he removed an amulet burning with a rich amber light. He took a full deep breath before he sent a cocky smile focused her way.

Fin, Duncan and even Ian all clutched or reached for an object that glowed.

Grainna's smile fell, her teeth ground together in frustration.

With a screech, she reached deep into the pit of her black heart and pulled out her dark power. She thrust her hands in the air, willing them all to drop to their knees.

The cocky smile upon Fin's face urged her on.

Blakely glanced around, and Grainna focused all her strength on him.

Duncan smiled, and Ian braced his legs. Fin shut his eyes as the ground began to shake.

The earth quaked when Fin opened his hands, and the walls supporting Grainna started to collapse.

"Hold on," he told the family. His warning could barely be heard above the roar of the falling stones from the building where Grainna and Steel stood.

"Holy Shit!" Blakely exclaimed.

Steel pulled her back from the wall, and kept her from plunging to earth. "Now what?" Steel asked.

Grainna glared at her enemies standing smug in her transient defeat. "This is not over," she warned.

Steel's anxious gaze searched around them. He covered his head when the bricks continued to fall.

Grainna clasped a deadly grip on Michael's throat and turned him toward her.

His eyes widened with panic when she stared into his questioning face. He struggled against her, but her strength kept him in place.

I'm immortal, he cried in his head.

"Do you really think I'd share that gift with you?" Grainna taunted him.

The light in his eyes started to fade as she kept air from reaching his lungs.

"You're nothing more than a fool." Grainna's nails dug into the flesh of his neck. She pressed her lips over his to take his last breath. His body buckled beside hers, and with his death, his essence filled her, giving her his knowledge, every skill, and all his power.

Above, the falcon screeched. Instead of filling the bird's head and bending it to her will, she stretched her arms.

The dress she wore floated to the ground as her features morphed. Black as a crow, with the strength and speed of the falcon, she changed from human to hawk.

She took to the air calling in triumph. Below her, the awestruck expressions of the MacCoinnichs and Blakely filled her black soul with pride.

"God's blood," she heard Ian exclaim before she flew away.

~~~~

Tara screamed. Sweat poured off her brow, her breaths spurted in short gasps. "Shit, shit, shit!"

Liz hid her smirk when the maid turned red at Tara's words. "Not much longer, Tara."

"Not. Without. Duncan!"

"You've been at this for too long."

Myra knelt at the foot of the bed along with her mother. The infant's head started to crown.

"You need to push," Lora instructed.

"No!" Tara screamed hysterically. Her head shifted from side to side on the pillows in protest.

318

"Dammit, Tara!" Liz cursed in her face. "Push!"

"The baby has to come, you can't wait for Duncan."

"Lora," Tara said between pants. "Can you hear them?"

Lora shook her head. Tara's labor had gone long into the night and the whole of the following day. The sun was already starting to set again.

With Tara's distraction, they weren't able to connect to the men. "They were nearly three days away, even if they turned back the moment we lost touch they wouldn't make it in time. You have to push."

Another pain wrapped around her, tearing a scream from of her lungs. "Dammit, Duncan, get your ass home!" She breathed through her next contraction.

Thirty long, hard minutes passed before Tara gave in and started to push. Myra held her shoulders and offered encouraging words.

Tara's hand clutched Lizzy's as she strained with the effort to bring her child into the world.

A loud crash sounded from the main hall, its echo vibrated every wall of the Keep. Lora shot Amber a telling look to find out what caused the noise.

"Okay, Tara, this is it. Push."

The next contraction arrived hard. Everyone held their breath while they watched.

Tara forced her remaining strength into the contraction.

Myra sprung to her feet when the door flung open and Duncan rushed in the room. His face switched from concern to awe at what he saw before him. His wife's eyes caught his for a second before Tara took a breath and pushed their child into the world.

For as long as Myra would live, she wouldn't forget the expression that passed over her brother's face when his son was born and the infant's cries filled the room.

The maid hurried to hand Lora a blanket.

Tara flopped back on the bed, trying to catch her breath.

Duncan took two wobbly steps in her direction. When Tara looked his way and extended a hand, he fell to her side. "I came as fast as I could."

Lora handed the bundle to Tara. "'Tis a boy, a beautiful, healthy boy."

Husband and wife pressed their heads together.

Myra choked back tears, as she and Lora quietly slipped from the room.

Myra ran down the hall, searching for Todd. "Where are they?" she asked a passing maid.

"Who, my lady?"

"Duncan has returned. Where are the others?"

"In the yard..."

Myra burst through the door. Todd was swiping dust off his pants. He was whole. Alive.

She saw her father patting him on the back and Fin smiling. They were all home. Safe.

She sent a quick prayer of thanks before she ran to him. A squeal was his only warning before she threw herself into his arms.

"You're home." His arms swallowed her, his lips met hers, and her body relaxed for the first time in days.

Todd rocked back and wiped the tears from

her eyes. "I have someone to come back home to, now."

"I love you."

He kissed her hard before returning her sentiment.

"Come." Myra led him toward the door where her father and Fin walked.

Lora and Liz were coming down the stairs when they entered the hall. A cry from above told the men of the birth.

Ian's face beamed. "Well?" he questioned his wife.

"A boy. Tara and Duncan have a son."

Simon scrambled down the stairs past his mom and flew into Fin's arms. "You made it."

"I told you I would." Fin laughed down at the head of the boy who clutched him around his waist.

"What's this?" Simon asked, noticing blood that oozed from the wound on Fin's arm.

"Nothing, 'tis fine."

Liz rounded on them frowning. "You need to have that dressed."

Fin smiled at her. "What is this? Concern for my well-being, Elizabeth?"

She stepped back.

He sent her a cocky grin.

"Whatever, MacCoinnich, get a nasty infection, gangrene, lose an arm. What do I care?" She turned to walk away.

His chuckle stopped her. "You do," he murmured.

Myra glanced at Todd and wondered if he noticed the tension between the two of them as she did.

Ian smiled on his family. "Fin, go tend your wound and be done with your squabbling. Tonight we celebrate," he announced.

"Is Grainna gone then?" Lora asked.

The men passed looks between them, their distress showing.

"Oh." Lora glanced at her husband. "Then we celebrate prematurely."

"Nay, my love. Tonight we celebrate the new life brought to this family. And Sir Blakely's and Myra's handfasting." He kissed Lora's troubled lips. "Tonight, we celebrate."

Todd pulled Myra close. "So handfasting is like a marriage, right?"

"Aye," she told him.

"So, we've been married for what, five days now?"

Myra sent a puzzled look. "Aye."

He wadded the gloves he held and tossed them to Ian, who caught them in surprise. Without ceremony, he dipped down and brought Myra up and into his arms.

"Todd, what are you doing?"

"Making up for lost time." He smiled down at her. "We'll be celebrating our honeymoon." He nodded to Fin who let out a laugh. "See you in a week, Dad." He winked at her father, who stood mouth agape.

Ian watched his daughter in the arms of her husband disappear up the stairs. "Tonight we celebrate." His heart swelled with pride.

He tried to stop his next thoughts, but couldn't.

Tomorrow we fight.

###

REDEEMING VOWS

BOOK THREE

BY
CATHERINE BYBEE

Chapter One

Liz snapped out of her daydream with Simon's voice ringing in her ears. He wasn't screaming from the front yard about his ball hoping over the fence. No, he was calling her in his head. Something even now, ten months after the first time he'd done so, she'd not grown used to.

Mom, come back to the keep. The shit is hitting the fan again.

Liz shook her head and surged to her feet. *How many times have I told you not to use language like that?*

I'm talking in my head, Mom. It doesn't count!

Liz lifted her skirt, ran to the door, and continued to argue with her son who was over a mile away.

It sure as hell does when you're talking to me.

Simon laughed. *Ha. You just swore.*

That's different, I'm an adult.

Whatever.

Liz could imagine the expression on her son's face. With eyes rolling back in his head and hands on his hips. *What's happening now?* she questioned, knowing he wouldn't have called her if it wasn't urgent.

Birds, hundreds of them. Grainna has to be in the mix. We all feel her evil.

Crap, hold on.

Like a cell phone, Liz tuned out of her son's thoughts and raced to the mare saddled and waiting outside the sanctuary of her hideaway.

"Come on, girl. We have somewhere to be," she coaxed while grasping the reins and hoisting up and into the saddle.

Hurry! Simon's voice pleaded while she watched the Scottish landscape race beside her.

The wind and rain drenched her gown and hair, grown long in her months in the sixteenth century. She searched frantically for a spell to ward away the birds so only the Druid witch remained when she finished her chant.

Liz pushed her horse faster, hearing her son's urgent voice in her head. Damn, she shouldn't have left him, she scolded herself.

Over the hill, the keep emerged strong, solid, and massive under a blanket of black.

Her horse stopped and whinnied at the chaos unfolding in front of their eyes. Crows filled the sky, thousands of them, blotting out the sun.

Liz's jaw hung open. "Son of a bitch!" she whispered before kicking her mount into a frantic run.

She started chanting long before she reached the gates.

"In this day and in this hour, I call upon the Ancient's power. Give us all the ability to see Grainna amongst all of these."

The closer she drew, the more powerful the effects of the chant became.

Birds dropped from the sky, dead, while servants fled the walls of the stone fortress of the MacCoinnichs'.

"Open the gates," she yelled from outside the huge wooden doors that blocked all unwelcomed visitors. "Open the damn gates!"

Stopping short of the wooden doors, Lizzy's horse strained against the reins and whinnied. Careful to hold her seat, and avoid landing on the ground, Liz continued her chant and watched the sky.

Finally, the barrier opened, and she had to still her horse with the dash of retreating people screaming and fleeing the inside of the gates.

Pushing her horse forward, she surveyed the courtyard and found her son standing next to Fin and the entire MacCoinnich family. All of them watched the sky. Tara, Myra and Amber held hands in the shadows, waiting.

Liz jumped off the mare and ran to the women, gasping for air.

"In this day and in this hour..." they all chanted, the only way to fend off the evil coming from the sky. Liz grasped their hands, strengthening and completing their Druid circle.

"Give us the ability," Liz said and waited for the others to repeat her words. "To see Grainna's true self amongst all these."

With each phrase, the sisters levitated from the ground, a side effect of any spell they wove together. No one knew why they hovered above the earth, and none of them knew how to fall back gracefully when they were done. Twice they repeated the words and like a plague, the crows began to drop.

As one, the sisters turned their heads to the sky as an inhuman screech of evil filled the air.

A solitary crow hovered. With one loud screech, it darted away.

Tara squeezed her hand before Liz let her gaze slip from the sky. Slowly the women let each other's hands go and slid to the ground. Myra fell on her behind and extended a hand to Tara to help her up.

Liz hardly took a breath before Fin stepped in front of her with hands perched on his hips.

"Where the hell were you?"

"Out." She turned away, intent on letting that be the end of their discussion, but Fin had other ideas.

His hand darted out and caught her shoulder. "Dammit, Elizabeth, you know better than to leave the keep without someone with you. Are you so selfish that you'd endanger everyone here for your own needs?"

His eyes expressed his anger.

She looked beyond him and over to her son who quickly diverted his attention to his shoes.

"I needed some time alone."

Taking a step closer, Fin lowered his voice so only the women heard. "Then take to a far tower here within these walls. You're of no use to any of us dead."

Liz felt her chest rise and color flame to her face. He was right, and she hated him for it.

Clenching her teeth, she turned and marched from the chaos. She didn't stop until she safely passed the threshold of her chambers. Tara followed her inside and gently closed the door behind them.

Without looking in her direction, Liz addressed her younger sister. "You agree with him, don't you?"

"You agree with him, too." When Tara didn't say more, Liz turned and stared at her.

"What if Grainna positioned that flock of evil

over only you? None of us are capable of taking her on alone." Tara stepped closer, taking Liz's hands.

"I'm suffocating here."

"I know." Tara pushed back a strand of Liz's hair and continued. "But stay close, Lizzy. I need you here. *We* need you here. You are the strongest of all of us."

"I'm not stronger than you."

"That's not true and you know it."

"I don't have an ability like yours or like the rest."

Liz referred to each and every one of the MacCoinnichs' gifts. Tara's ability to move and manipulate everything that grows might have been a new power, but it was something Liz's baby sister had already learned to use to her advantage. Tara's husband, Duncan, could cast a flame larger and stronger than anything imagined by twenty-first century fiction writers. Simon spoke to animals. Ian directed the weather with a mere thought. Myra moved objects with her mind. Even Amber, the youngest of the MacCoinnichs, was an empath who could sense events long before they happened.

No, compared to Tara and the rest, Liz felt inferior, like a cast off.

As if sensing her concern, Tara continued. "You are the one who comes up with every chant, every spell that keeps Grainna at bay."

"Any of you could do that."

"Really? I don't think so."

"All of us are Druids, Tara. We all have the ability." Liz moved to the large fireplace and held out her hands. Sparks flew into the hearth and flames leapt to warm the room.

"Look at you. If I had told you a year ago that you were able to start a fire without a match, you would've had me committed. Now you prance around, spread your hands and *voila...* flames." Tara stepped behind her. "I know you're unhappy here. But until this is finished, until we destroy Grainna and find the stones, you're stuck here."

Hearing the words aloud felt so final. It wasn't that she hated the MacCoinnichs; she simply didn't have any control over her own life. With Fin hovering close by, it was as if she couldn't breathe. In order to return to her century, they needed the sacred stones. Grainna had three of them in her possession. The MacCoinnichs held the other three.

"I know."

"Think of Simon. If Grainna caught you alone, killed you..." Tara's voice dropped away. "What would he do without you?"

Closing her eyes, Liz turned. Tara was right. They all were right.

About the author

New York Times bestselling author Catherine Bybee was raised in Washington State, but after graduating high school, she moved to Southern California in hopes of becoming a movie star. After growing bored with waiting tables, she returned to school and became a registered nurse, spending most of her career in urban emergency rooms. She now writes full time and has penned the novels Wife by Wednesday, Married by Monday, and Not Quite Dating. Bybee lives with her husband and two teenage sons in Southern California.

Connect with Catherine Bybee Online:
Website: http://www.catherinebybee.com
My blog: http://catherinebybee.blogspot.com
Facebook:
https://www.facebook.com/pages/Catherine-Bybee-Romance-Author/128537653855577
Goodreads:
http://www.goodreads.com/author/show/2905789.Catherine_Bybee
Twitter: https://twitter.com/catherinebybee
Email: catherinebybee@yahoo.com

Discover other titles by Catherine Bybee

Contemporary Romance
Weekday Bride Series:
Wife by Wednesday
Married By Monday

Not Quite Series:
Not Quite Dating

Paranormal Romance
MacCoinnich Time Travel Series:
Binding Vows
Silent Vows
Redeeming Vows
Highland Shifter

Ritter Werewolves Series:
Before the Moon Rises
Embracing the Wolf

Novellas:
Possessive
Soul Mate

Erotic Titles:
Kiltworthy
Kilt-A-Licious

30391189R00192

Made in the USA
Charleston, SC
14 June 2014